MW00529164

What They're Saying About *The Russian Job*

"Phillip Sheppard The Specialist's *The Russian Job* is a sophisticated spy novel that digs deep into today's global and political issues. It touches on redemption, hope, and reassurance that evil cannot prevail.

The reader will be hooked from the first paragraph as you dive into this thrilling action-packed world that will keep you wanting more. You will be on edge with The Specialist as he tracks down all the leads to the mind-blowing conclusion. A heart-racing, edge-of-your-seat ride that will keep you guessing until the very end.

The Specialist always answers the call to chase the devils back to where they belong. When a mystery brings him back into the world, he thought he left behind it turns everything on its head. Aaron Cohen, Senior Vice President of Derivates and Global Acquisitions enters a train but never exits it. The Specialist is called in to make sense of what could've possibly gone wrong. This disappearance suggests a kidnapping took place and begins to open up a giant global conspiracy where Aaron Cohen could be the pawn in a dangerous game. The truth may be more than The Specialist can handle as the twists and turns bring him closer to a ticking clock that may blow up in his face.

A main theme throughout the novel is redemption which was in a big part inspired by Sheppard's time on Survivor Redemption.

Sheppard would like to see his newest book turned into a major motion picture with the following actors and actresses Michael B. Jordan as The Specialist, Annie Monroe as Yifat, Viola Davis as Diana Heartly, and Shawn Yue as Zhang. This would be his dream cast."

—Jasmine Willis, *The Tribune*
State-award-winning independent journalist

THE RUSSIAN JOB

Phillip William Sheppard

Published by Stealth R US

930 Euclid Street, #101, Santa Monica, CA 90403

310-310-0310

ISBN: 978-1-80128-057-0

Printed in the United States

Disclaimer

This book is a work of fiction. Names, characters, locations, events, places, organizations and businesses are either the product of the author's imagination or used fictitiously. Any resemblance to actual persons living or dead, events or locales is entirely coincidental except the Protagonist "Phillip Sheppard: The Specialist."

This book is dedicated to my son, Marcus Alexander Sheppard

Motivation

"What is the fear of living? It's being preeminently afraid of

dying. It is not doing what you came here to do, out of timidity

and spinelessness. The antidote is to take full responsibility

for yourself– for the time you take up and the space you

occupy. If you don't know what you're here to do, then just do

some good."

—Maya Angelou

The Specialist—is the One and Only

The Specialist has honed his skills as an expert from his military training in special ops with the Pentagon, Defense Investigative Service, Home Land Security and Department of State, conducting worldwide background and criminal investigations with other Federal Agencies, and has developed a keen ability to work with other elements of the arm forces, due to his exceptional ability to gain the confidence of other elements of NSA, CIA, FBI, and International organizations who have supported the USA as part of our core alliance both known publicly and those of hidden cells all over the world, he is the first person to be called when all appears lost.

Contents

What They're Saying About *The Russian Job*................i

Motivation.. ix

The Specialist—is the One and Only x

Foreword 1

Chapter 1...3

Chapter 2 22

Chapter 3.. 45

Chapter 4 58

Chapter 5 77

Chapter 6 90

Chapter 7 101

Chapter 8 114

Chapter 9 128

Chapter 10..141

Chapter 11 152

Chapter 12..161

Chapter 13.. 176

Chapter 14.. 188

Chapter 15.. 203

Chapter 16..218

Chapter 17..228

Chapter 18..244

Chapter 19..259

Chapter 20 276

Acknowledgments...289

Special Thanks 290

About the Author 291

Foreword

Having the opportunity to meet Phillip Sheppard, *The Specialist*, at a past charity event was truly an honor. He is a man full of adventure, intelligence, and charisma, with a charm and personality that feel contagious. *Watching* him on a nationally televised reality show provided me with my first impressions, but watching the very last episode allowed me to draw more distinct conclusions about who the man really is. Phillip's energetic personality radiates toward others. His sharp mind works constantly to analyze the situation, scan the environment, decipher those around him, and furnish a plan to make the best of all possible situations.

That's why I like this book so much. It captures his essence. Being asked to read *The Specialist: The Russian Job* was an honor equal to meeting the man himself. As a published author (Your Winner Within), I know the eff ort involved in writing a book, and this novel truly surpassed my expectations. Once I picked the book up and began reading, I couldn't put it down. Loaded with excitement, anticipation, challenging situations and unanswered questions, this gem made me yearn to read faster, just to enjoy the final outcome. From the beginning, I tried predicting the finish, but the unexpected conclusion produced more than surprise; it served up a jaw dropping shock! The characters seem so real; I could actually visualize them and all the situations they encountered. This is a "must read." This book will answer all your questions about who The Specialist really is. As I read it, I couldn't help but think about how proud I felt of Phillip. In writing this fictional work, he has fulfilled some lofty personal expectations.

It must be great to be **The Specialist**. —

Holly Hoffman, author
Survivor Contestant: *Nicaragua, Survivor* Season 21 Finalist
Motivational Speaker

Chapter 1

"Found it?"

The voice boomed from my earpiece. I merely breathed out a *yes* as I glanced down at my task at hand, which was staring back at me.

Tick, Tock! Tick, Tock!

The sound was all too familiar to my ears. I bent down to inspect what I had to deal with, and the time stamp ticking away glared back at me. Fiery eyed, red and glowing, the blinking red light never ceased to amaze me. It was high. The countdown to finishing something always felt like a competition with myself. My challenging personality found an adrenaline rush anytime the tick-tocks sounded... echoed... bellowing a victory that I knew I would turn into defeat. The sound of a blaring ring was melody to me. They moved me, and the agent in me who had to retire a while ago danced in tune with it.

"It'll be a difficult task; you got this?" The voice came off again.

"Give me five minutes," I declared. "Child's play," I added with pride.

The air around me on the building's rooftop was rasping through me, sending waves of fear, rush, and excitement. I looked around the space. There was nobody. I had made sure that I locked the door behind me. "Nobody can know about this," I was briefed before coming here. The people in the building went about their routine without an ounce of inkling that there was a bomb on the rooftop that could blow up anytime, ending their existence in mere seconds.

"This is critical, specialist." The man mustered again, "Tell me you don't need a backup."

"I don't," I repeated dryly. "Crucial is what I do, my man."

There was silence on the other end. Without bidding a farewell, I disconnected the call. My knee that was touching the cemented floor had scuffed. A while ago, on my way here, a pesky pebble twisted my ankle, and I had knocked into a stone wall. The fall had torn my well-fitted dress pants, and now, the harsh floor was inflicting red rashes on my exposed knee, burning to the touch and painful. But did my injuries ever matter to me? No! Best in the game, 'The Specialist' always did what was beneficial for others. To safeguard and protect my people was the priority. It always has been.

04:59

The ticking time now indicated five minutes. Blinking away, intensifying my nerves, I quickly pulled out the tools from my satchel and went to work. It was time to make good on my word. The clock beeped to warn me that time was slipping by me, and I darted my eyes from side to side to examine which wire I needed to cut to disarm the bomb.

"The Specialist is on the job. There's no way the bomb will blow up."

"One of these days, he'd die pulling a stunt like that. You mark my words."

The two most contradicting statements of the people who had put me on this life-threatening job began to echo in my head. My hands shivered but momentarily. It always happened the first second I stared down at the explosive device in front of me. Sometimes, it was the wind chill, other times the scorching sun. It was never the nerves...no! I took pride in having a steady hand at disarming bombs or dislocating bones.

A pair of pliers was secured in one hand, and the other one pinched to take a grip of the aimed wire. I drew in a sharp breath. The sun had aided greatly in sweating up my face. I could vividly see some drops on the box that was hidden inside a large tire on the rooftop. , Mixed with the whistling of the dry wind, the sound that the cut made felt like a symphony to my ears. The red timer stopped blinking, indicating that I had successfully put an end to the danger that awaited the inhabitants of the building.

"Ahh! The Specialist. Of course, why am I surprised?"

A voice came from behind me, and I stood up in the next instant. Turning around, I came face to face with the man whose organization had allegedly planted the explosives. I knew him from my time in the force. Tall, tanned, and well-built, he was the spitting image of a movie's protagonist. As intelligent as he was, sadly, he had put his mind to use for the wrong reasons.

I smiled at the intruder, "Still picking locks, I see."

He laughed, throwing his head back. "I do more than that, my righteous counterpart. Need I remind?"

I walked closer to him, and with the reduced distance, his tall stature failed in comparison. Our eyes no longer met at one level, and I had to look down to talk to him. I quite liked that. It was a different kind of high. "Your rap sheet is quite fascinating, I am aware. However, I have much more pressing affairs to attend, and I can't waste any more time here as you gloat over your sorry evilness," I said, walking past him to make my exit.

Suddenly, I felt a hard grip on my shoulder. With one force, I was swiveled, and before I could blink, the man stroke a harsh jab across my face. I stumbled over backward with the sudden blow, and my nose started to bleed. A throbbing and numbing sensation spiraled across my face.

"This was for your heroic mission, my friend... courtesy, The Boss."

I wiped the blood on my coat's sleeve, shading it crimson. Although the dark blue color hid the bloodstain, the reddish hue on my perfectly tailored suit made me squeamish.

"It's a sign of a battle won. It's like a badge of honor on your uniform. How could you not find happiness in that? Pride even?"

Many would ask me, wondering why I crinkled my nose every time, even some dust settled on my outfit. Ever the prim and proper gentleman that I was, I had my finicky attributes. A clean suit was one of them. I inwardly smiled. This man would have to pay for the cost of laundry, and perhaps a little more than that. Gaining back my balance, I walked toward him and smiled brightly at him.

"Pardon me... my bad," I said in a hushed whisper.

He glared at me, but I could see a small smile playing across his lips. Poor chap... He had this crazy idea in his head that he had won—time to rectify the misconception. Without saying anything else, I hit him straight in the nose, held his shoulder, and slammed my knee in his stomach with full force. He fell on the ground and doubled over with pain, as an involuntary scream escaped his lips that parted the wind around us. I walked closer to where he fell on the ground and bent over his body, nearing my face toward his. The sound of his ragged breaths pumped adrenaline through me.

"And this is for staining my suit, dear old Bradford," I said in a menacing tone. Words gritted in more anger than I intended. I was done with the rude chap who dared to think that he could defeat me with a surprise blow and an unannounced intrusion, but this man truly had a death wish.

He stood up again and gripped me by he neck, making another mistake of thinking he could choke me. "You're not walking away, Specialist... not today." He breathed in my ear, "I have dreamed of this. Not being able to kill you has haunted me for far too long to let this opportunity slide by."

I forced a smile as the air closed in on me. My breathing was restricted, and I struggled to catch some air. "Don't be a fool..." I choked my words, "the sorry likes of you can't kill The Specialist."

"It looks like I'm already halfway done, old man. Cough up a storm."

That was it. My fighter instincts kicked in, and my training came rushing to me. Although I came here vowing not to shed blood, this man was making it hard for me to abide by the commitment I made to myself. Stiffing my body, I braced myself for the impact, and with force, I threw back my head, striking him across his face. His grip loosened as he stumbled back. I coughed loudly to gain back my breaths as I watched him fighting through the pain I had just inflicted on him. I had hardly reformed myself. When I saw him reaching for his pocket, clearly aiming to retrieve a weapon. Quick as a cat that I was, I charged toward him, and in one swift motion, I twisted his arm, and the gun he so gracefully managed to pull fell on the ground. I picked it in an instant and pointed it at his head. Knelt, he had his hands up in the air in surrender. His face was now radiating fear and regret.

"Give me some names, and I'll let you go," I reasoned with him.

"If I gave you any names, they'll kill me. Might as well be you," he said, defeated.

"Tsk tsk! Such a sad story. Not interested, mate... names, now!"

"No!" He denied, "You don't kill without reason, I'm aware."

"Sweet of you to have such high regard for me, my vanquished foe." I scoffed, smiling, "But this isn't the answer I'm looking for. Tell me some names of your accomplices and walk free." I gritted, loading the gun for good effect.

To my surprise and his dismay, the man smirked. "You don't have it in you, Specialist. Not anymore. You are a 'has-been'...retired, dusted away in a corner, picking measly cases to kill boredom." He gave out a laugh. "I pity you. If a random kill that shall do no good to your life is something you need to feel like the hero you no longer are, then by all means... fire away."

Stunned with his words and how they stung me, I almost put my hand down. His sideway mocking smile held my arm in position, and before I could think it over, I pulled the trigger. The deafening sound of the gunshot echoed in the silence, and I looked wide-eyed as his body fell to the ground, lifeless. What lay before me now was a pool of blood and his brain scattered across the cemented floor like an abstract painting—gawking at me, judging my choices, and laughing at how my nerves failed me. It was my nerves, was it now? The gunshot was never needed. I tried not to let undeserving blood to flow, and yet there it was... something that I could have avoided... something that should not have happened. I sighed. Perhaps he was right. I might not deserve the title of The Specialist anymore.

Wiping my bloodied hands on my dress pants, I started walking to the door, preparing for my descent from the building. My suit was a lost cause anyway. Tiny droplets of blood had painted my neatly suited persona crimson. Breathing out to rid myself of any guilt, I climbed down the stairs, prepared to retire myself for the day. I spotted my black 718 Cayman GT4 from a distance. It was hard to miss. The car exerted power, suave, and class. My phone began to ring the minute I sat inside, and I tapped on my Bluetooth to answer the call.

"Mr. Sheppard, I hope it is not a bad time," the person on the other side said.

I took in a breath to calm myself down before I spoke up, "May I know who am I speaking to?"

"Michelson... we interacted a year ago about an arsenal case," the man explained.

I nodded. "I remember, but I'll have you know that I've retired from the force already," I said, my tone unintentionally getting bitter. The words of my deceased evil counterpart had stung harder than I thought. It is more painful when you are not at the age of retiring but forced to do so. I thought I was fine. I thought that I was leading a life that I wanted at the prime age of 39... that I enjoyed doing what I did now. But the words of a dead man haunting inside my head were singing a different song... a painful melody of failure and defeat.

"I am aware, Mr. Sheppard. There is, however, nobody I can trust with this."

I brushed a hand through my hair. My head was throbbing with pain at this point. "Can this wait a day or so? I have some other urgent matters I need to attend to."

"I won't take up much of your time. The case I want you to handle is of Aaron Cohen's kidnapping."

The name instantly perked my interest up. "Cohen? From the JPI International Securities?" I asked.

"Yes! That one..."

"I'm listening," I said, turning my full attention on him.

"Mr. Sheppard, we shall meet soon. I'll hand over all the details about the case to you in person. I'm afraid that the phone's frequency could be taped."

I nodded in agreement. "Very well. I was heading home to attend a meeting. I can swing by..."

"...The Gold Club," The man finished my sentence, "I am playing a game there. Why don't you join in, and we can go over the details?"

"Sounds good," I said and hung up the phone. Quickly setting the address in the navigation system, I drove off to meet with Michelson.

***

"Over here, Mr. Sheppard," Michelson waved me over, who was standing in the middle of the golf course, with a golf club in his hands.

I took a rental one from a counter in the corner as I marched toward him. I had taken off my suit's jacket, which had a noticeable amount of blood on it, while my white shirt remained stainless. Sleeves rolled up; it was probably the first time that I had gone to a place in anything but a three-piece suit.

"So, Mr. Michelson, you were going to brief me about Aaron Cohen?" I reminded him, getting right to the point.

He smiled. "Let's see if you can score first?" He pointed at the golf club in my hands.

I sighed; the things I did to find my life's high again. "If defeat is what you came here for, I'll be more than happy to oblige."

The next hour was spent battling on the golf course. We exchanged some wits and old anecdotes. I shone on the scoreboard, and Michelson acted like the good sport he was. This was something I had to take up during my undercover assignments. An old suspect of mine was a golfer, and I spent days upon days here at the course to make him a good accomplice.

"It is not fair how good you are," Michelson chimed in at one point during the game.

I had laughed as I made another long stride. "It pays to be The Specialist," I had stated proudly.

Soon, we were sitting in the club's cafeteria, sipping coffee and biting into sandwiches.

"Aaron Cohen," I started again. "What do you know about the case?"

Michelson backed into his chair with his coffee mug in his hands. "He was kidnapped from a train. He got on a train from Munich to Heidelberg but never left it."

"What do you mean never left it?" I asked curiously.

"There is footage," Michelson took a sip from his coffee. "He can be seen getting on the train, but nobody could find anything on him getting out."

"He can't disappear into thin air." I raised my eyebrow. "Even if he was kidnapped, someone left with him from the train... whether in a mask, him in a body bag, or luggage... something."

Michelson smiled. "That is why you are here, Mr. Sheppard. There's nobody who can solve unsolvable quite as you do."

"Flattery won't make me take it up," I said dryly. "I want more details. You are aware of what I look for in a case, and it's not praising."

"Fair enough." Michelson nodded, putting his coffee mug back down on the table. "One more piece of information I can share is that there are people from his work who saw him in a heated argument with someone."

"Tell me more..."

"Dear old Aaron, you know what they say, involve yourself with the big shots."

"You can stop right there, Hex." Aaron put up his hands, but it was not in surrender. He just didn't have the energy for it after a long day at work.

The crowd who had gathered listening in on their argument already had their phones out, filming a heated scene, an interesting exchange of wits, and snarky remarks—what a scene to behold for the intrigued passers-by and those who knew Aaron Cohen all too well.

"I'll stop when you stop." The man seethed with anger, gritting his teeth with each word as he took a calculated step toward Aaron with a menacing look in his eyes.

"The digging for more answers continues. Big money often brings bigger investigations, and I'm not stopping for anything, at any threat you throw my way," Aaron said confidently, taking another step closer to the man. Aaron didn't want to come off as scared. He didn't look at it anyway. His stature was tall and mounting over the relatively smaller man, who was failing miserably at his attempts at intimidating him.

The man smiled. Despite the smaller size, it was visible that he had a certain level of power in the palm of his hands that he was not afraid of. There was a much superior back supporting him to stand figuratively taller than he looked. His confidence triumphed in Aaron's prideful stance.

"Back down, Cohen. You are already in deep waters. You don't wanna drown here. Do you? It's not worth it." Hex, as someone on the scene heard it, was now trying sincerely to grant Aaron with some words of wisdom. To the unaware gawking eyes in the crowd, it almost felt like the smaller man cared. The reality was different—much more chaotic than what was transpiring at the moment on the surface.

"Hunting sharks, my nemesis... I do that as a sport. You gotta risk drowning to take one down."

Hex took another step and stared at Aaron. "You're stepping too far. You'll be eaten alive."

Aaron took another step as well, closing the small gap between the two of them only to mere inches now. He gave a smile to Hex. "Threats have never worked on me, Hex. They didn't work when I took down a million-dollar fraud, and they sure as heck won't work now."

"You don't know who you are messing with," Hex glared at him, warning him again. "You'll lose more than your life. Your days of darkness have begun. Look over your shoulder for the lurking shadows as you walk down the streets of your precious tall building. One might just devour you."

Aaron smiled. "There will be a candlelight dinner served in my wake when what you say happens to me for real. Don't forget to come by the buffet and devour me." He smirked at the smaller man and walked away.

***

I took in a mouthful of my coffee, which was cold by now as I listened to Michelson narrating the story of the day when Aaron Cohen got into an argument with a man supposedly called Hex, as eyewitnesses on the scene confirmed.

"Hex, you said," I started, putting down my mug back on the table. "If he was the one threatening Aaron Cohen before he was supposedly abducted, why don't we start there? Arrest him."

Michelson leaned forward, placing his elbows on the table. "He used an alias. Hex was not his name. We tried looking for him in the database. It's almost impossible to track him down now."

I stroke my chin, trying to figure all the details out. The case was intriguing. Things were not clear, and there was an obvious need for digging deeper to retrieve answers. I had a reputation for that... extract answers from unexpected places. "How about those in the audience? They must have a video."

Michelson sighed. "If only we as humans didn't fear death to such an extent, things would be much easier for the likes of the detectives and whatnot."

"Yes, I'm aware." I nodded. "Almost too often, many pieces of evidence are lost in fear of those who are in possession of the final straw needed to take down evil. It's always the fear halting progress toward the good."

"Precisely, Specialist." Michelson said, "Every witness we had to that argument went into hiding. Some officers already tried reaching them, and those who did speak only shared brief details. Nobody, however, dared to share a video they had recorded. Everything was either deleted out of fear or made to be deleted by someone."

I leaned back in the chair, propping my foot over my leg. I had still not made up my mind about whether or not I would be taking up the case. It was hard to solve, which meant it would be interesting. Deep mysteries and unknown territories always intrigued me. I took a high out of such victories. However, every case I took up after retiring from the force brought a fresh sense of longing and loss.

"You're trying to savor your glory days," some would mock, and I would feel the reality of the statement hit me hard, with a force that weakened my nerves.

"Specialist, there's nobody else who could figure this out." Michelson interrupted my lugubrious thoughts. "There is a large network at play. It's instilled a certain level of fear in those who saw Aaron that day when he got into an argument and even on the day when he disappeared. They don't want to speak about him. It's why we are left with zero evidence." He looked at me with warmth and plea in his eyes. Leaning forward, he continued in hushed words. "No evidence, the mafia-like crowd... isn't that your specialty, Specialist?"

I took in a sharp breath and tapped on the table with my finger. "The day he was abducted, tell me what you know about that day."

Michelson took his storytelling stance again, leaned back, relaxed, and lit up his cigar. "There was a man who knew Aaron." He started between taking in drags of smoke out of the cigar and blowing out the steam into the cold air. "He shared a few details with us that day."

"I'm listening..."

***

Antonio left his office early that day. He had an invite for a family dinner, for which he was already late. He pulled his suit's jacket in place by adjusting his shoulders as he stepped out of the building. At the curb, he spotted Aaron, one of the most well versed and highly informed employees of their company, waiting for the valet to bring around his car. It was strange for Antonio to find him leaving work this early. He was usually the first one in and the last one out.

"Good evening!" Antonio greeted Aaron. "Cohen, heading home early, are we? Last I checked, the sun still rose from the east today."

Aaron laughed. "On the contrary, I have to catch a train to Heidelberg."

"Oh!" Antonio smiled. "You're taking your car to the station?"

"No, I'll take it home, park it there, and head to the station by cab," Aaron answered.

Antonio scratched his head and looked at his watch. He knew he was cutting it short, and some people were going to be angry with him, but he decided to go for it anyway. "Why don't I come with you? You can take your car home, and then I'll drop you at the station."

"Oh, that'd be helpful." Aaron smiled, happy with the proposition.

When his car finally came, he got in, and Antonio followed him on his own. A quick stop was made at Aaron's home, where he informed his daughter where he was going.

"A few weeks at the most," Aaron told his daughter. "It may take me some more time, but I'll be back. Wait up for me, alright!"

"Of course, you would be back, dad. I'll be here."

Antonio saw him smile at his daughter as he kissed her on the forehead to bid goodbye. Antonio didn't hear him state any details, but he was slightly puzzled at what he meant when he insisted that he'd be back. Was there something else at play there? After his brief farewell to his daughter, they were off to the station in Antonio's car. Antonio took him to the station, where he bid his farewell to a distressed Aaron, who looked back and forth between him and the approaching train in a tensed manner.

"More than what a CCTV could catch, I have you to vouch for me."

"Pardon?" Antonio asked, puzzled at what Aaron was saying.

"I am going to Heidelberg. I boarded the train... you saw it. Tell them that," Aaron requested. Antonio was about to ask what was going on, but Aaron stopped him from speaking. "Let's not indulge in my words any longer for now. I know it is confusing. I am not making much sense right now. Perhaps you may understand it later."

"Aaron, if there's a danger, you're heading into that we're not aware of, please let me know," Antonio said seriously.

Aaron smiled. "I appreciate the concern, but there is no danger. Just remember what I said." With that, he walked away as the train made a stop at the platform. Before entering, he turned around one last time and looked at Antonio more intensely. "Be my witness."

***

I coughed loudly as the smoke from the cigar got in my face. Picking up a glass of water, I gulped down the cold liquid, quenching my thirst, all the while trying to drink in the story Michelson had just finished narrating. The more he shared, the more intrigued I got with the case. The question that ringed the loudest in my head was... Was Aaron Cohen aware of his impending kidnapping? Followed closely by another... How did he disappear from the train?

I needed answers. By now, I had figured out that I had tried out every single avenue from Michelson. He was out of answers I needed to find. This had started to feel like a riddle that I wanted desperately to solve. No clues, no evidence, just a vague story that I had to rely on for the answer, and nobody was there to tell me if my guesses were right. It was a matter of physically diving in and digging up into the depth of reality.

"So, what do you think?" Michelson asked, "Interested at all?"

"Fascinated, but not quite sure." I answered, "I am a retired agent. How much risk could I afford?"

"The Specialist never fears. That's one thing I can vouch for blindly," Michelson said with absolute confidence. The truth be told, he was right.

It wasn't the fear of harm befalling me, rather the fear of testing failure. I was afraid that if I failed to deliver, I would lose faith in myself. I was afraid that the reflection staring me back in the mirror would mock me for being a cowardice, incompetent, and has-been agent. There was nothing I feared more than my mirror image looking down at me... Nothing at all.

"I have a few more questions," I said. Perhaps I was stalling my final decision.

Michelson dabbed his cigar in the ashtray, putting it out. He leaned forward to look at me. I was hit with a pungent smell of tobacco that had taken over his aura. "I wish I had more answers for you, but I'm afraid that I don't." He took in a deep breath before continuing further. "Look, the only reason you were chosen for this mission is that we know you're the only one who can solve this. We have hit a dead-end, and I'm aware how brilliant The Specialist is at breaking down those walls that forbid entrance and finding new ways on roads that seem to lead nowhere." He looked at me intently. "Please, Mr. Sheppard. We need you on this case."

I sighed. "I am in," I finally said before my racing mind could make me change my decision. "Let's solve this mystery."

Chapter 2

"We can have a few men from the force accompany you to Atlanta."

"That won't be necessary. I work best alone."

"The Specialist... there is only one, of course!"

I remembered the parting words of Michelson at the airport as I looked out the window. The city lights of Atlanta came into view as the plane began its descend. This wasn't the first time I had taken the red-eye in a state of emergency. No! I had flown longer hauls and traveled to deserted far and beyond regions when the case required it. However, this case held a strange sense of excitement for me. I couldn't quite place it. Perhaps it was the first real case I took on after my retirement.

As a private agent, one often does not entrust you with chaotic cases, regardless of how sans of faults your track record is. Breaking in and Entering, B&Es as they call it had been quite the popular one in my portfolio post my farewell to the force. Although my pride forbade me from admitting it out loud, I was bored with them.

"You just like swimming with the sharks... blindly, without oxygen back up. Is it not your high, Specialist? It is what will get you killed one day."

An enemy had once mocked me, and I memorized those words, for they held the most truth about me. I wasn't sure how he meant it as an insult. Better praise had never been sung in my honor. Shortly after the final announcement of the pilot, the plane landed at the location that I was sure held many possibilities for me. The airport's familiar scent hit me with a sense of nostalgia, and I clutched on to the handle of my hand carry as I made my way through the arrivals and into the city of history, art, and grand museums.

"Mr. Sheppard," I heard a tall man, clad in a well-fit three-piece suit call out to me. He had my name card in his hands, which meant he had not seen me before. I wondered how he was able to recognize me. Perhaps he was shown my picture. "I hope you had a pleasant flight!" The man said, extending his hand toward me.

"We encountered some turbulence. It was a good ride," I replied, shaking his hand.

The man stared me down with an impressed smile. The night had aged and turned quite dark. The street was partially empty and not well-lit. I couldn't make out the man's features properly, perhaps because I was tired or maybe it really was too dark, but I could tell that the man was just about my age, a little over thirty-nine, inching closer to forty. His brown hair was neatly gelled back in place, and he had the perfect-tanned, well-toned physique. His eyes were, however, what caught my attention the most. He held a glimmer in them, almost as if he was meeting with an idol of his that he had admired all his life.

"They inquired, 'how I would recognize you, Mr. Sheppard,'" the man continued, answering my earlier wonderment. "I told them that I would. Your tales of victories, triumph, and defeat; they're all so fascinating. I painted a picture in my head - suave and epitome of elegance. I must say you match the visions quite closely."

I passed a smile at the man. "Let's not dwell in pleasantries much longer, shall we?"

The man nodded. "This way, sir! Mr. Michelson has sent a car for you. It'll take you to your hotel." He informed me and opened the door to a stretch limousine.

I was never one to be impressed by the worldly marvels, but I appreciated Michelson for making things more comfortable for me. "There is this hotel," I handed a small piece of paper to the man who now sat on the driver's seat. "I believe there's a train station around its quarters. Some people on long haul journeys often take a stop here and stay in this hotel." I explained.

"This is where we're going," the man announced. "Mr. Michelson informed me that you'd wanna stay there or at least visit."

I smiled. Michelson once identified himself as a fan. "In the events that I'm puzzled of the next move that I need to make, I ask myself: what would The Specialist do? It opens new avenues for me."

He would often tell me, and with how much attention to detail the man had paid on my way of workings, he was truly making true of his words. The limo took us to the hotel where I was supposed to stay. The rest of the drive was spent in almost silence, other than the man occasionally telling me about some of my solved cases that he had read. In exchange, I reciprocated with smiles and some hms and ohs.

When the hotel came in sight, I smiled to myself. My first lead lay there. My parched soul danced on the prospect as I made my way through the intimately decorated lobby. The hotel was not spacious, but it held all the luxuries of an extravagant stay-in experience. I took a glance around the small elegant space. The lobby that I had walked in held one large rug in the center, on which a round table was placed with a large vase on top. On either side of the table, four chairs were situated, two on each side with a small wooden table between the two chairs. Right above the center round table, a giant chandelier was hanging; and above the entire seating area, a beautiful skylight was put in place, giving the place a rather dreamy look. I could only imagine how breathtaking the lobby must look in the light of day. When the sun would shine through the skylight, the inhabitants of the intimate place must bathe in the glory of the mighty star. Perhaps that was why this place was so famous between travelers in transit and even those who had come to explore the historic city of Atlanta.

Adjacent to the small seating area for the waiting guests, the reception was located. Behind the tall guy whose name tag read Thomas, wearing a usual hotel uniform – a white dress shirt with navy blue waistcoat – an enormous and beautiful painting hung. It was of the city's landscape, surrounded by numerous dark shadows of trees. On the left wall to the entrance, a chest like a piece of furniture was situated. Though I could not make out what it was, probably a mix between a cupboard and a chest, it was a beautiful piece of art, much like what the city was famous for. The walls were painted in a shade of caramel, white, and slightly tan. It appeared to be a mixture of all those, I gathered.

On the right side to the main entrance, a bank of elevators was situated, three in a total of relatively very small size. Lightning of the main lobby was quite dull, as if it was intended to give the intimate effect that was usually associated with the city. Taking in my surroundings, I finally made my way toward the reception to be greeted with a polite smile.

"Good evening, Sir!" The man at the reception greeted me. "How may I help you?"

"Good evening," I responded. "I have a reservation under this name," I informed, sliding my ID across the counter.

"Of course," the man said, picking up the card.

I heard a few clicks here and there as he tried to look me up in his database before he finally turned to me with a key card.

"Here are your keys, Mr. Sheppard."

"Thank you," I nodded, taking the key card from his hands.

"I was asked to inform you that Mr. Andrews is awaiting your presence in the restaurant on the first floor. Once you are settled in, you can find him there." The man explained, and I nodded as I walked to the elevators, with a bellhop on my tail, bringing my one piece of luggage with me. He had insisted on assisting, despite my denial of the service, and I had conceded.

I entered my room and took a quick scan around the space. Although the room was small, it was quite luxurious. A double bed was placed in the center with two nightstands on either side. There was a wall-mounted smart TV right opposite the bed, with a writing table of sort underneath it. On the side, where a floor-length window was overlooking the bright city lights, there was a small seating area; two chairs and a center table. In my years of traveling as a special agent of the force, I had lived in far more extravagant hotel rooms. However, it was always just a vessel to recharge my energies to be prepared for the next day—nothing more, nothing less. I took in a sharp breath as if I was trying to gather all my lost energy from the flight. I put my suitcase in a corner, quickly freshened up, and walked out of the room to meet with Mr. Andrews.

Mr. Andrews was the hotel's manager. Michelson had briefed me regarding his aid that I would need in the case. I needed to access the data from the surveillance room, which, of course, without my status of being a member of the force, would be hard to gain without inside help.

"We had some witnesses on the scene inform us that he got out in Atlanta," Michelson had informed me. "We think that there must be some clues you might find there."

That was all the information I needed to conclude that Aaron must have made a stop at Atlanta and stayed in the hotel nearest to the station. I found that in the restaurant where the manager was seated in a secluded corner booth, sipping away on his expensive scotch. I made my way toward him, and my tall presence in his space instantly caught his attention.

"Mr. Sheppard, I was expecting you. Such a pleasure to meet you in person finally," Mr. Andrews said, standing to greet me with a handshake.

"Likewise, Mr. Andrews," I responded, taking a seat opposite him.

"What will you take, Specialist?" Mr. Andrews asked.

"The surveillance footage of April 3rd," I answered, to which the manager laughed.

"I was told you don't waste time." He said, "Fair enough! That's where we'll head then." He gulped down the beverage remaining in his glass and stood up. "Come this way, please!"

I took the cue and followed him as he led the way. Through the narrow corridors, we made our way to a room somewhere in the deserted corners of the hotel, where despite the silence and seclusion, the loud sound of beeping of servers was manic and deafening. We made our way inside the surveillance room, where a man was snoozing over the console, and another one was clicking on the monitors, sitting guard to the various hallways and street entrance.

"Mr. Andrews, what brings you down here?" The man who was awake stood up to greet Mr. Andrews.

"This man is with me. He is part of a special force," Mr. Andrews introduced me. "He wants to see the footage of..." He turned to me and raised his eyebrow.

"April 3rd," I finished for him.

"Yes! That one. So, I'm leaving him in your hands. Assist him however he likes," Mr. Andrews said, and the employee nodded at the order. When Mr. Andrews left, the man sat on his chair again and looked up at me.

"Which area are you looking for?"

"Main entrance," I said. "My man never made it inside. He does not have any history of checking in here," I explained.

The man nodded and turned to his screen. He searched his database for the date I had mentioned and clicked on the video. The window was long. Twenty-four hours to be exact. I advised the man to fast forward as I took a seat next to him and carefully focused on the screen.

The video featured nothing but many people coming in and going out of the hotel. Bellhops were taking in the luggage or putting them away in the trunk. There was some occasional sleeping spotted on the job of the front doorman, who would look around at the deserted street to make sure nobody was witnessing the scene, sit down, and shut his eyes. I almost laughed at the antics. Other than that, the video had nothing. A few minutes in, and I was already yawning.

"Wait! Pause it," I exclaimed suddenly as I noticed something. I looked at the time stamp on the screen and noticed that there was a clear jump cut in it. "Rewind," I said.

The man listened to me and did what I asked. Sure enough, around the time when the guard had decided to take a nap, there was an hour or so cut after that.

"9:00 pm There's no video after that until 10:30 pm. Were the cameras shut during that time?"

"No, sir!" The man shook his head, shocked at what he was finding out. "I am not sure where the footage is."

"Were you on duty that day?" I asked him.

"Unfortunately, no! I had a morning shift that day," the man explained. "It was prescheduled," he added.

I could tell that he was afraid I was going to suspect his involvement in this. "Who else has access to the surveillance room?" I further inquired.

"Just me and him," he said, pointing out at the snoozing man. "But we don't have the key to erasing data. You may ask Mr. Andrews about that. None of us has the key to make changes in the stored surveillance data," the man defended himself.

I nodded, feeling defeated. In due time, I would look into the matter of who erased the footage. For now, my priority was finding an alternative way where I might find the video of that time. Perhaps there was a camera on the street that might have caught it. I silently hoped as I bid goodbye to the man on the surveillance monitors and walked out of the room. I would walk on the street, get some fresh air, find some clues, search for a camera somewhere, anything really, or maybe just the cold breeze might help me reboot my system and think more clearly. I forged a plan in my head as I walked out of the hotel.

As if my lucky stars were conspiring to aid me, the second I stepped out of the hotel, I spotted a shop across the street, and sure enough, there was a camera that seemed to be facing the entrance of the hotel.

"Bingo!" I smiled. "Things just got interesting."

"Fine evening, brother!" The tall African-American man, standing behind a desk, greeted me as I entered the store, which possibly had access to the footage that the fortunate camera outside must have caught.

The ding of the bell that chimed in as I opened the door still lulled in the silence. I nodded my greetings and proceeded on the critical subject at hand. "Good sir, where do you keep your data of that CCTV camera situated right at your main entrance?" I asked.

The man raised an eyebrow and answered me. "We have a surveillance room at the back," he said, pointing behind him.

Perhaps it was my immaculate dressing that presented me as an agent, despite not being one anymore. "That's perfect!" I smiled. "You mind showing me to it? I'm looking for one particular day's data."

The man opened his mouth to refuse my request, but I produced my ID card before that. Michelson had been generous enough to conjure up a temporary one that would aid me in my endeavors in this case.

"Oh, you're an officer of the force. You should have just said so, my man," the cashier said, smiling, and gestured me to the back of the store.

The lights in the room were fairly dim. The setup of this room was unlike the one in the hotel. It was small and cramped. There were two computer screens, operated by one employee, who was sipping on his night's coffee. He leaned back in his chair, unbothered by the screen. It made sense to me now that even if there had been a kidnapping caught by those cameras, it could have easily been ignored, given the state of attention the employee was paying to the screens.

"Neal, what's up, bro?" The short, petite guy got up as we entered the room.

The man from the front desk, who was supposedly named Neal, explained why we were there and then turned to me. "Just state the date and time to him. He'll retrieve the data for you," he said, patted my back, and left. He couldn't leave the store unattended.

"April 3rd," I said without wasting time. "Between 9 pm to 11 pm," I added.

The short guy nodded, clicked a few buttons, and pulled up a screen that showed the hotel's front entrance as clear as day or at least as clear as the poor quality of CCTV recording allowed.

I took a seat next to him and directed my whole focus on the screen.

"Just a bunch of snooty riches going in and out." The guy interrupted, "You looking for someone specific?"

"Not quite!" I answered, without taking my eyes off the screen. "I have intel that there was some criminal activity around this time that day. Looking to catch the culprits in the act, so I may have a lead."

"Neat," the guy muttered, uninterested at this point. He picked up his coffee mug and went back to his unfazed stance.

"Pause!" I suddenly yelled after many minutes into the video.

The guy was startled but listened to what I had asked. I smiled when Aaron Cohen appeared on the screen. Someone else who knew what was about to happen now as I did would think I was a sadist at smiling at the prospect. I got that praise many times from people.

"You take pleasure in sorrows, my friend." They would say. "It's scary how happy you are at the prospect of evil, just so you could cleanse it away through your good."

I never minded such remarks. It was rather odd how my conscious mind always took them as high regard for my expertise.

"Woah, woah, woah!" The guy screamed. "They just abducted that man." The guy exclaimed when the footage suddenly turned into an action movie, with Cohen being taken by three tall men.

"Rewind," I ordered, ignoring his exasperation. He did as I told him, and I grinned. "Bingo!" I exclaimed.

The video played to reveal three tall, heavy, and well-built men, taking hold of Aaron Cohen a few steps away from the hotel's entrance. There was a guard at the door, but the video revealed that the deed was done out of the way of his sight. The men did it discreetly. One of them placed a hand over Aaron's mouth, which instantly made him limp and grew unconscious. The other two held him from either side, and then they dragged him out of there. I assumed there must be a car ready for them somewhere near the hotel, but it couldn't be seen in the video.

"Rewind," I ordered again. This time around, I asked him to zoom in on the scene. When the screen provided me with a better scene, I was able to spot that one of the assailants had a visible half-sleeve tattoo. "Zoom in on his arm," I ordered the guy, and he did. "Woah!" I gasped. "This is wild."

"What?" The guy was intrigued.

"Does not concern you." I said, "Here, give me a copy of this, will you?" I handed him my USB.

Although the guy looked visibly annoyed, he abided by what I asked of him. I grabbed my USB and left the surveillance room.

"Got what you're looking for?" Neal asked as I walked out.

I went to him and shook his hand. "Thank you for your help, my man! Here..." I said, pulling out a crisp bill and slid across the desk. "For all your troubles."

"No need, brother!" Neal said, but he picked up the bill and put it away in his jeans pocket.

"But kids gotta eat." I smiled and bid my goodbye as I left.

My mind went back to the tattoo I had spotted on the assailant's arm as I walked out of the store to my hotel. I remembered the first time I had seen it. It was the night of a celebration. I had solved yet another unsolvable case when my protégé, Dave, came up to me.

"Specialist, an amazing solve." He praised.

I raised my glass at him and nodded. "What do you have there?" I asked as I saw him with some files.

He extended them toward me, opening one of them to a picture of a tall, ginger man. He wore a hoodie with rolled-up sleeves, and instantly, something that was the most eye-catching, his unique tattoo caught my attention.

"Cool ink," I said. "Is it like a cult symbol or something? Looks like it."

"I believe so as well," Dave said. "I tried digging up on it, but I met many dead ends. All I know is that it's a Russian thing."

"And you want me to dig deeper?" I asked, smiling.

"You're the master gravedigger, aren't you?"

I remember I had laughed back then at the comment, but I had dug, and I dug deep. My extensive research eventually led me to a conclusion. The tattoo of a star with many points belonged to a Russian mafia called 'The Bratva.' Although my interest in that case of Dave was cut short when more pressing matters came about, my research had concluded that the Bratva mafia was extensive, deeply networked, and had its roots set all around the world.

Now, looking at the same pointed star-like tattoo instantly flashed that memory back at me, and my agent mind danced at the prospect and possibilities that lay ahead for this case. I went to my hotel room, made sure I had privacy and pulled out my phone.

"Specialist, here I thought we might not speak again." Came an annoyed woman's voice from the other end.

"Daphne! It's good to hear your voice again. How are you?" I asked with a smirk.

"Sleeping!" Daphne responded in annoyance.

"Ahh! Perfect time. You're your most pleasant self when in slumber." I mocked.

"What do you want?"

"Are we still angry about Africa?" I just had to bring it up. It was fun to irritate her.

"You shot me, you old man." Daphne spat. "I couldn't even lift my arm for six months."

Daphne, who worked with the force as an undercover agent, finding intel on the detectives' cases, was once accompanying me to Africa for a case. She was sent in to gather information as an escort. She was meant to seduce our prime suspects and retrieve some intel. As always, she had managed to do her job right. However, during the showdown, I had shot her in the arm by mistake, which haunted me to this day, for I was famous for being an amazing shot. She never forgave me for that. Our relationship stirred to a fun, banter type from that point onward. She would say she hated me but never faltered in helping me.

"Let me make it up to you by giving you an intriguing task." I joked and could practically see her signature eye-roll through the phone.

"Just tell me so I can get it over with."

I smiled. "That's the Daphne I know. I am sending some footage over to you. Go through it and tell me all you know about The Bratva Russian mafia."

"Why do you need this?"

"It's for research. Call me curious," I replied, teasing her. "Besides, last I heard, you were pretty close with the Bratva, weren't you?"

"Save the compliments, Specialist. Flattery shall do you no good."

I laughed. "Fair enough, I'm currently in Atlanta, so do me a solid and find me places here that Bratoks or Shestoyorkas frequent."

"Well, unlike you, I'm already aquatinted with that information, old friend," Daphne said proudly. "There are many places in Atlanta that the Russians like visiting. But you know how these places are... exclusive to Russians. And last time I checked, you ain't one."

"There must be someplace, Daffy," I insisted. "There has to be someplace in Atlanta where outsiders are allowed to walk in, have a little drink, chat perhaps."

"You sound desperate." I could finally hear a smile in Daphne's smile. Oh, how this woman liked my misery. "Kamchatka, Atlanta Chapter... that's a Russian bar from Moscow that you can find here. Non-Russians are allowed in. You can go in, grab a couple of drinks if you like, and talk to some Russians about your little research project if you must."

"That is great!" I smiled. "Thank..."

"Good night!" She said, and hung up before I could even mouth my gratitude to her.

I sighed. It didn't matter. I had the intel I was looking for, and there was no time to waste. "The Specialist is nothing if not proactive." Those who knew me would say, and I intended to uphold my reputation.

I immediately made my way to the lobby and asked for Ed from the front desk. Ed was the driver who drove me here. Mr. Andrews had told me that he would be my driver during my stay here in Atlanta. The receptionist told me he was right outside after giving him a call. I thanked him and walked out of the hotel. By the front entrance, a beautiful red Ford Mustang Mach E was parked, with Ed standing, leaning against it, his hands folded, but his posture upright and alert.

"Good evening, Mr. Sheppard. Where are we headed?"

"Good evening, Ed, my ride changed," I said, and Ed smiled.

"The limo was a rental to bring you here. This is for use alone until you are here." He clarified.

I nodded and sat inside without further questioning. Never big on the electric rides, I refrained from commenting on it. "Are you aware of Kamchatka?" I asked Ed the second he took hold of the steering wheel.

"The Atlanta Chapter, yes, I've seen the place. It's the site of many Russian mob activities, I've heard."

I nodded. "That's what I'm looking for. I'm about to listen to a Podcast. Tell me when we're there." I put on my Bluetooth and turned up to The Privacy, Security, and the OSINT Show with Michael Bazzell. I liked this one because of how closely it related to my field of work. It was fun to listen to the various ways of online spying and how things were changing with the altering times.

"Mr. Sheppard, we're here." The audio had got to an intriguing point when I heard Ed's voice announce.

I put away my Bluetooth headphones and thanked him for driving me there as I stepped out of the car. Instantly, I was taken in by the rustic, vintage Victorian style of the bar from the outside. A tall iron gate with grill separations that allowed the view of the inside welcomed me in. Stepping in, I was greeted by loud decor… neon lights displaying the bar's name and heavy furniture with bamboo style tabletops and carved wooded stools. The bar itself offered a variety of drinks, all shelved on a grand placement of rowdy cases, decorated in dim yet shimmering lights. Overall, the place was given a dark theme, with a very small number of people scattered around. It made sense why it was a hot spot for many Russian mafia lords to meet and chat.

I took my seat in one of the booths instead of at the bar and looked around the intimate space. A young couple was sitting at one of the booths adjacent to me. I could hear them faintly speaking in Russian. While I couldn't understand them, I could tell they must be words of endearment from the giddy smile on the girl's face and a passionate sparkle in the boy's eyes. Three men were seated on the bar stools, one of them drinking away his sorrows, one eyeing a lonely girl sitting one stool away from him, and one of them singing his woes to the bartender in a very movie-like fashion. My attention, however, was caught by a man sitting alone at another booth. He had a large pint of beer on his table and two empty glasses, indicating he had been here for a while.

"You'd find a man there. My research reveals he frequents there a lot and has connections in Bratva. He would probably have the same tattoo on his arm. All of the higher-ups in the mafia do."

I remembered Daphne's words. After she hung up, she had sent me a voice note to share some more information with me. She had sounded just as annoyed on the audio, and I had merely smiled, thanking her for cooperation. Sitting there, I tried to look for the tattoo on the guy's arm. Even though it was dark, I spotted some ink peeking out of his long-sleeved Henley. But I needed to be sure before I approached him with my questions. So I decided to go to the bar and ask around the well-informed bartender.

"Good evening, sir! What can I get you?" The bartender greeted me in a chirpy tone as he shook and mixed a drink in his hands.

I took a seat on the tall barstool and smiled at him. "I'm unaware of your Russian drinks, my mate! Get your best beer," I said.

"Coming right up!" The bartender said and turned around as he got busy with my drink.

I took that as my opportunity to ask my questions. I had heard and experienced myself that bartenders often shared the most intricate of details when they were in their element, shaking drinks, and whatnot. I propped my elbows on the counter and leaned forward. I cleared my throat, "Say, Teado..." I said, reading his name tag. "You get a lot of Russians here?"

"It's a Russian bar, is it not?" The bartender said, "We get all kinds of characters here."

"I see. Care to give me one, for instance?"

"Like that big guy over there..." Teado pointed in the direction of the same man I was eyeing earlier.

I turned around to look at the tall, heavy man, with sleeve tatts, bald head, and dark shades on even when he was indoors.

"This unfriendly blob happens to be part of a mafia, or so we've heard. He just does not talk to people. He comes in, drinks in silence, and leaves." The bartender chuckled. "It's rather fun, actually. We usually have a pool going on about him every single day. See who he gets mad at that night. He always finds one person or another to be angry at. Here you go!" He ended his explanation, sliding my beer across the counter to me.

I took my beer in my hands and stood up. A plan was quickly formulated in my head. I knew that he would not share details with me, but perhaps if he thought I was part of his group, he might. And so, the next couple of hours were spent bonding with the man. I shared my stories on the force, twisting it and making it sound like I was on the opposite side—the same as he was. I slowly relaxed into the conversation and made him feel he could trust me. At last, I pulled out my USB and laptop from my bag and propped up the clip.

"My family is looking for this guy... long unresolved issues and whatnot. Say, have you seen this man? The one with the tattoo. I can't let them take away my guy. He's mine to kill. I get to choose his sufferings."

"Oh, man!" The tall guy, who was named Yaroslav, gasped after carefully examining the footage. "I would stray clear of him." He said, turning the laptop screen back toward me.

"I have my network, my man! I ain't scared of anybody," I said, trying to match his tone.

The man stared me down for a while before he sighed. "He's a renowned Obshchak in the Bratva. I don't know what you intend to accomplish, but let me clarify, your network, be it anything, I'm sure his deep-rooted one triumphs it."

"Let me be the one to decide that," I said, standing up, prepared to take my leave. "If you could just tell me where I could find him?"

"New York!" The guy answered, with no hesitation this time.

I nodded a quick thank you at him as I turned around to leave. "I don't possess a care in the world for you, my man!" Before I could leave, the man halted me with his words. I turned around, and he was smiling at him.

"All that I shared with you, I did so because I might just do a happy dance if the Bratva folks kill you in cold blood. That is high."

I pressed a forced smile and walked out of the bar. It was quite late now, which was why I had sent Ed away sometime during the night. Although he had insisted on staying, I warned him not to argue and asked him to leave and go sleep. I quickly called an

Uber, who asked me to come to a street at the back of the bar. Good! Perhaps I could use the walk to formulate a plan for New York and how I'd track down the Obshchak. Steady steps ahead, I felt a shadow lurking behind me, but I found nobody when I turned around. Throughout my way to Uber, the feeling of someone following me continued to linger in the dead silence of the night surrounding me and didn't even leave when I sat in the car to drive back to the hotel. I shook my head. Whoever it was sure had a death wish. I would have to see to it that it was fulfilled.

Chapter 3

He flipped through his notes, quite the material he had gathered. The bosses shall be proud; he thought to himself as he made his way to the casino they had asked him to meet them at. The place was crowded. There was a dull light surrounding the gambling area of the small space. While all the tables were occupied by serious players, rowdy men groping half-naked girls and drizzling alcohol flying around, there was one table in a secluded corner, which was home to five well-suited men, drinking away in silence, with a card game laid out in front of them that hardly any of them was playing. Hushed conversations could be heard from the corner, which seemed restricted to any outsider.

The man, holding a file in his hands, made his way to the corner table. He cleared his throat to catch the attention of the five men. The one in the center looked him dead in the eyes. He wore a fitted three-piece suit. His head was covered with a top hat, and he additionally had dark black specs on, which left little to no find of his face. The small part that was exposed held a stubble, making it impossible to read his features. His signature jewelry, a gold watch, a thick gold chain, and one shining silver earring proudly sported that he was angry and debonair. The man reeked of mystery, embedded with darkness laid deep within.

"Ahh! My trusted spy on The Specialist! Make me happy, my man. Tell me what you have on The Specialist?" The boss asked him.

He gulped and slid the file across the table toward him. "As you suspected, Sir, The Specialist is working on Aaron Cohen's case."

The boss nodded and opened the file to read the notes that his trusted spy had made on the whereabouts and activities of The Specialist. "New York, huh!"

"He's off to find the Obshchak," the spy added.

"I see!" The boss passed a sinister smile. "You know what you have to do."

The spy nodded, "Always, sir! The Specialist would not see it coming."

"He better not." The boss reminded him. "The Specialist never takes lightly to the spies."

"I am aware," the spy answered. A hint of fear residing his features but all too subtle to come to the notice of the boss. "Trust me; he shall not see it coming."

***

The tall buildings, skyscrapers, and city lights greeted me as we entered the vicinity of the great New York City. The city that never slept was still as crowded and filled with chaos at the late nightly hour as it was on the busiest working hours. It was a long 14-hour drive, and I had driven here with Ed almost without a stop, other than the few for filling gas, using the restroom, or grabbing something to eat. I could have taken a flight; all my expenses were paid for. However, I always liked the thrill of being on the road more than flying across the ocean. On the road, I didn't know what enemy I'd encounter, who would be following me, or who was on my tail with my death wish on their palms. This was the thrill I had craved since I left the force, and I never let go of a chance to get a small taste of it again. Additionally, Ed had insisted on coming along. To accommodate him, I had thought that it was best to drive to New York.

"We're here, Sir!" Ed announced as the car stopped in front of the Four Squares hotel and the grand building's entrance welcomed me.

"You have a room here, Ed?" I asked as I stepped out of the car.

"Yes, Mr. Sheppard, Mr. Michelson has made arrangements for me as well," he responded.

I nodded. "Very well, then. Let's regroup in the morning and leave for our daily adventure."

Ed smiled at me. "I am waiting with bated breath, Sir."

"Pleasant night, Ed," I said, bidding goodbye to him as I made my way to the reception. I had been here many times, so I didn't stop to take in the view. Although a few things had changed in the main lobby, such as the addition of an indoor fountain, there weren't many changes from the last time I was here for a case. Ahhh! What a difficult solve that had been! I relished in the memory of the glory days as I entered the elevator to head up to my room. The night's slumber might not make an appearance, but a peaceful rest should have to take over my body, for I needed my energies rejuvenated for tomorrow. The Obshchak awaited.

The crack of dawn soon arrived, and with it, my morning alarm chimed in – a call from Michelson, who wished to get up to speed regarding the last couple of days' events.

"Your judgment has to be right. I believe it."

Michelson said, showing full faith in me when I told him about my hunch. "It was a pretty painting. It had such a magical symbolism that it instantly grabbed my attention. It is almost like it belongs to a group, a class, or even an ancient clan. It's what lured me in. Although not sure entirely, I have reasons to think that the art hails from the wilderness of the mythical lands of Riverrains," I said.

Michelson refrained from asking further questions. He had understood all of my codes and didn't find the need to inquire about the meanings. For someone from the force himself, he was aware of the regularly used terminologies. While many online calls were encrypted, I was working against the powerful forces of Russia and couldn't risk getting the frequencies of my calls tapped. The code words would have to do for now for all the calls I made.

"I wish you all the luck. I have no doubt you shall be able to procure the desired painting from Riverrains." Michelson said.

I nodded. The call was disconnected when I heard a knock on the door. I got up to answer, pulling out my gun from the nightstand. A habit you pick being in the force; never open the door unarmed when on a mission. With the gun tucked away behind my back, I opened the door to find room service wheeling in my breakfast. Ahh! Michelson had really thought of everything. I tipped the waiter as he walked out, and I shut the door behind him. I decided to do some research while I ate my breakfast. Ed was required to pick me up to take me to the place where, as per my intel, the Obshchak frequented when in New York. Few clicks here and there, suddenly I landed on something that stood out to me instantly.

"Wait a sec..." I muttered to myself. "This girl, she's Aaron's daughter?" I looked at the picture on one of Aaron's social media friend's pages.

Apparently, the person who had uploaded the photo was Aaron's daughter's friend. The picture was taken on a golf course, which looked to be a post-victory photo-op. *"Beat your dad at golf... Sorry, Cohen."* The caption read and below was a comment by none other than Aaron, stating that he'd redeem himself in the next match.

The strange victory of a young girl against a seasoned player was not the most astonishing part of the said post. No! What had caught me off-guard was that the description of the girl I had theorized to be involved in the kidnapping of Aaron Cohen matched exactly how his daughter looked like. In my pursuit to investigate the abduction of Aaron Cohen, I had met with a number of people, both in Atlanta and back home.

"It has to be an internal job," they would say. "See if you can find who knew where Aaron was off to." This didn't make my task any easier, for many were aware of Aaron's voyage, his co-workers, his daughter, and perhaps some friends as well. That one faithful day, I had visited a local coffee shop where Aaron was seen hanging around on a regular basis. The shop's owner knew Aaron quite well, for he was a regular at his business. Although it seemed that it was only on the surface because when asked some in-depth questions about Aaron, the owner could not answer them as he didn't possess the said personal knowledge.

"He often sits here alone on that table," the owner had pointed out to a corner where there was a secluded booth. "But when he is with a girl, they sit here," he said, gesturing at a center table.

"Who's that girl you talk of?" I asked curiously.

"I'm not sure, but she looks much younger than him. I have often seen the same girl with a few other men as well—tall, well-built, almost scary-looking men."

It was those lines of the coffee shop's owner that had hit me. I had immediately asked him to describe how the girl looked like, and he had voiced her sketch from memory. *She is a beautiful, petite-looking brunette with big, piercing brown eyes. She is white-skinned. Her lips are plumed, nose straight, and structured cheekbones. In context, I have noticed that she looks a lot like Aaron himself. A pretty man with a pretty girl.* Following that, I had inquired a few street vendors and other passers-by about the girl.

I asked if they had seen a girl matching the description around those quarters, and those who frequented the area or were residents backed my hunch. The girl was witnessed with strange men. Many labeled them as foreigners. Some even claimed that they were Russians. This solidified my belief that there had to be a girl involved in the kidnapping. Now, sitting here, looking at Aaron's daughter's picture matching the description of the woman I thought possibly aided in his abduction had me shocked to my core.

I sighed, plopping the last bite of my egg-whites in my mouth. Somewhere during my wandering thoughts, I had finished my breakfast. It was now time to head out. I gave my last look at Aaron's daughter before I shut down the laptop. It was a matter of another time. For now, I needed to focus on finding the Obshchak. Perhaps that shall open the case wide open, or at least, I hoped it would.

***

"Ed, pull over to the side of the curb," I asked Ed as I spotted a black SUV.

Daphne had shared with me some details of the vehicle that the Obshchak I was looking for drove -

tinted glass, a blank nameplate, and bright silver rims. While it felt like any other SUV around those areas, this one stood out because it was found in front of the same bar that Daphne had informed me about the Obshchak visiting regularly.

I stepped out of the car to examine the car more carefully—top-notch, scratch-less, and a beauty. I looked over to the solid iron gate behind the vehicle and found it closed.

"Sir, the bar does not open until 7 in the evening." Ed came behind me to inform, and I roughly turned toward him. "I am aware. It's open, though, just so you know."

"Pardon me?" Ed asked, confused.

"My friend, it's often dark places like these that do their dirty work when it's not open for business. Inside, there're tons of activities happening, and we're here to investigate."

I could see that Ed had some more questions, but a sudden commotion stopped him from voicing it. A man appeared out of the narrow alley, possibly coming out of the closed bar's backdoor. He was tall, muscular, and had the same Bratva tattoo proudly exposed through a sleeveless tank he wore. He additionally had sleeve tattoos, but his clan pride tattoo was more prominent than the others. He was white but had developed some tan lines under the sunlight. His eyes were piercing blue, with a strange touch of black residing within them. It was rather off to look at him.

"It's closed, fellas!" The tall Obshchak informed as he prepared to walk away, but I stopped him.

"Actually, we're here to talk to you," I said, and he stopped, turning around to look at me. Good! At least I had his attention. "You're Nikolai Balagula if I'm not wrong?"

"Yes!" The man responded. "Look, I'm running a little late, so why don't you give me your contact info, and I'll hopefully call ya later, okay?"

I shook my head, "No need. I just wanted to inquire about your Obshchak duties. That's all."

The man stared me down, and his blue eyes seemed to be piercing right through me. There was a hint of fear in them as if he was afraid of the title or someone knowing who he was. The next thing I knew, the man pushed me away and sprinted to his car, quickly getting in and driving away. All that was felt was a brisk wind as his car rushed past me.

"Ed, start the car. Hurry!" I ordered as I stabilized myself and got in.

His car was larger in size, so naturally, it required a bigger space on the road, which was why we were able to catch up to it, despite the obvious head start that he got. Only a few feet apart, Ed and I continued to follow the black SUV of the Obshchak. With sharp turns and loud speeding screeches, the crowded streets of the New York city displayed an epic battle of the chase as our car stayed in Nikolai's tail. Suddenly, our car crashed into a street vendor's cart while turning, who was selling hotdogs. I quickly got out to apologize to the poor vendor when another car halted in front of me.

"What in the world?" A Chinese man had stepped out of the car, shouting at the scene.

Ed had apparently hit the back of his car.

"I'm so sorry! Here..." I pulled out my card and handed it to the Chinese man and the hotdog vendor. "Please contact me to claim expenses for your damage, but I can't possibly stop right now. I'm chasing after someone who is possibly involved in the kidnapping of a known man, and most likely even worse crimes," I briefly explained and went back to my car.

"Hold on." I felt a hand on my shoulder. "Who's this man you speak of?"

"I don't have time for this."

"Then tell me quickly," the man seemed firm in his demand.

I sighed, "Aaron Cohen." I saw the man's expressions change suddenly as if he was trying to formulate a plan.

"Come on... I know a shortcut. We can corner him from the front," the Chinese man said as he got into his car, skidded around as the car made a loud sound, and went in the opposite direction.

Although puzzled by what had happened, I didn't question it as I was running on a thin time thread. I got into my own car and had Ed drive fast to chase after the SUV again. Sure enough, after a block or two, the Obshchak abruptly stopped with a screech as I saw the Chinese man's car on the other side. I exhaled in relief and got out of the car.

"You should not have made a run for it. I just wanted to talk," I said to the Obshchak as he stepped out of his car.

My eyes suddenly fell on the gun he was holding, and instinctively, I clutched onto my own in my suit's pocket. I saw the man smile, looking back and forth between the Chinese man and me.

"Don't worry; the bullet is not for you. It's for me."

"Wha..." I had barely said the word when the Obshchak held the gun over his head and shot himself. His brains blew out on the street, blood smeared everywhere, as his lifeless body fell on the road with a loud thud.

"Oh, fuck! He shot himself," the Chinese man exclaimed.

My mouth was hung open in shock. Although I had seen my fair share of suicides to avoid confrontations in all my years of service, this hit me quite hard. I was known in the field to have an amazing intuition. However, I didn't see this one coming. It took me a while to compose my senses, and then I bent down to check his pockets for some clues. Wallet, keys, phone... pretty ordinary stuff. In his left pocket, I found a piece of folded paper. When I opened it, it was revealed as a printout of a ticket— to Hong Kong, scheduled for the next morning.

"Ahh! The man was heading to Hong Kong," the Chinese man, who for whatever reason was still standing there, chimed in.

I nodded at him and turned around to make my exit when the man stopped me again.

"I am an agent myself. I want to land a hand to you in this case."

I stepped back. Looking at him, I smiled. "I really appreciate the offer, but I work best alone."

"Don't we all?" The man threw his hands in the air and smiled. "But, my friend, two heads are always better than one."

"Not for me!" I simply responded and turned away again, but his words halted me.

"I knew Aaron Cohen."

I stared him down to find a glimpse of a bluff in his eyes, but those deep brown eyes only displayed honesty. "How?" I asked him.

"He was my financier. He was a good man, or is a good man! I'm sorry for my use of was." The Chinese man looked seriously troubled at the thought of Aaron's past news. "Look, my point is, I have a personal stake here. I can be of help."

As my thoughts ran haywire, trying to decide whether I wanted his help or not, he extended his hand toward me, holding out his card.

"I'm Zhang. Trust me; you won't regret this."

I took his card, scratching my head. Zhang was a spy in a reputable intelligence agency with many years of service. He looked to be my age and was still on active duty. Although I had the necessary temporary identifications I'd need to get into and investigate anything; I could probably use the help of an actual active spy with me. I was still not sure if I could trust Zhang, but the benefits outweighed the costs in my head. Perhaps it would not hurt to involve him after all.

Chapter 4

"Monsieur Sheppard, how pleasing to hear from you." The cheerful voice of Captain Banville chimed in through my earpiece. "How may I be of your service, Ser?"

"Likewise, my man!" I replied. I briefly turned around to find Zhang engaged in a conversation with Ed at a near distance, leaning against my car. I shook the skeptical thoughts about the Chinese man out of my head. My priority was to get on the ship that was currently set to voyage to Hong Kong from New York. "Say, I hear your ship, The RMS Odyssey is docked at the New York port and is leaving shortly on a voyage to Hong Kong. Right?" I asked the captain—no time to waste.

"Yes, ami. You never falter... always the eloquent." Captain Banville praised.

"If you could, could you please grant me space for two passengers to board your prestigious liner? It's a rather critical matter that I need to deal with." I requested Banville.

"Oh, oui, Ser... but I can. You are always welcome aboard. Any time, Specialist." Captain Banville replied enthusiastically. "It'll be my honor, Monsieur, to host you."

"Ahh, yes! But you shall not inform anyone of my presence there. I wish for my stay to be as discreet as you can make it." I instantly clarified, and Captain Banville agreed.

Captain Banville and I had made many journeys together. Anytime I needed to gather intel for a case from many different countries, I would travel by his ship. This granted me not only long stays to work on the case but also an opportunity to sneak into many cities. I was fortunate that I caught one ship leaving for Hong Kong right on time. When he hung up, I walked back to where Ed and Zhang were standing. They stopped talking as I appeared.

"We're leaving now," I addressed Zhang. "We have a ship to catch."

"Ship? Aren't we in a hurry?" Zhang asked.

"We're not. We don't have a lead, and our ship's voyage shall grant us that. We'll be making a few stops along the way." I explained to him and turned to Ed. "Thank you, my friend, for all your help. I'm afraid I'll have to head on alone from here."

"It was my pleasure, Mr. Sheppard. I hope you find success in all your endeavors." Ed smiled.

I nodded at him, shook his hand, and bid him farewell. Zhang offered to take us to the port in his car, and I agreed. Soon enough, we were on the docks, faced with the tall luxury-liner called Odyssey. The title was proudly painted across her magnificent ceramic white body in glistening black color. The ship on the outside was a beautiful sight to behold. She was not as large as the likes of Titanic but was marvelous enough to stand tall like a queen, afloat on the mighty ocean.

"Are you aware that Odyssey means epic or adventurous journey?" Zhang halted my process of taking in the beauty of Odyssey with his sudden quip.

I turned to look at him. Judgment was evident on my face. "I've been around. I think I'm aware." I barely gave him my full attention before I turned to look at the ship again. "An epic journey. It has always been the same with you, dear old Odyssey." I said, smiling as I stepped ahead toward the wharf to get on board. Our adventures awaited us.

***

The sea breeze rasped through, gently caressing my face, and I felt an eerie calm settling within me. We had been cruising across the vast ocean for a couple of days, only making one stop since we left New York just about a week ago. I eyed the approaching port of Tel Aviv, Israel ahead, and the wheels in my brain started turning at full speed. One strategy formed and another discarded. I continued to formulate and rehearse a plan until a voice interrupted my intricate activity.

"Upon the deck again, I see. Thinking of life and whatnot." Zhang smirked at me, standing by my side but looking at the moving waves of the ocean.

"Perhaps you ranting to me about Chengdu once again bored me." I turned to look at him; seriousness displayed on my face, but with a subtle hint of a friendly snark. "A man has to find some peace."

"Oh, here?" Zhang gasped. "The damn waves are too loud for my liking. Come on; my mouth siren can't be as disturbing as the mighty sea."

"Preferences, my friend. What you find loud, I tend to take calm in. I have always taken calmly in chaos. Harmony disrupts me."

Zhang raised his eyebrow to look at me with a strange look before he focused on the waves again. "You're a strange man, Specialist. It'll take years to crack through the exterior and find your real soul."

I took in a sharp breath, letting the wind soothe my senses. "Many have tried. Nobody knows what lies within."

Zhang patted my back and smiled. "We got plenty of time left on the sea. Maybe the salty water shall aid me in this impossible quest."

I watched as Zhang walked away and an involuntary smile appeared on my face. For the past few days, we had collaborated on Aaron Cohen's case, as we each shared our experience with the man and on our respective fields. Our nights were often spent in my cabin, where we popped open a bottle of scotch as we dwelled in the intricacies of the case we were handling. Every time Zhang talked about his past, I listened carefully, observing his hand gestures and eye movements.

Every little word he uttered was decoded in my head intensely. I realized that I was looking for clues whereby I could prove that he had an ulterior motive in the case. Perhaps he was sent by my enemies to destroy me. However, the one observation I made most vividly was that while my brain scanned for clues, trying to prove his evil status, his expressions showed the very same. He was trying to analyze my words just as carefully, which showed that he didn't trust me either. I found that to be comforting. At least we were on the same page.

Despite the lack of trust we had in each other, I willingly let him work the case with me, for I figured that he could be of help since he knew Aaron better than I did. Under rocky circumstances, we had no choice but to be civil with one another. All the while, we continued to walk around as if there were eggshells placed near us. We were both careful in our approach with each other and made sure never to let our guard down.

I had heard from many of my colleagues back in the days, *"Sea turns enemies into friends."* They'd say. *"When you don't have an escape insight, for the vast spreads of water surrounds you, you're forced to co-exist with your traveling partner. Bonds are forged over nightly drinks, midst the residing fear of a possible storm, and the serenity of the majestic ocean. When you surface, you realize that you no longer possess the same loath for the other man. It's evaporated somewhere into the chilly sea breeze."*

The words today held great meaning for me, for I was slowly starting to see past my suspicions and beginning to like the short 5'6" Chinese man, who wore a hoodie over a dress shirt like it was his symbol.

His eyes, though, were a mirror to his ethnicity; the deep brown in them told a story of his past woes. Black-haired and white-skinned, the man was conventionally handsome. But what stroke me the most about him was how smart he was. He had his unique way of thinking. He was never too serious yet always figured things out rather quickly. He had certainly made my journey more entertaining, and while I continued to be vigilant around him, I was no longer completely opposed to the idea of him being my partner.

Far in the distance, I could see the sun rising slowly as the Tel Aviv port neared us. The ship, although had docked at other places, Zhang and I never left to explore. However, I had talked to one of my contacts in Mossad, who happened to have some useful intel about our case. Fortunately for me, the vessel was already scheduled to dock in Tel Aviv for some time, where my contact resided. That granted me an opportunity to meet with him and discuss the case. Surely, he must have been in possession of useful information, given that he was a member of the Mossad. The ship closed in on the shore, and I made my way to Zhang's cabin, who I was sure must have gone back to bed. I knocked on the door, and a sleepy Zhang opened it.

"It's dawn, my sleep time." Zhang scrunched up his nose in annoyance.

I rolled my eyes. "We're docked in Tel Aviv for just one day. No time to waste. Get changed. We're heading out." I explained and walked away to change as Zhang's arguing voice followed me until it was out of my earshot.

I quickly changed into a fresh three-piece suit—encrusted with self-print lines, dark blue in color, with a crisp white shirt. I headed to the exit, where the ship was docked at the wharf. Many passengers were coming in and going out. Those who could enter the city were dressed in fancy clothes, wearing excited smiles on their faces, and heading out to explore the city for a day. I found Zhang standing there in a corner, sleep evident in his eyes, and annoyance in his features. I ignored his disapproving stance and walked out of the ship onto the wharf to enter the city of Tel Aviv.

"At least tell me what are we doing here?" Zhang came up behind me and asked.

"We're meeting someone I knew back in the day. An agent with the Mossad. He has some intel," I explained as we walked out of the port, and I quickly hailed a cab over.

"Wait, we're not heading to a hotel or something to freshen up?"

I raised my eyebrow at him. "We're quite literally coming from our temporary home. What more freshening up do you require?"

Zhang sighed. "Fine! Let's go talk to this man."

Right then, the cab stopped, and I gave the driver a slip on which the address was written just as we got in. The driver took a glance at it, nodded at me, and drove off. In a matter of half an hour, given the lack of traffic on the road at that time of the day, we reached a historic looking building. Immediately, I recognized the place. It was a bar called Bar-a-Vin, located at the intersection of Rothschild Boulevard and Herzl Street, one of the first sites you see when entering the city of Tel Aviv.

"The wine they serve here just dances around your tongue, and the French history so deeply embodying it's walls just puts you in the olden, calm Parisian mood. One could talk here. The music is soothing, not too loud that you need to yell out your words."

I remembered my old pal, Alexender Abramczyk, who we were meeting today, used to say this about the bar. I had only ever gotten a chance to visit the place a few times over the years, and I knew instantly after the first time that he was right. I looked over at Zhang, who stood beside me, taking in his scene. I gestured for him to follow along, and he started walking by my side as we entered the bar.

Like always, the bar was not crowded. Dim lights and candles lit at places. It gave a scenic and calming ambiance to the place. Slow melodious songs, playing in the background, were adding to the warmth and peace in the air. I spotted Alex in a corner booth, with a glass of Chardonnay in his hands, sipping in silence, as he flipped through the pages of a book he was currently quite engrossed in. I could see from a distance that the tall, muscular man had not aged a day in the time I had last seen him. Other than the full beard that he had grown now, he was the same. Dark brown hair, hazel eyes, fair skin that had gone a golden shade of tan in the sun, and same intimidating persona.

I gestured for Zhang to follow me as we made our way toward Alex, who put his book aside and stood to greet us when we came in his view.

"Ahh, The Specialist! It's been long." Alex greeted me with a big smile, shaking my hand. "Take a seat; we have lots to discuss."

As we sat down, Alex asked us what we'd like to drink and ordered that for us. He looked over at Zhang with a questioning look, and I shook my head.

"It's fine. He's with me. We can trust him," I said, even surprising myself at the words.

After catching up on things we had missed, I soon turned our conversation to the subject at hand - Aaron Cohen's mysterious abduction.

"Things aren't so simple. It goes deeper than the kidnapping of Aaron Cohen," Alex said, propping his elbows on the table and leaning forward to look at me. "I hear many whispers around the streets. They might be rumors or nothing at all. They might just be what you call Chinese whispers, no offense," he said, turning to Zhang, who merely shook his head, gesturing for him to continue. "But, my friends, there's never smoke without fire."

"What kind of rumors?" I asked curiously.

"There are some agents of the forces or former agents of big reputable agencies. My contacts informed me that many notable names from intelligence services have gone rogue." Alex paused to take a sip from his drink and sighed. "I hear they are forming their secret intelligence society."

"What for?" Zhang chimed in. "Could they not have done their dirty work from within? Sounds more effective that way."

"One would think so, yes!" Alex said, "But it's always easier to hide in the dungeons to commit a crime than to do it right under the prying eyes."

"This agency you speak of, all of it can't be for just one man," I interjected. "I realize that with such a prominent post at the JPI Securities, Aaron was important, but to form agencies, with rogue members of notable forces joining in, it all sounds too extravagant for one man."

"You are right," Alex said, leaning back on the couch. "It's not just for Aaron. Something much bigger is at play here. His kidnapping is also a part of that extensive game."

"Care to venture on that?" I requested. While I enjoyed riddles and solving puzzles, I was impatient today. I needed vivid answers and fast.

Alex sighed. "I wish I had all the information for you, but as I said, they are rumors at this point. Of course, I'll dig deeper into this secret Intelligence Society that the rogue agents have formed." He gave me a warm smile. "You'd be the first to be in that loop, Specialist."

I nodded, knowing that it was premature to expect full intel at this point. "Those notable men you spoke of," I started. "Could you name a few for me?"

Suddenly, I saw Alex's eyes change a shade, turning into sympathy as he looked at me intently. It was as if the topic held information that could hurt me. I remained calm as I waited for him to answer me.

Alex came forward, leaning on the table, and neared his head toward me again. "Many names came up, Sheppard, but one stood out to me. It shall to you as well. One name, whose involvement in the newly forged Intelligence Society's hierarchy had me seething. Perhaps it might rage you even more."

"Who's that?" I asked, getting impatient now.

"Dimitri Yahontov."

As the words escaped Alex's mouth, the world around me seized to exist momentarily. The still scene surrounding me went numb, and the music in the background faded away into unknown oblivion. The name lingered in the air as a sharp reminder of what the said man had done.

"It's not the adventures in the force that will kill you, no! You'll survive the wounds. You'll live past the gunshots, the injuries, and even the handicaps you may encounter. It is the troubled past that cripples you beyond standing. It is the hard and painful memories that break you beyond repair. It is the reminder of what's gone that destroys you beyond mending."

I remembered what my father used to say. He was right. Never had there been an injury that I endured during the service that had shaken me to my core to a tragic extent. However, some memories of what I had lost had managed to inflict so much damage to me that I still reeled from the aftermath. They broke me; they destroyed me. They even crippled me for a long while. The name of Dimitri Yahontov was one such memory that brought about a fresh set of sorrows for me.

"Who's Dimitri?" Zhang finally asked, confused.

"The man who killed my father so mercilessly," I said without thinking. The words just blurted out of me, despite my careful stance of putting my personal life under wraps.

"Woah, man! I'm so sorry!" Zhang said sympathetically.

No! I didn't want that. I never wanted sympathy. I decided to change the subject. "Are you sure about his involvement?" I asked Alex.

"Nothing is for sure as of yet, Sheppard. However, my men are looking into it. I'll inform you as soon as I get more intel."

I nodded. "Very well. Tell me, do you know anything about this man?" I said, sliding the ID card across the table toward Alex, of the Obshchak that I retrieved out of his pocket back in New York after he had killed himself.

Alex carefully examined the picture on the card before he spoke up, "He's the Obshchak in the Bratva. This is what I wanted to discuss with you."

"Pardon me?" I was confused.

"This man, a high-ranking over-lord in the Russian mafia..."

"I know who he is... or was!" I interrupted Alex. "I was given his information by someone in Atlanta.

I sought him out in New York, but before I could get anything out of him, he killed himself."

"Of course, he did," Alex didn't sound surprised. "He was heading for Hong Kong, right?"

"Yes!" I nodded. "How do you know that?"

"Because there's a very extensive network of Russians at play in Hong Kong, the information of which he could not share with you. That is why he shot himself," Alex said, looking at me intently. "The matter is that serious, Specialist. Many superior Bratva members meet there every few months. It is their hub; Cybercrimes, stealing through deeply encrypted channels, manipulating with the security systems to gain access to critical intelligence information. Anything that is done, it's almost always done from Hong Kong. In fact, I heard that."

"Good afternoon, messieurs! Are we all happy here, or do you require something?"

A waitress, dressed in the usual white dress shirt and black pencil skirt uniform, interrupted Alex with her forced, enthusiastic greeting. I formed my best fake smile and looked at her.

"No, thank you. Just some privacy shall do."

"Oui, Ser! Je suis désolé. Merci!"

For whatever reason, the woman spoke in full French and walked away, smiling at us. I knew enough French to know it was not an insult. I focused my attention back on Alex and asked him to continue.

"There is a secret meeting with the triad taking place in Hong Kong in a few days. Or at least that's what my sources tell me." Alex finished his sentence.

Perfect! I thought to myself. We were set to reach Hong Kong in a matter of days, hopefully, right in time when this secret meeting was supposedly scheduled. I was sure that this would grant me great clues, which would aid me in solving the case. I stood up, gulping down my drink, and slamming the glass on the table.

"Thank you for hosting us, Alex!" I said, extending my hand to shake his. I pulled a few dollars from my wallet and put them on the table. "For the waitress. I might have been rude," I said as Alex stood up to bid me goodbye.

Our ship would leave the docks in a couple of hours. I had a few more places to go before we left, so I bid my farewell to Alex and walked out of the bar. In a matter of a few hours, I was done with the shopping I intended to do, and we were boarding the ship again. The next time I shall walk the wharf, I would be setting foot in Hong Kong. I rejoiced at the exciting prospect as we made our way in the vessel.

***

"With the distance, who knew the Russian mafia would be operating primarily from there, eh?" Zhang asked, leaning back on the deck chair he was seated on, taking a sip from his glass of scotch.

I inhaled the fresh air and closed my eyes. After coming back to the ship, Zhang and I had slept. This was why we found ourselves wide awake when the sky turned dark, and the ship went silent. I marched to the upper deck to let the sea breeze soothe my tensed nerves, and shortly after, Zhang followed, with a bottle of scotch and two glasses in his hands. We sat down on the wooden deck chairs as we drank in silence, occasionally exchanging a few words. It was the first time in years that I had felt myself relax and take it easy.

"That's the thing about being on the force. You discover such interesting things." I responded, sighing. "I miss that rush."

"What's your story, Specialist?"

The sudden words startled me as I looked to my side. "Pardon me?"

"You don't look old enough to be retired. Must you not still be working actively? In the force?" Zhang sounded curious.

I turned around and looked up at the sky. The night was dark, and the sky was covered with thick spreads of clouds. One couldn't find any star twinkling their bright light down on us. I inhaled in a sharp breath. "Sometimes, you're made to do things that you don't want to do. Retiring from active duty was one of them."

"But why? As far as I've gathered, you're an outstanding agent. I don't see why you were made to retire so early in your career."

His question was valid. I would have wondered the same thing. I sat up straight at his questioning words, took a mouthful of scotch, as I needed some alcohol in my system to find the strength to answer to Zhang, placed the glass down on the wooden floor, and focused my attention on him. I cleared my throat before I started.

"Long ago, I was working on a case that required investigating an extensive network of a secret terrorist organization. We had intel about the group targeting crucial intelligence information in Germany that could cause mass destruction. The case was hard, the nights were long, and the days were stormy. Back then, my way of working was lethal. I often went in and bang bang bang, killed it all inside." I paused briefly as I looked at Zhang, who was so deeply engrossed in my story. It was strange how I enjoyed reminiscing about my past, even if it was painful to do so. Taking in another sip from my glass, I began again. "One day, I was requested by one of the higher-ups in the organization to meet with him at his headquarters. Truth be told, I had agreed to the meeting only because I went in with the idea of killing him. It is like, plan for a hunt of a lion in its absence. Chances are, it'll devour you before you could even think of your well-formulated plan. That was what I believed in."

"You're a lot like me," Zhang said, raising his glass in my direction.

I nodded in acknowledgment and continued, "However, when I got there, the man proposed a deal. He asked me to back out in exchange for him sparing my life. He assured me that he could kill me in the blink of an eye, so I should better listen to him. Naturally, I said no! It wasn't the first time that a powerful member of a dangerous organization had threatened me with my or my loved ones' life. I was used to it. But, he then proceeded to show me a video, and with that, my world changed."

"What was in the video?" Zhang asked me.

"My boss and the member of the terrorist organization, chatting over a game of poker like two best buds."

"What?" Zhang was shocked. "A superior in the force was his friend?"

"The superior most, yes!" I sighed. "I had heard of corrupt officers in the police, army men, and even agents in security and intelligence agencies before, but it still gutted me to see one man who I respected so much turned out to be the bad guy."

"What happened then?" Zhang was impatient.

"I was not sure what he intended to achieve by showing me proof of his close friendship with a serviceman, but then it all made sense when he threatened me with something I could never have expected."

"What was that?" Zhang asked.

I looked up at the sky again, as if pleading to the heavens to make what I was about to say a bad nightmare, and I would wake up to a day where my reality today would remain a bad dream and nothing more. Sucking in a breath, I continued, "Dishonorable Discharge. That man threatened that he had the superior most officer in his pocket, and if I didn't back down, he would have me discharged from the force dishonorably, tarnishing my years of service. My hard work and honesty would then be accountable for nothing."

"That's messed up!" Zhang chimed in. Being an agent himself, he was aware that a dishonorable discharge from a force was worse than a life sentence or even execution for an agent. "So, you retired instead?"

I nodded. "I couldn't stand being a former army man and an active member of an intelligence agency and turn a blind eye to such a mass crime. I retired from my post because I decided I would conduct my investigation on the case, without the sword of DD lurking over my head."

"So could you?" Zhang asked. "I mean, did you investigate then?"

I sighed. "I did everything I could. But it turns out, without a badge, you're accounted for almost nothing. A lot of access that I had previously was then lost. That's when I realized that I could not do anything but become a private agent."

"Do you regret it? Retiring, I mean." Zhang went for the hard question.

I fell back in the deck chair again and closed my eyes. "Yes! It was a brash decision. A coward one too. But what's done is done. I don't dwell on the past."

"You shouldn't," Zhang said, lying in his chair. "Besides, you have such a sweet juicy case to solve now."

I almost laughed. "Lucky that Aaron got kidnapped."

"The poor guy, but thank you, dear Aaron, for getting abducted."

The quiet deck echoed with our laughter as we continued to talk about our past and what the future held for us. Perhaps bringing Zhang here wasn't such a bad idea after all.

Chapter 5

"Thank you for hosting us, Captain Banville." I shook the captain's hand as we were about to head out of the ship.

"De rien, ami. It was my pleasure." Captain Banville smiled with enthusiasm.

We parted our ways, walked through the exit onto the wharf, and finally entered the grand city of Hong Kong. As soon as I stepped inside the vicinity of the city that was most famous for the world's most thriving economies and being a hub for international trade and investment, I was taken aback by its life, brightness, and an eerie calm embedded in the fast-paced life of this cosmopolitan city.

Whenever I came to Hong Kong, I always felt a strange energy that the city's streets, tall skyscrapers, and rapid moving cars and trains embodied. It was hard to describe, but the city had a unique life and personality. The most beautiful part of the city was that as much as it was a fast-moving concrete jungle, it had it's peaceful, laid-back life to it as well. Far in the distance, hidden away with tall buildings, one could still see lush forest-covered mountains, hiking trails, beautiful beaches, islands, and traditional fishing villages. All of this made Hong Kong truly a one-of-a-kind experience.

I breathed in a sigh to take in the city's peacefully rasping wind as Zhang nudged me.

"Where to, sir?" He joked.

I pulled out my phone. "The arrangements have officially been seized from Michelson's end, given that we continue to change plans as we go. I guess I'll find a hotel nearby." I suggested.

"Nah uh! We're not going to a hotel." Zhang was quick to deny my recommendation. "We don't exactly blend in. We should go to a secret location to not attract any attention."

"We could be tourists," I pointed out. "There are many roaming around here."

Zhang stared me down. "Have you ever looked at yourself, Specialist? You dress like you're attending a wedding or on your way to give a heartfelt eulogy at a funeral."

"It never hurts to dress immaculately."

"It might in this situation... now come on, I know a place," Zhang said as he asked me to follow him.

"Where are we headed?" I asked him as he hailed a cab from the street in the next block of the busy Nathan Road.

It had to do with Hong Kong's rule of only loading passengers in the cab at a point where there was a single yellow line on the street.

"To a hideout," Zhang answered my question as we sat in the cab. "It is used by the Ministry of State Security, also abbreviated to MSS."

"I am aware," I nodded at him. "I appreciate your quick thinking."

"Hey, you're not the only agent around here, my man!" Zhang quipped as we laughed, conversing about the weather in the city or other tourist destinations we could visit if we found the time, as we waited out the drive to get to where he was taking us.

***

"This is quite the place," I exclaimed as we entered a room that looked like a storage facility. It had minimal furniture such as a two-seater couch, two mattresses on the floor, and one round table that held a lamp, which was the only source of light in the room.

"The best I could do," Zhang said as he slumped down on the couch.

I shook my head. "I mean it. No sarcasm in my words."

Zhang didn't answer, for he had already laid his head down, his eyes covered with his arm. After the time that I had spent on the ship with him, I had learned that he didn't compromise on his sleep. I sighed as I pulled out my phone, sitting down on one of the two mattresses. I scrolled through my contacts to find someone who resided in Hong Kong, someone who could help me get an invite to the party.

"This meeting, it'll take place during an exclusive party thrown by a corrupt Hong Kong politician, which is why it's almost impossible to get in without an invite. As per my intel, the triad is meeting with the Bratva Pakhan there. There are just too many loops at play. The only way to untangle them and follow the trail of clues is that you need to secure an invite to the party."

I remembered what Alex had informed me when he called me later after our meeting in Tel Aviv. We were already back on the ship when he ringed me again to tell me about the new developments he had found. If only he had made getting an invite that easy as well. I sighed. There was no contact on my list that I could reach for help. I tossed my phone aside and lay back on the mattress, spent from the journey here. Perhaps getting a quick shut-eye won't hurt.

"A few years ago, I came to Hong Kong for a mission."

My eyes shot open when I heard Zhang's voice. He still had his arm over his eyes, but he was talking, so I waited for him to continue.

"There was this armed robbery at one of the largest banks here in Hong Kong. The trail went deeper, and the robbery was linked to an underground mafia. In digging for evidence, I ended up befriending an enemy of the mafia lord."

"For the case, right? Because you were undercover?" I interjected.

"I'm afraid not," Zhang said as he sat up and looked at me. There was a hint of guilt evident on his face. "This man, who ran an operation of another gang, approached me when he found out that I was the lead detective on the armed robbery case. He gave me all the intel I then used to dismantle the whole gang involved in the string of internal intelligence crimes. He made things easier for me."

"You do know that he was only helping you because he wanted to take down his enemy. It doesn't make him the good guy here, Zhang," I said as I feared where the story was going.

"I knew that, and I had every intention of arresting him once we were done with our mission... but,"

"But...?"

"I let him walk because I agreed with his work," Zhang confessed and hid his face in his palms.

"Zhang, that is..."

"Look, I know..." Zhang interrupted me. "I should have put him behind bars. But this was their entire work. They used illegal means for good. I remember how this man hated law enforcement agencies. 'They don't do jackshit,' he would say. I know his means were wrong, but his motive was broadly right."

I shook my head. I didn't have time for this. "You do you, my man! Why are you telling me this?"

"Because that man knows Hong Kong and all of its important people better than we ever can."

"So?" I asked.

"He knows the politician who's throwing the party. He knows the organizers, I'm sure. He can get us invites. So, if your high moral compass allows us, I can contact him and take his aid in this case."

I listened to Zhang and thought about what he was saying. Although I didn't agree with the notion of doing the right through the wrong ways, we didn't have a choice but to ask for his good-evil friend's help. I sighed. "Let's involve the criminal in taking down some more criminals," I said, slumping my shoulders.

"Don't be so melodramatic. It's not as catastrophic as you're making it out to be. Just an invite, dear Specialist."

I smiled. Perhaps it wasn't the end of the world, after all.

***

After a peaceful rest, Zhang and I found ourselves outside the venue where the said secret party was set to take place. The place from the outside was decorated with expensive lightning, glittering away, adding a bright hue into the darkness of the night. Although it was a grand ball-like place, once inside, the scene instantaneously changed into something that was mirroring a casino. People were dressed in expensive clothes, with some adorning masks of silver and gold covering their faces.

At one corner of the grand hall, there was a bar with numerous kinds of drinks proudly showcased for the partygoers to quench from. While most of the hall was empty, providing a large space for people to dance their hearts out, there was one place secluded for those with an itch for a good gamble. Casino tables that seated a group of people on each, playing cards, were scattered around the small intimate space.

Greetings were made along the grovel path as we stepped ahead through the decorated path toward the gambling corner. Dainty fairy lights hanging dazzlingly added an extensive amount of color, brightness, and serenity in the extravagant hall. It was as though the people who had organized the event went the extra mile to mask the darkness that resided in the well-lit walls of the hall. It was a rouse, a facade. The dance of the devil is never quite obvious. It's often orchestrated midst the twirls of the beautiful angels. Such was the case of this party.

A sweet melody was drifting through the environment, with a heavy disco ball dancing to its beat, hung right above the wide-spread floor, designated for those with a spring in their step and an inkling of the art of dance. We weaved our way through the crowd of champagne-baring waiters, slow dancing couples, and others chattering away to what I was looking for.

"Table no. 7. All the important people you wish to exchange a word or two with, you'll find at table no. 7."

Zhang's contact in the mafia had informed. That man was a former triad member and currently operated a secret network in Hong Kong. His intel was right, and so were his connections to get us in the party. He had given us names and fake identities that allowed us inside because the names were already on the guest list. Zhang and I walked toward the table that probably had the triads and Pakhans seated.

"Good evening, gentlemen!" I greeted.

The man in the center looked up briefly before he turned his attention to the hand of cards in the front, not acknowledging our presence. I gestured for Zhang to take the empty seat next to a tall, beautiful brunette, as I sat on one of the chairs next to the man who wore a top hat. I stomped a wad of cash on the table, indicating that I was a serious player here only to gamble and for nothing else. I glanced around the table and immediately caught that the group was playing Black Jack. Ahh! Perfect. I had immense experience in the game as I had gone to my fair share of casino nights as an undercover agent.

"Your bet, sir?" The dealer asked.

"All in," I answered as the dealer took the money and gave me four tall piles of chips.

The game began in silence as I continued to observe each one on the table. They all looked shady, to say the least. Almost all of them had visible tattoos, except for one, who might have it as well, but his all-black three-piece suited debonair prevented me from seeing if he had any. Three of them were of Chinese descent, and I instantly knew that they were the ones representing the triad. The rest of them looked to be from everywhere, the U.S.A., perhaps Germany, and even Japan. Mostly, though, they looked Russians.

Someone who caught my attention the most was the beautiful woman sitting at the table. She was Russian and looked quite familiar. Dark brown hair, hazel eyes, and a pouty smile placed across her puckered lips. What stood out to me the most was how the woman was behaving with the men, seductive, flirty, and almost manipulative.

"How are you doing tonight, darling?"

I heard Zhang talk to the woman and tried staring at him. I knew at that moment that he had mistaken the Russian woman for the Obshchak. Given that he only knew that we were looking for a Russian contact, it was natural for him to mistake her for that. However, I knew she was not the Obshchak. Anything but that.

"I'm trying to win a game against these handsome gentlemen, so I'd rather not be disturbed." The woman rejected Zhang's advances, and I sighed in relief. Perhaps he'd stop fake-flirting with her now.

"Oh, but it's so much more fun outside here. Why don't we head out somewhere quieter?"

I watched as the Russian woman turned back and focused on the other man. She passed a flirty smile at him. It was strange how the woman was blatantly ignoring Zhang but was interested in every other man on the table. It almost felt as if she had some ulterior motive attached to her flirtatious quips. Zhang, however, was not ready to give up. He continued to persuade her despite her constant denials. I watched as the triad and Pakhan members started to look suspicious. Two of them began to take notice of Zhang's persistence as I saw them halt their game and focus their attention on Zhang's and the Russian woman's exchanges. I tried my luck at gesturing for him to stop talking but to no avail. He continued the action without fail.

"He has a gun," one of the men spewed loudly as they all stood up. "This man, he has a gun."

I immediately checked my pocket and mentally smacked my head. In my efforts to signal Zhang, I had become oblivious to the gun secured in my top pocket. "I'm a foreigner. I need to protect myself," I tried to argue as the triads and Pakhans started marching my way. Before I could form another thought, one of them threw a harsh punch across my jaw, and I stumbled backward, my gun falling to the ground in the process.

"Hey, no need to be all violent now," Zhang interjected.

The Russian man turned to him. "You're with this chump?" He seethed. "Tell me, are you all in cahoots? I bet this skunk is with you as well."

"I don't know these men." The brunette held up her hands. "This man was just shamelessly flirting with me."

The Russian man laughed. "Oh, I have seen this staged crap before. You're a whore, aren't you?" The man walked closer to her. "They hired you to seduce us? Is it not true?"

"No, I have nothing to do with them. I was just..."

I continued to witness the fight from a distance as I tried to formulate an exit plan. As if my lucky stars were working in my favor, a triad shot one of the Russians, and the man who was currently engrossed in chastising the Russian girl turned around, his focus broken.

"This Russian woman was your hire. It all makes sense now." The Chinese triad who had shot the Russian man yelled.

With the gunshot, the normal partygoers began to freak out and run haywire in every direction. Screams could be heard in the atmosphere that once was ringing with a melodious tone. As the brawl between the triad and Pakhan intensified, I took this opportunity to walk toward Zhang, who stood a few steps away next to the Russian girl. In the next moment, I decided to take the girl with us. I needed to make sure if my hunch was right and if this girl had an ulterior motive for all of her actions. I put my hand over the girl's face and dragged her out, as she tried screaming, but Zhang lent me a hand, and we walked out of the party, amidst the commotion.

Once on the street, in a deserted alley, Zhang retrieved a rope and a tape from his bag. He tied the girl's hands and put tape over her mouth. He then pulled out his phone, and I heard him talk to someone about sending us a car to take us back to the MSS. We couldn't possibly take a cab with an abducted girl accompanying us. The car was sent by the same man who had given us an invitation to the party. Soon the car arrived, and we were off. I looked over at the girl, who had by now stopped struggling and had her head laid back. I sighed. If only our cover wasn't blown. I could only hope now that this girl would tell us something useful. I could only hope.

***

"You, idiots! You guys blew everything."

The girl started shouting as soon as we had her tied to the chair back in our hideout. We had peeled the tape off her mouth for her to talk. Gone was the seductive girl who seemed to be tone-deft and knew nothing but relentlessly flirting with the men. The woman who sat in front of us now looked to be intelligent, well-articulated, and strong, raging with anger. Her eyes were accusing and fiery with loath.

"What are you talking about?" I asked, confused.

"Because of your stupidity, my investigation was derailed. Had you not barged in there, I would have gotten something out of those men." The woman seethed.

"Wait a minute; you're an agent?"

The girl seemed to ignore the question. "My name is Yifat. I was undercover for the past month, mingling with the mafia, to obtain some intel on their activities. I have some personal reasons for doing so." The woman, who told her name as Yifat, shared with us, although I felt she was careful with her words. She only said what was necessary.

"That was why you didn't come with me?" Zhang chimed in.

"Is it so important for your men's ego to hear me say I only rejected your advances for a case, and not because I wasn't charmed by your antics?" The girl raised her eyebrow, and I almost laughed at that.

"Hey, I was only flirting for the case as well." Zhang hung his hands in the air.

Yifat rolled her eyes. "Be that as it may, you guys ruined my chances with the mafia. My cover is blown because of you."

"You still didn't tell us why you were on the mission? Are you an agent?" I ignored her accusations and tried to bring her back on the subject. "Why were you investigating the mafia?"

The Russian woman sighed. "It's because of Aaron Cohen."

Chapter 6

The room was engulfed in silence. After casually taking the name of Aaron Cohen, the woman went quiet. Zhang and I continued to request her to speak, but it was as though she had gone into a trance. Her gaze was fixated on one spot, and she refused even to acknowledge our presence, let alone respond to any of our questions.

The night lamp's bulb flickered. "Tighten the screws, will you?" I asked Zhang. The sound was only adding to the dark silence that was already slowly devouring the room, as Aaron Cohen's name lingered in the quiet atmosphere, sitting heavy on our senses. "Miss Yifat, will you please speak now?" I tried again after giving her a few minutes to get ready. Oh, how difficult this woman was, I thought to myself.

"Why should I help you at all when you cost me my whole mission?" She spat out in anger. Her features displayed aggression, rage, and even hurt.

I sighed. This was not the time to feel sympathy for her. No, it was time to get her to talk. "Because you're not in a place to negotiate," I said, gesturing toward the restraints she was currently in.

"You think that, but dear sir, I never give anyone an authority to rule over my mind." She proudly stated, "Shackle me in restraints of iron and steel if you will. Still, I won't allow you to control my mind. Never." She was still just as stern in her stance.

I threw my hands in the air, exasperated at her stubborn attitude. "Look, we can all get out of this if you are corporate with us. You obviously have some connection with Aaron Cohen, and you're likely an agent or something. I still don't know why you were undercover in the first place," I said, trying to inspire an epiphany that would grant me the reason for her undercover mission, for clearly, the woman was not ready to share it herself. "If you could just tell us who you are, it can help us both." I requested one last time.

Yifat shifted in her chair, her wrists twisting under the restraints. I felt an ache inside my heart at its sight.

However, before I could act on it, she spoke up again, "Why are you so interested in Aaron Cohen? Are you...? Wait," she paused and stared me up and down as if she was trying to analyze something in me. "Are you The Specialist?" She asked me curiously.

"Yes!" I said, raising my eyebrow. "Have you heard of me?"

"Quite the opposite, no!" She almost laughed as if she was mocking me. "When your name came up as someone who could find Aaron Cohen, I had my reservations, for I knew nothing of you and your work."

"Hold on, did you hire me?" I was taken aback. "How do I not know you then?"

"My family did. We never met." Yifat specified. "I was never sure if you could solve the case. In fact, for the longest time, I was reluctant to even have them hire you."

I stepped back as her words were hitting me strangely. The girl seemed to have good connections with the Bratva and even the triad, given that she was playing an undercover agent herself. It was rather unacceptable that the woman of her knowledge didn't know who I was.

"Were you afraid that the Specialist won't be able to solve the case? Or was it the fear that he might solve it that bothered you?"

That was it. It suddenly hit me what I had found strange in her explanation when Zhang said those words. I looked at her more carefully. It was as though my brain rebooted. All the stress and exhaustion wore off, and as if the fog was lifted, I could see her face more clearly. I was reminded of where I had seen her before. This was the girl who I had thought was involved with Aaron Cohen's abduction. She was his daughter.

"Are you seriously accusing me of having a hand in my own father's kidnapping?" She almost sounded hurt, but I was more focused on her admission of her relationship with the victim.

I was afraid she would not accept it easily. "So, you're Yifat Emuna, Aaron Cohen's daughter?" I asked, wanting to reaffirm it.

"The one and only," she sighed.

"Might I ask, why have you been so under wraps when it comes to this case? Why did I have to talk to third parties regarding your father when you could be the one briefing me over it?" I was still skeptical about what I had initially found out. The girl I had linked with Aaron's abduction matched her description. Her discreet presence in the case didn't help matters in making me warier of her.

"Because I knew nothing of my father's whereabouts, his activities in those days, or the company he kept." She confessed.

I could see the color of her face turn from a series of raging emotions displayed on it into a shade of guilt and shame.

"Could you please untie me? I'm cramping." She requested.

I looked over at Zhang with a raised eyebrow, and he merely nodded. I went with my intuition that told me that the girl would not try something smart at this point. I went over to the chair she was tied in and loosened her restraints. She twisted her wrists to promote her blood flow as she stood up, rubbing her neck. I granted her some time to get stabilized before I could interrogate her further.

"You didn't want to hire me because you didn't know me," I asked her. My mind was still working on the theory that she could be involved, and her reluctance toward me as an agent to find her father was furthering my suspicions.

"At first, yes," she said, throwing her hands in the air and trying to get them moving after they had been tied up for some time. "But it was my research on you that raised my disinclination toward you, Specialist."

My mouth was hung open. I liked to think I had a clean slate, crystal clear, and void of bad marks. What could she have found out? "Surely, you could not have found me to be a serial killer or something. What was so bad that it made you timid about working with me?"

"A tale for another time," she said, trying to walk around, uninterested in what I was asking her.

I sighed. It was best if I asked her something that she would answer, less controversial perhaps. "Were you and your father not close?" I tried my luck with that question.

She shook her head as she sat on the couch, leaning back. "Not in the last days before he went missing. We had a fallout, details of which I'd refrain from sharing for now. So, despite having a good relationship throughout my life, things weren't on the best terms toward the end."

"That's convenient." I blurted the subtle accusation, despite not having the intention of doing so.

To my surprise, she caught it. "This is the last time I'm taking this blatant blame," she warned. "I love my father dearly, and I'll do everything in my power to bring him back. I have so much to say to him. So many things are left unsaid."

I conceded. Like the way I had learned to trust Zhang, I shall come around to trusting her as well. Perhaps for now, what was best for the case was to work together. I walked closer to her and extended my hand toward her.

"Truce?"

Yifat thought for a bit before she gave her hand in mine to shake. "Truce," she exclaimed with a smile. "I guess we don't have an option but to work together. If my family hired you, there must be a reason."

"And if you've been undercover for a month, there must be a lot of intel with you that you've gathered, which could aid us greatly in the pursuit of this case." I smiled.

She was about to answer when we got distracted by Zhang's phone ringing. I could only hear one side of the conversation, so all I could hear was a series of "roger that," "Sure!" "Right on, sir!"

When he finally hung up, he turned to look at me. "I've been called back for another mission by my boss." He informed us, "I won't be able to continue with you from here on."

"Oh, why? You've been of great help here in Hong Kong," I said, realizing that Zhang's presence was essential to the case and that he would be missed.

"I know, mate!" Zhang said, patting me on the back. "It was a pleasure working with you."

"Likewise! It was great while it lasted," I said, bidding my goodbyes.

Zhang shook his head. "No, no! Don't act like this is a farewell, and don't you dare try and eliminate me from the case. I might be going away, but I will be working on the case. I'm following on a lead on my own and will keep you posted," Zhang said, smiling.

I nodded with a short smile. "Please receive my gratitude for your unwavering service these past many weeks."

"Oh, don't be so formal, my dear Specialist," Zhang said as he gave me a giant hug. He waved a final goodbye to both Yifat and me and was off.

I took in a sharp breath and turned to Yifat, who looked almost emotional, witnessing the scene before her. "Now, shall we discuss what we each know about the case so far?" I proposed, and she nodded at that.

We took our seats back on the couch before I began telling her as much as I deemed I could trust her with. Even after knowing that she was Aaron's daughter, I still had my guard up and continued to have my suspicions regarding her motives. Once I was done, I nudged her to share her side of the intel. She cleared her throat.

"I know my fair share of details about the politician who had organized the party where you came swooping in and ruined my mission." She started, not forgoing the snarl in her tone.

I sighed and let her be. We did cause hindrance in her mission. Her anger was justified to a large extent. "Who's this politician you speak of?" I asked her.

"Kennyon Cheung," she answered.

I instantly knew who she was talking about. I had heard tales of his corruption over numerous news channels. I had heard that he had many cases filed against him in the court of law. He was one who had links with the underworld gangs. He provided aid to other countries to obtain arms and ammunition for destructive purposes. He was accused of having a hand in many terrorist attacks, not only in his own country but also in other countries. The mention of his name alone told me a lot. However, I needed to know more. Much more.

"So, what do you know about Cheung?" I nudged her to continue with her story.

"Do you have some water here? I have this bad taste in my mouth from the duct tape you so mercilessly fettered around me," she said, scrunching up her nose in disgust.

"Of course, I'll get you a bottle right away," I said, standing up, almost rolling my eyes at her melodramatic complaints. I pulled out a bottle of water from my backpack and handed it to her.

She snatched it away, twisted the cap open, and chugged it in one breath. "Fancy!" She exclaimed breathless, looking at the almost empty water bottle. "No tap water for the rich Specialist, I see!"

Once again, I moved past her remark and decided to bring her back on the subject. "You were telling me about Kennyon Cheung."

"Ahh! Yes. You're quite persistent," she sighed and said. "There is a major meeting between both Triads and Pakhans, along with his presence. I'm not sure about the whereabouts or the date yet, but I do know that a meeting is going to take place soon and somewhere discreet."

"I figured that on my own." I sounded annoyed unintentionally. "If he was the one throwing a party for the gangs, it must've been for a reason. Their meeting does not come as new information, Yifat."

"Oh, but that's not the whole information, my impatient acquaintance." Yifat was quick to dismiss my snarl. "The said meeting is not organized by Kennyon, but rather the Triads. They are the ones who are bringing the Russians on the table to face each other and to face Cheung."

I scratched my head, confused at what was the meaning of all this. "Why is Cheung so open about giving the Triads this much power?"

"Because he's pro Beijing. The man is a traitor. He opposes the concept of free Hong Kong quite openly." Yifat explained, gulping down some more water. "I see why you don't go for tap water. It tastes different."

I nodded. "Expensive things are often better... not because they are, but because we perceive that they are. It's only psychological."

Yifat rolled her eyes. "What else do you want to know?"

I stood up, for I was getting too agitated in one place with all the new developments pouring in. I paced around the room, trying to make sense of everything and figuring out what more could I ask for from Yifat. "What I don't get is, why do Russians want to meet with Triads so badly? I mean, why are they so interested in the local Chinese politics?"

"I've been wondering the same thing."

When Yifat's voice came ringing in and breaking the eerie silence, that was when I realized that I was talking out loud about what I was merely thinking in my head. I turned to look at her, who had found a comfortable spot on the couch and made it home.

"What does all of this have to do with Aaron Cohen?" I asked, this time not by accident.

She sighed, shrugged her shoulders, threw her hands in the air, and stood up. She walked closer to where I was standing and looked at me seriously. "I've wracked my brain in thinking about this for quite some time, in hopes that this would lead me to my father."

"Then?" I nudged her further. "You don't try to find answers anymore?"

"I do, every single day, I do!" She breathed out, frustrated with her situation. "Truth be told, now I only concern myself with searching for those answers that directly pertain to my father."

"What do you mean?" I asked, more confused than ever.

"I mean, I don't care about the Chinese gangs, Russian mafia, or Hong Kong politics. I don't care what bizarre string attaches these high-profile catastrophic manics." She sighed and paused for a while.

I saw her tucking a loose strand of hair behind her ear and breathing out sadly before continuing.

"Now, all I care about is finding my father. I can't investigate deeper, for the life of me when my father is in danger. I just want to strive harder to make his return home possible. That is all."

I felt my heart hurt for her pain. I nodded at her with compassion in my eyes. "It is possible. We will bring Aaron Cohen home safe and sound. I promise!"

Chapter 7

The one lone clock on the wall in our secret hideout displayed nine in the evening. The room had suddenly gone silent after our conversation as the stress of Aaron's sudden unexplained disappearance sat heavily on our tensed nerves. The only prevalent sound in the room was of the tick-tocks of the wall clock and the irritating flickering of the bulb, loosely fitted in the lamp.

"Nothing short of a horror movie this place is, I tell you." Yifat finally broke the silence as she gestured toward the lamp. "There has to be a fix for this creepy bulb."

I turned to look at the lamp and smiled. "Zhang tried. Nothing works for this persistent beauty," I joked.

"I'm starving, in case you can't hear the groveling of my stomach amidst the sweet melody of your dear bulb," Yifat pouted.

I stood up. "Oh, I hear it! Just didn't feel like it's a gentleman's attribute to point out."

"And let the girl starve? How's that a trait of a gentleman?" Yifat stood up as well, raising her eyebrow at me.

I laughed. "Let's head out then. I know a place here that serves excellent sushi."

"No! We're heading to a place of my choice," Yifat argued as she walked ahead of me with a purpose in her step.

"Why should I compromise?" I mused.

Yifat briefly turned around to look at me as she unlatched the storage place's door. "Because I have gathered intel from my successful undercover mission that some Russians frequent this restaurant. That's called killing two birds with one stone, Specialist." She winked.

I was impressed, but I still had some confusion. "I thought you don't care about anything other than saving your father."

"This is about saving my father," Yifat said with confidence. "Like you, I agree that the thread might connect to Russia, given the Bratva tattoo you saw on the CCTV tapes. I want to follow that lead. Perhaps we might find a connecting point that guides us to the end we sought to achieve."

I walked closer to her and pulled up the metal door, which I knew might be heavy for her to lift. "I like that we're on the same page about the Russian leader," I said as we walked out of the storage facility-like military hideout.

"I know karate."

I halted at her words, turning to look at her, confusion evident on my face. "Are you warning me or something?" Strangely, I felt challenged by the sudden declaration.

"No! Just telling you that I could have lifted that door quite easily. Piece of cake," Yifat clarified. "But also, yes, you may take it as a warning too."

I laughed at her shrug of the shoulder and nodded. "Duly noted. Shall we?" I asked as she walked in front of me, leading the way, for she knew where we were going. I rarely followed anyone's lead, but my overpowering persona, know-it-all mind, and deep-rooted pride always surrendered when I felt the person leading me matched the level of my intelligence and could mirror my skill set. In ages, I had found someone whose words echoed of wisdom and whose persona was glazed with uber-intelligence. I knew that working on Aaron Cohen's case with Yifat would be fun, and I looked forward to it.

***

The cab stopped on Wyndham street, 63, in central Hong Kong, in front of a restaurant whose board dangling outside read: 'Ivan The Kozak.' The board was lit in bright, colorful LED lightings, and the name instantly told me that it was a Russian restaurant. The name lauded its origin quite distinctly. Ivan is a common term used all over Russia, had its roots in Slavic, and meant *God is Gracious*. Kozak was the proud surname of many

Russians, for it was associated with rebellion, being a fighter, and being a hero. I had heard that Russians took the name as grand praise when someone called them Kozak. It was a symbol of pride for many commoners in the country.

I turned to Yifat as we stepped out of the cab after I had paid for the ride. "No wonder the likes of Pakhans frequent here. The name alone exerts power."

Yifat shrugged. "I'm nothing if through... come on."

We headed inside, and while I had visited Hong Kong quite a few times over the years, I had never been to this restaurant. Tall floor-length windows were covering most of the walls. A few remained without the large glass windows and featured many different variants of the Russian culture. Paintings drawn of their heritage, tapestry hung on the walls, and ancient-style shelves hung in every space, adorning vintage crockery. The restaurant was painted in shades of dark red and bright white. There were booth seats at some corners, while the standard tables and chairs were characteristically scattered around in the center of the restaurant. Overall, the place offered good light, but there lurked a dark aura in the atmosphere, perhaps because of the presence of a few that was our prime reason for coming here - The Pakhans dining in one of the booth seats in a secluded corner.

"Table for two, please! It would be lovely if it could be near those gentlemen." I went to the man standing in front of the entrance, slid a crisp bill toward him on the podium as I discretely gestured toward the booth that the Russians were dining in.

The man nodded, smiling. "This way, Xiānshēng."

Fortunately for us, the table near the Russian men, currently consuming the traditional bowl of Shchi and a large pie of Pirog, was empty. Once we sat down, I could hear them talking, in hushed whispers, barely audible over the faint music playing in the background, but I could make out from their expressions that what they were speaking of was not casual dinner conversation, but rather a crucial discussion of something important.

"Can you hear them?" Yifat asked me as we settled in our seats.

I briefly turned my face to their table, making sure not to attract any attention, before I focused on Yifat again. "Hardly," I groaned in annoyance. "Aren't Russians supposed to be loud people? How unauthentic of them." I watched as Yifat played around with the knife on the table, drawing invisible circles on the wooden surface. "Discretion, my friend, makes you do the things most unlike yourself." I gestured for the waiter to come over and take our order. "Those damn Pakhans have given me an appetite for Pirog," I exclaimed, to which Yifat agreed. So that was what we ordered. Once the waiter left, I decided to bring her back on the question that she had denied answering earlier. "What did you find out about me in your research?" I just couldn't let it go. Call it pride, need to please, or even ego, but I did take pride in my work, which was why when it was questioned, I strived to prove to the other person why I was titled The Specialist in the first place.

Yifat picked up the napkin from the table and spread it out on her lap as she smiled. "They told me you could come off self-absorbed at times, and they weren't wrong."

"Hey," I raised my hands in the air. "I've earned this, have I not?" I defended myself.

"I guess so." She shrugged. "Regardless, it's still not the time."

I hung my head. "Why the dismissal? You're making me curious."

"Well, you're the specialist. Conjure up the answers on your own." She snickered.

I could visibly hear her smart sarcasm in her tone. I was about to answer her with my comeback when the waiter came over with a jug of Medovukha and filled our glasses. He settled the jug down on the table and left.

"Now I know what the hype was all about," Yifat said as she took a sip from her drink. "So sweet, I could fly."

"Would not have taken you to be so dramatic," I mocked with a friendly snicker.

Yifat gulped down a mouthful and looked at me seriously. "I'm too high on honey to care, Specialist."

I laughed. "You're a strange woman."

"Hold on," Yifat said, raising a finger at me and placing her glass down on the table. She dug into her bag and produced a mirror. She handed it to me, and I raised my eyebrow, confused at what I was supposed to do with it. "Look at yourself in the mirror."

"Excuse me?" I asked.

"Stare into the eyes of what truly is strange," she stated with sass to her tone and witty shrug to her shoulder.

I busted out in laughter. "See, I told you, dramatic and extra."

She rolled her eyes and waved me off, merely enjoying her drink. Suddenly, my eyes fell on the mirror, which was one of those zoomed-in mirrors that were used for a better view. Was it called a concave mirror? I didn't know, and I didn't care. I had caught sight of the Pakhan's booth behind us in the mirror. One of the men was giving a piece of paper to the other men. Gratitude to the mirror, I could evocatively see what was written on the paper.

"Sklad dom." I breathed.

"Pardon?" Yifat asked, confused.

I placed down the mirror on the table and tried to bring down my huff. "It's a code, Yifat. This man just handed a piece of paper that says Warehouse in a Russian code."

"Oh!" Yifat exclaimed. "But how do we know which warehouse are they talking about?"

I didn't answer her right away. Instead, I directed all my attention to their conversation in hopes that I'd hear something that could lead us to the warehouse they were referring to. The group conversed mostly in Russian, with hints of English here and there in some of their words. Although my Russian was not fluent, I knew enough to be able to catch a possible clue.

Or at least that's what I told myself. To my relief, among other words, I overheard one word quite distinctly: Des Voeux. I was aware that was the name of a road that had a grand storage facility, and I figured what the group meant by a warehouse could be just a storage room. At least I hoped it was true.

"Des Voeux, come on, we need to head there," I said.

"But our dinner?" Yifat pointed out. "Those Russians are smart, you know. If we left like this in such a huff, they might take notice of it." She picked up her fork and danced it around her empty plate. "Plus, I'm still famished." She pouted.

I smiled. "Fine, we can eat first!"

We settled back in our seats as we waited for our food. All the while, I remained focused on the conversation of the Pakhans. As soon as our food arrived, the Russians were done with theirs, and they prepared to leave. I turned to Yifat and glared at her, scolding her with my eyes that she would have missed this opportunity.

"Relax!" She said, propping a fork full of Pirog in her mouth. "If they were talking about a warehouse, they must be heading there. We should leave after some time. They would be done with whatever they intended to do there by then," she said while chewing on the crusty goodness of the Russian pie.

I nodded, realizing that she was right. I dug into my food, more relaxed now than before, and no longer huffing the forced morsels into my mouth, no longer eating on the edge of destruction. I intended to enjoy my dinner, let the Russians do their dirty work, and we shall investigate later... all in due time, I thought.

***

On the Des Voeux street, our cab halted in front of a grand storage facility. The night had aged dark by now, the streets were deserted, and there were no prying eyes, ready to suspect our arrival. Once inside, I found the place to be an authentic facility that most common people used to store their valuables. There was a front desk right at the entrance, behind which a clerk sat; his head down on the desk, arms stretched, and face hidden. Faint sounds of his snores echoed in the silence. It was a good thing. We were saved from forging an excuse to be scurrying around the storage rooms without having one to our name. A glass door led to a hallway, which had a series of identical blue doors on either side of its wall, all used by commoners, I assumed.

"Great! Let's play scavenger hunt to find the desired door now." Yifat sounded annoyed as we walked deeper in the hallway, looking on both sides to catch a clue of what room it could be.

"Dom," I exclaimed in excitement as I spotted the words written on one of the doors. A small slip like paper was pasted over the surface at the top right corner, which read in small font the same word I had read on the paperback in the restaurant. "This is the one," I said.

"Russian food has treated you well," Yifat mused.

I shrugged off as I thought over a way to enter.

"Look, it's not locked." As if reading my mind, Yifat gestured toward the open lock at the bottom of the door, and I instinctively took a step back.

"Does this mean someone's still inside?" I raised my eyebrow, preparing an escape and fighting strategy both in my head.

Yifat didn't answer. She stepped forward and placed her ear against the door to listen. "I don't hear anything," she declared.

"I guess we just have to find out," I said as I reached for my gun and held it tightly in my hands, securing my grip on it and getting in position.

Yifat stood behind me as I lifted the door with a loud shuttering sound, and an empty room revealed itself with nobody inside. We entered, pulling the door down behind us, and breathed a sigh of relief as I put away my gun back in my pocket.

"Who leaves such an important room open? Dumb Pakhans," Yifat snickered, glancing around the room.

"That's what makes me wonder if this was a setup." I pondered on the possibility. Thoughts of a backup showing up at any moment and ending our lives, catching us off-guard, lingered in the back of my mind. They had played it nicely and lured us in a deserted corner. How swell! I gulped as I continued to forge plans in my head, all the while looking around the room.

"What is here, anyway?" Yifat started to look around, walking toward one of the many cardboard boxes scattered all around the room.

I took her lead and went in the opposite direction to check in another box.

"Weapons," she gasped. "Wow! There are so many weapons," she said, pulling out a long assault rifle from the box.

I briefly looked at her because I was too focused on examining the substance in the box I was looking in. Packets upon packets of white powder and pills were filled in the box to the brim. I picked up one of the packets and brought it close to my nose. Instantly, I knew what it was... pure cocaine.

"Looks like this place is merely a storage room for their illegal possessions," I said, holding out the packet of cocaine in front of Yifat.

"This place is reeking of drugs." Yifat scrunched up her nose. "It's almost as if it's mixed into the confide air of the room. What is all of this for? Consumption?" She questioned sarcastically.

I shook my head. "If only. These people are most likely smugglers."

"And weapons." She secured her grip on the rifle she was holding as it started to sit heavy in her hand and looked into more boxes. "There are just so many of them. What are they planning? A mass terrorist attack or something?"

I could hear a sense of fear in her tone and knew it was justified, given that I was afraid of the same thing. "It's hard to say, but this is not good," I said more to myself than to her as I circled the room, looking into the boxes. All of them held the same things, loads upon loads of guns and endless packets of drugs.

"These people... they seem dangerous," I heard Yifat behind me, but I didn't turn around or answer her.

I agreed, but the more I thought over how dangerous these people were, the more questions it raised in my head. To kidnap someone, you need motive and association with the person. Was Aaron in any way associated with these treacherous men? If so, was he involved in illegal activities? If he was, why did they kidnap him if he was on their side?

"You seem to be in a trance," Yifat interrupted my wandering thoughts with her words as I turned around to look at her. She was a walking embodiment of her father, not a spitting image, but many of her ways mirrored him to a large extent.

My racing questions could be answered by her, but I knew this was a dead end. I could not possibly mouth my suspicions to her, for I knew she was in a vulnerable place. Her guilt of becoming estranged with her father right before his abduction had closed her mind to the idea of her father being involved with the lurking evil spirits. I sighed. No! She would not cooperate. I knew that much.

"Hello!" Yifat snapped her fingers in front of him to break my lugubrious thoughts.

Finally, I breathed out. "Let's get out of here," I suggested, trying to divert her attention from wondering what I was thinking. "Staying here any longer is not void of risks," I said, heading for the exit.

"I know you have a hunch already," Yifat seized me in my place. "It's fine if you don't wish to share it right now. I just hope your hunch leads us to my father."

I turned around to look at her and could see pain evident in her beautiful eyes. I nodded, despite myself, "I hope for the same thing, Yifat."

Chapter 8

"Your silence rings of good things, I was told." Yifat penetrated the heavy ice that was formed between us in the cab as we headed back to the hideout from the warehouse. "People in my family, when talked about you, said that when you go quiet, it means your mind is working in overdrive, forging a million plans, soaring through the hurdles, and nearing close to your destination."

I briefly turned to her and passed a smile. "People say all sorts of things. Rarely there's truth in those words. I'm merely tired."

"I'm not going back to that bizarre box of a place," Yifat declared, changing the subject almost instantly. "That damn bulb will for sure give me nightmares."

"There's no other discreet place in Hong Kong that I know of," I told her, and she shook her head.

"Maybe you wish to stay discreet. I, on the other hand, wish to stay somewhere comfortable." She retorted.

"Where would Miss Emuna like to stay then?" I raised my eyebrow, unintentionally groaning the words out.

"Parks Hotel," Yifat declared. "I already have a room there. I've been here for the past month, remember."

I nodded and instructed the cab driver to drop her at the hotel first. When the car stopped by the curb in front of the hotel's main entrance, Yifat turned to me.

"Once again, I'm holding out my breath for the turning wheels in your head to lead to Aaron Cohen," Yifat said, with her eyes displaying a mixed set of emotions - hope and faith embedded in doubts and feelings of hurt.

I remained motionless and didn't respond as I watched her leave the car and enter the hotel without giving me another glance. I asked the driver to head to our initially inputted destination as I lay back in the seat, closing my eyes. My thoughts ran haywire and rogue, forming some plans and rejecting a few.

I fantasized in my head about an ideal solution and then dismissed the notion on the grounds of realistic boundaries stopping my fantasies. Nothing seemed to stand out in my head as the perfect plan to follow on how to get to Aaron Cohen. Amid this never-ending train of thoughts, the street finally arrived where the military hideout was situated. I paid the driver and tipped a little extra as I got out, headed into the hideout, and slumped on the mattress bed.

"In times when you don't know what to do, when you have a million ideas running through your head, just remember one thing, go for your first thought because often the inception of all ideas is your gut feeling, your instinct. In jumbled notions, the start of a puzzle is most like the answer to your mystery."

The words of my mentor from when I had first started in the force echoed in my head as I had closed my eyes to catch some sleep. Instantly, I shot up, having made up my mind. I went to my suitcases, emptied my backpack, ridding it of everything I had brought with me here, and filled it with some of the necessary stakeout equipment; binoculars, Bluetooth microphone, night-vision goggles, a Range-R device, a crawling camera bug, and many other amenities that made surveillance from a distance easier.

I zipped up the bag, hung it over my back, and left. The night had turned the darkest shade of black. That meant the righteous were tucked away in their beds, slumbering away peacefully, while the evil lurked around on the filthy nook and cranny of the city. The devil always danced in the darkness. That was why the best time to catch the evil was now. I couldn't wait for the sun. This needed to be done now.

***

"Xièxiè!" I said, thanking the manager at the car rental company, which to my surprise, was still open at this hour. I secured the keys in my hands as I walked toward my rented car for the rest of my stay here in Hong Kong. It was a sweet Porsche 718 Cayman, which I was quite grateful for, given that it mirrored my car back home. The minute I settled into its warm, plush leather seats, I felt home.

The salesman at the rental company told me that not many people rented this car, given the high price tag. Maybe that was the reason why the car felt new and unused. Parking by the curb on a deserted road, I did a quick Google search, inputted the location in the GPS, and drove off to my destination that was awaiting my arrival, hopefully with bated breath, bearing answers to my relentless wonderings. In no time, I found myself in central Hong Kong, outside the listed residence of Kennyon Cheung, the politician who, at this point, seemed to be the link to all my mysteries. Although finding his address was not the hardest part, given that it was one search away, getting close to somewhere I could find some clues posed itself as the hardest challenge.

"Not my first stakeout," I reminded myself as I parked my car quite at a distance from his government-allotted house. I didn't want to attract any attention and surely didn't want to be caught on the camera. I rolled down my window and took a glance at the street. There was no life in sight, except for one lone stray dog barking at a distant corner. Good! His barks would muffle any noise I might make in the process. I opened my stakeout bag and pulled out my camera bug as I stepped out of the car. This tiny device was equipped with a microphone, and while the camera produced distorted imagery, it's fascinating features were that it was controlled by a remote, caught signals up to 200 feet away, and could crawl under the tiniest of spaces because of its minuscule size.

I turned on the bug, placed it on the ground, and pulled out my remote control to reel it inside Cheung's house. The bug effortlessly crawled through the fences and stopped at the main entrance's stairs, the faint squeaky sounds fading away over the loud barking of the dog. Once the bug was in place, I sat back in my car, closed my window, and pulled out my Range-R device. This device signaled about the movements behind walls when turned on, which made it easier for those who had it in their possession to track their target. Now, all I had to do was sit back and wait for Cheung to make an appearance. Of course, I could have left the bug on as well instead of using Range-R, but I didn't know how long the stakeout would take. The battery would have drained by then. The movement-detection device was a better option.

I leaned my head on the seat of the car. It was too comfortable to stay alert. I closed my eyes and found myself drifting off into a slumber when I felt my Range-R device buzzing. I shot up, knowing that the signal-meant Cheung was moving inside his home, or was it someone else? Perhaps a servant? Another guest? I held my breath and pleaded with the higher-ups for the movement to belong to Cheung and this operation to grant me with something positive to return with. I immediately turned on the earpiece connected to the bug, which now stood by the stairs to the main entrance, and braced myself to listen.

Nothing! There was absolute silence, and I felt my hopes diminishing with each passing minute. Suddenly, I felt my Range-R device buzzing more loudly and looked up to see who it was. A man, dressed in a casual hoodie and sweatpants, with his hood set over his head, so his face was not visible to me, was entering the house of Cheung, using his set of keys. I pulled out my binoculars and watched him go to the main entrance. I gritted my teeth, crossed my fingers that the man would not step on my bug. Fortunately, he stepped up the stairs, and my bug survived. Phew! I sighed in relief and, once again, focused my attention on listening.

The hooded man rang the doorbell, and the door flung open almost instantly as if the person on the other side was waiting for his arrival.

"No phone, yes!"

I almost jumped when, all of a sudden, the voice came booming into my ear, but I quickly celebrated in my head at the success of my plan. I could hear them. Luck had worked in my favor. I held my breath in, afraid that I might do something that would alert them toward me, or even the bug currently sitting near them. I pulled out my phone to take notes of what they were saying.

"Dinner at 23:00 hours. Make sure the food does not have oil. Harper is meeting with me tomorrow at

8 to discuss some points about North's bridge construction."

I heard Cheung give instructions to the man. I smiled to myself... A code, a definite code, I immediately recognized the encrypted conversation. "Could be the place where this meeting is happening that Yifat was talking about." I thought to myself. Regardless, I'd get to decoding the message once the exchange ended.

"See you Monday," the man in the hoodie said and walked away as Cheung went back inside.

I ducked down in my car so the man could pass without noticing. My car had tinted glass, so the insides could not be seen anyway. It was just a precaution. Once the man left and Cheung was tucked away inside his evil's den, I pulled out my notepad to write a few things down.

In encrypted messages, numbers, and names of people, anything was the key. In Cheung's words, there were two numbers stated – 23 and 8. And the names that were mentioned were Harper and North's bridge. Something that stood out to me was his specification not to put any oil in the food, so I made sure to keep that in prominence as well when decoding. I pulled up my search engine on my phone and typed the numbers with the names in relevance to Hong Kong, granted that I already had a hunch that the encrypted message could be the address of a location.

"23 Oil Harper North, Hong Kong," I typed a combo, and to my absolute surprise, the first search came up as a hotel's name. "Harbor Grand Hong Kong," I breathed. The words and numbers checked out, as the address of the hotel had those in it. I smiled; maybe this was the place where the meeting was taking place. I quickly searched about what services the hotel offered, and sure enough, there were grand ballrooms in the hotel. T

he perfect place to conduct secret missions in hiding, with a mask of normalcy placed perfectly on the surface, while the depths carried heinous crimes, tucked away from the sight of those enforcing the law and the public's judging eyes. I dug a little deeper and found out that there was a grand party, hosted by some of the top political leaders of Hong Kong, happening in one of the ballrooms of the Harbor Grand Hong Kong Hotel on Monday, which was the day after tomorrow, starting sharp at 8 in the evening.

"Bingo!" I exclaimed proudly. The encrypted message was successfully decoded, and I had found myself a lead. Now all I had to do was to find my invite to the exclusive party, and I might end up finding more useful answers. Immediately, another strategy was forged in my mind as I drove back to my hideout to catch some sleep. I had one day to acquire the invite. It shall not be a task. I was confident of that.

***

"Found any leads?"

The voice on the other end held urgency in its tone. I merely breathed a no as my eyes were still heavy with a deep sleep that I was woken up from. My alarm never rang, or did it? I was not sure. There were no windows in the hideout I was residing in, so there was no way to know if it was day or night without waking up and checking the time.

"Seems like you partied hard last night with your friends. Sleeping in till 10? How unlike the Specialist."

My eyes shot open. What? Was it already 10 in the morning? My phone flipped out of my grip in the process. I patted my mattress to look for it, but I was too disoriented to function. It was the loud hellos of the caller chiming in the quiet that granted me with the whereabouts of the phone. Picking it up, I finally spoke a coherent sentence. "Nothing of that sort, Yifat. I was up late last night looking into the case," I clarified, which was the truth, but not the whole truth.

It was Monday at last. The day that the meeting between the Triads, Pakhans, and Cheung was taking place at Harbor Grand. All of yesterday, I had kept it to myself and conjured up ways of not only procuring an invitation to the party but also forming strategies of how I would acquire the intel I needed from the meeting.

"That was my first question, Specialist... did you find any leads?"

I sighed. In formulating plans, one of the biggest challenges had been dodging Yifat. I had no idea why, but I had intentionally kept her out of the loop regarding my plans. "I have some friends in Hong

Kong. I'm taking a little downtime away from the case to hang out with them," I had told her, and while it was a good enough excuse, she had still called me several times over the last two days to inquire about my whereabouts. How was she not an agent herself? I wondered every time she seemed suspicious about my words. Regardless, the day had finally come, and once I was done with today, I might involve her, depending on what I'd find.

"No!" I answered her, "I guess one can't party and work at the same time. My brain isn't working all the same."

"You're getting old, Specialist. Rest up." Yifat said and hung up.

I breathed out in relief and tossed my phone aside. I had to do a lot of preparations for today. The first order of business was formulating a good story for my undercover character, as not to raise suspicions. Fortunately, the hard part was out of the way, which was to obtain an invite. I had called Zhang, who had conjured up an invite for me despite being occupied. I stood up, went to my backpack, and pulled out the invitation card. "Rez Milano." I read the name of the card. "I can't wait to have Triads and Pakhans meet you."

The day went by, and the night soon ringed in. I found myself outside Harbor Grand at 8 sharp. I gave a final tuck to my bow tie and brushed away the small wrinkles formed on my suit due to sitting in the car as I made my way inside. This ballroom, much like the last one, was grand yet decorated in an intimate setting, extravagant enough for the riches to bask in its glory, while classy in a sense to appeal to those minds with a taste of elegance and subtlety.

The grand hall spread to a distance that the other end was hard to spot. Crystal chandeliers circled down from the arching sky-blue ceiling, which gave an illusion of the open sky. The bright lights that lit the room were illuminating the glimmering golden walls, and the floor was so polished that it looked like a thin spread of ice over a lake, almost mimicking a clear glass. It wasn't only the ballroom. The women in attendance sparkled like an open box of jewels, embodied in shades of emerald, ruby, and amethyst, swirling before me. As I walked through the crowd, scattered away in their cozy corners, their low chatters accompanying wafts of rose, hyacinth, and jasmine held me captive, even if momentarily, for I was on a mission of my own. My mind did not wish to bow down to such distractions. Not today!

At a distant corner of the ballroom, a little secluded from the rest of the crowd, I spotted a group of men, conversing amongst themselves. I instantly knew this was the group bearing the members of Triads and Pakhans. Any doubts that I had washed away when I saw Cheung's head ducking out and coming into my focus. The politician was engaged in a serious conversation with the group, rarely exchanging a small smile here and there. Perfect! With my target locked, it was easy for me to drive my plan into motion.

"Good evening, Xiānshēng," a beautiful Chinese woman greeted me as I made my way toward the group, trotting ahead with casual steps as if I was looking around exploring the place so as not to attract attention.

I smiled to myself. I had planned to flirt with the very same woman, for she was sitting next to my targeted table. Fate was working in my favor. "Hi, Madam, good evening," I said as I took a seat with her. Before she could say anything, I made sure I was in earshot of the table behind me, and sure enough, I heard one of the Chinese quite clearly over the faint music playing in the background when he said, "Come forthright, and I'll bear witness to the greatest concert of this era."

Ignoring that, as I figured they were just making casual talk and there was no code hidden in his words, I diverted my attention to the woman in front of me, who was merely smiling at me as if I was a unique art piece.

"Nǐ hěn shuài," the woman said something in mandarin, and I shook my head, gesturing to her that I didn't speak the language.

She nodded. "I only look," she said, smiling.

While I found it weird, even creepy, I took it as a blessing in disguise. This way, I won't miss anything important from the table behind me.

"They have a great deal to offer. Hear them out."

I heard Cheung propose, and my ears were instantly perked up. Yes, speak of the deal, reveal the truth.

"Two hundred million dollars," one of the Triads declared, and I almost spat out the drink I had just sipped.

The girl raised her eyebrow, handing me a napkin. I thanked her with a smile and focused my attention on the group again.

"He's worth more. You don't even know how much money he has earned us in the past. Not 200 million. No!" One of the Russians exclaimed, and I inwardly gasped, wondering if they were talking about Aaron and what did they mean by him earning them money.

To my dismay, my wandering thoughts were soon pulled into a loop, and my questions were answered when the politician spoke again. "Aaron could not have possibly stolen you more than what we're offering. I refuse to believe that."

I brushed a hand through my hair. No, I could not believe that my hunch had been right. Aaron Cohen was a dirty financier. I didn't have enough time to dwell on the new development when the Russian man laughed.

"Oh, sir, if you have to ask such questions, I assure you, you don't deserve to take Aaron Cohen in your possession."

I chugged my whole drink down as my senses were slowly getting numb, and I needed to rehydrate myself. Now I knew why they chose a busy ball event to discuss this. Most of the people here were foreigners, not even knowing English. Often in such events, dirty games could be tucked away under thick, expensive fur carpets and stashed up on grand chandeliers.

"Let us be the judge of that." The politician sounded annoyed. "Name your price."

"You want a drink?" Right then, the woman raised my empty glass toward me to ask.

I sighed. This was not the moment for unnecessary distractions. I nodded so she would leave, and I could focus on the conversation again.

"You just can't put a price on somethings, my friend."

I heard the sound of the chair back up and held my breath. Was the deal off?

"$2 Billion."

I heard the politician and closed my fists tightly. Waiting with bated breath, I anticipated an affirmative answer. The offered money should have to be more than what Aaron stole for them. It just had to be.

"Drink." The Chinese woman was back, and I merely snatched the glass away from her. She started saying something in her language, but I didn't say anything this time, for the Russians had uttered the word I was waiting to hear.

"Deal."

Chapter 9

When I parked my car outside my hideout, I was drained off every last ounce of energy residing within me. For the longest time, I remained seated in my car, trying to process everything. My nerves had gone numb, and I couldn't think straight. Come the morning sun; I shall figure out how to rescue Aaron. For now, that lone mattress on the floor was calling out to me. Sleep had my thoughts clouded, and my muscles weakened. That was all I could think of at the moment and all I intended to do. I got out of the car with a purpose in my step. Head lowered and eyes half-closed, I made my way toward the gate of my hideout.

"Out partying again?"

I was startled at the voice, unexpected and catching me off-guard. My trance was broken as I came face to face with Yifat standing there.

Arms crossed and eyebrows raised, she passed me a judgmental glare, which held questions and accusations both. I sighed, not having the energy to take on a confrontation. I merely nodded.

"Yes, and I'm tired. I'll talk to you tomorrow," I said as I moved past her to get inside, but she stopped me again with her words.

"How's Harbor Grand Hong Kong from the inside? I've heard great things about its lavish ballrooms in particular."

I turned around and looked at her, puzzled. How did this woman figure things out? And so quickly? Here I was, still wondering how easily she managed to learn the location of the hideout when she only came here once, with her eyes covered the entire time. It really was a mystery to me. I still tried to play it my naive, unknowing self.

"I'm sorry?" I said, questioning her.

She passed a smile at me as she walked closer. I said, "I have heard great things about the hotel. Tell me, do the grand ballrooms live up to the hypes? Rumors rarely are true, you know."

"What are you talking about?" I asked her again.

"Oh, dear Specialist, you really thought that you'd go and follow the leads you've collected without me, and I wouldn't know?" She sounded serious but then suddenly gave out a laugh. "I told you about the meeting. I told you that the Triads and Pakhans are meeting under Cheung's supervision, and you still left me out of your big mission to follow the lead I initially provided you with."

I sighed. Perhaps it was wrong of me. However, this was not the place to talk about such details. So I gestured for her to come inside with me. Once we were in, we sat on the couch, and she turned to me, looking almost hurt.

"This might just be a job for you, but to me, it's a quest, a life-altering mission, which success or failure can give or snatch my father away. How could you have left me out of this?"

I listened to Yifat carefully; my heart feeling her pain. The woman had no idea about what I had found, and while I had dreaded revealing the news to her earlier, I now realized that what her father did wouldn't matter to her. She would still want to be involved in the process of saving him.

"I'm sorry," I said sincerely. "I should have involved you in the mission."

Yifat leaned forward and placed her elbows on her knees. She tucked her hair behind her ears as she looked at me intently. "Look, it's fine if you go to places alone if that's what you deem necessary for the mission. What bothers me is why you did it."

"I don't follow," I said, raising my eyebrow.

"The lack of trust, Specialist... you did it because you don't trust me." She sounded hurt.

I shook my head. "I don't know you well enough to form an opinion, Yifat." I defended myself.

"Oh, but you have formed opinions, alright. You didn't exclude me because you don't know me. No! You did so because of the opinion you've formed of me. You did not involve me because you think I have something to do with my father's kidnapping," she said, more as a statement than a question, as if she had made her mind that I suspected her.

I took a deep breath. It was best to bring the truth to the table so we could talk about it and move on. "Alright, you're accurate in your assumptions that I have had my doubts regarding your involvement in the abduction of Aaron Cohen. But I have my reasons to suspect you."

She crossed her arms and leaned back. "Really, like what?"

"For starters, you get defensive when I bring it up."

"That's because you accuse me of having my father abducted." She almost shouted, "I don't get defensive; I simply defend myself."

I understood her point, so I nodded and moved on. "Another reason that I don't trust you or that I didn't involve you is that you have a conflict of interest."

"What do you mean?" She curled her lips in confusion. "You're saying I'll be biased because the victim is my father?"

"Yes!" I said without fail. "You wouldn't realize that your father could have done something wrong on his part and that he could be involved in some fraud."

Yifat threw her hands on the side as she came forward and sat on the edge of the couch to focus on me. "You think I can't see that? Heck, I'm more sure than you that my father must be dirty in some way that so many dangerous people are on his tail. What you don't realize is that it does not matter to me." She sighed. "Don't blame the victim, they say, and my father is a victim here. Regardless of what he has done, he still deserves to be saved because what they did to him is criminal. That is all I know. End of story. No questions asked."

I leaned back, realizing the sense and logic in her words. She was right. It didn't matter what his father did or how he got himself involved with some dangerous people. He needed saving, and that should be our only concern. I looked at her, this time with guilt evident in my eyes.

"You are right. I shouldn't have brought this up," I said sincerely. "Your father's past deeds should not alter my actions toward solving this case."

Yifat brushed a hand on her face and sighed. "I wanted to be a part of this case."

I stood up as a show of my declaration of the promise I was about to make. I raised my hand as if I was taking a pledge. "I promise, from this point onward, I shall never exclude you from any details pertaining to the case," I said and waited in the very same statue-like stance until she gave out a laugh.

"Alright, Specialist... You're forgiven," she finally said, and in response, I bowed down and influenced another round of loud laughter out of her.

I went to sit next to her on the couch and breathed out in relief. Silence took over, and I relaxed in the calmness after enduring a horrible stormy night. It was like the sun was out, casting its peaceful light on me.

Yifat looked around and scrunched up her nose. "This place is almost unlivable," she said. "Get yourself a hotel. We're here indefinitely anyway."

I lay my head on the back of the couch and closed my eyes. "I like it here. This reminds me of my days on the force."

"You never told me," Yifat said, and I briefly looked at her.

Exhaustion was still sitting heavy over me. I was not in the mood to indulge her in my life's story. "Perhaps another time, Yifat." I breathed.

She rolled her eyes. "I tend to look forward, Specialist. I seldom bring up the days that have gone by."

I shifted my head a little to look at her. "What do you mean?"

"I don't care about your past," she said in a careless manner. "Tell me about what you found out on this little mission of yours." She insisted.

I groaned. Here I was looking to get out of that conversation, but I could understand why she was impatient. I sat up straight and cleared my throat. I began telling her everything I had found out back at the politician's house and how I came about receiving the invite to the party where the meeting was set to take place and everything I heard in the meeting. I watched the shades on her face change when I mentioned that her father was a dirty financier, but she quickly moved past it and focused on the information I was sharing. Finally, when I told her that there was an exchange of Aaron Cohen taking place between the Pakhans and the Triads, her interest was piqued.

"The place and that day and time," she spoke for the first time since I had started talking. "Are you sure it is what you think it is? I mean, it was narrated in code, right?"

I extended my arm to pick up water from the table in the front as I felt my throat drying up. I took a few sips before I continued, "I have figured out their system by now. They disguise it in a casual statement, where the keywords and numbers are thrown in the exact way they are, without a change. That is usually the address, date, and time." I clarified. I could see she was still wary of it, but she nodded anyway.

"You're the agent. I trust your instincts," she said, extending her hand in front of me. "Can I get some water as well?"

"Sure," I handed her the bottle and watched her drink it in its entirety in one gulp.

She wiped her mouth on her long sleeves before turning to look at me. "What was the place again?"

"Pok Fu Lam," I answered. "I did some research and found out that there's a deserted and secluded hiking trail on the mountains overlooking the road. I presume it had to be where the exchange must be happening."

She nodded, agreeing with me. "And did you happen to catch the day?"

"Most likely, it's this Friday," I said. "The group mentioned the day many times in their conversation.

That, and the time, 10 p.m... They kept answering each other's questions the same way. 'I'll get back to you by 10 p.m.' They kept saying this one line. Again, it's a hunch, but I have a strong belief that it'll check out."

Yifat looked a little worried. "You're really proposing for us to head to that place when the exchange is happening to save my father?"

I nodded. "We still don't know where they are keeping him, and who knows how long it'll take for us to figure it out. This is our chance. Aaron Cohen might be right there. The exchange has presented us with a great opportunity."

Yifat nodded. "Alright!" She stood up and brushed a hand over her wrinkled dress. "We have three days to forge some successful strategies to go about this mission. Let's catch some sleep and meet for breakfast to discuss." She suggested.

I shook my head in affirmation and led her to the exit. Unlatching the door, I stopped her before she left. "We'll get him back," I assured her, knowing this was not just a job for her like she mentioned it was for me.

She smiled. "I know!"

***

"Drinks a night before our big mission?" Yifat raised her eyebrows when I broke out a fancy bottle of bourbon. "Driving a little on the wild side, aren't we?"

"I'm throwing caution to the wind." I raised my glass. "We have earned it after working relentlessly for three days straight."

"I'll cheer to that," she said as she clinked her glass with mine, and we took a mouthful in—letting the first few drops burn our scratchy throats from all the talking we had to do, exchanging theories and whatnot.

It took a while before the liquid began to soothe our tensed nerves and calm us down. It was a down night after a few days of exhausting casework, and I thought we needed a little break. It was quite unlike me. People who knew me and my ways were aware that I often spent my nights before a showdown, either exercising, rehearsing my plans in my head, or merely sleeping. However, this time, it just felt right, like I needed this more than I needed a peaceful slumber.

"So, why did you retire from the force?" Yifat asked me out of nowhere, throwing me off-guard with her sudden question.

I almost choked on the bourbon I had just consumed. Clearing my throat, I looked at her inquisitively. "I thought you only look ahead. You know, you said that you don't concern yourself with the matters of the past." I reminded her of what she had said a few days ago.

"Not when there's a chance I'm about to be passed... a story of yesterday myself," Yifat said dramatically, taking another sip of her drink. "This will cloud my senses for sure tomorrow. Oh well..."

She shrugged. "It's better that way. At least I won't feel my end so vividly."

"Oh, it won't come down to that," I said, raising my glass. "Don't you worry... I'll be there to protect you if need be."

Yifat rolled her eyes. "I can protect myself, Specialist."

"I said if need be," I clarified.

"Your story, Mr. Sheppard. I'm not letting you off the hook, so don't try to change the subject." Yifat brought us back to the topic

I had no choice but to start telling her about where I was from and why I retired from the force so early. "I'm a veteran from the army..." I started, diving into my life's details, bit by bit, making sure only indulging her in what I was comfortable with.

"You're one with high morals. I like it," she said, toasting me in respect when I finally stopped talking. "Not many like you exist these days."

"I try!" I said, bowing with a smile. "It's your turn now, Miss Emuna."

"Pardon me?" She said, almost slurping her words.

I could tell that the drink had set nicely in her system. "Your story..." I said. "I know nothing of you."

"What do you want to know?" Yifat leaned back, gripping her glass between her fingers, and crossed her legs, as if ready to narrate a long tale filled with many twists and turns.

"For starters, I'm quite intrigued by why you had a fallout with your father right before he was abducted," I asked her.

She sighed. "My father and I had different visions for my future." She started, "Ever since I was a little girl, I was a very good student; straight A's, always on the top of my class, always super skilled in sports. There was no area where I didn't excel. And like any father, my dad had this notion that my intelligence deserved to be used in the places that he deemed were right and useful. In that way, he cared less about what I wanted to do with my life."

"What did your father want you to do?" I asked her, nudging her to continue as I felt she was trailing off.

"He wanted everything; learn Karate, learn as many languages as I could, and worst of all... study law or medicine. He had my future path set out for me long before I could even have a mind of my own." She paused, looked at her empty glass, and extended it in front of me. "Could you top me up?"

Although Yifat was getting a little drunk, I nodded and filled her glass, knowing that the only way she was finding the strength to speak of her past was under the influence of alcohol.

"I take it that you didn't want to do any of that?" I said, handing her the glass back.

"No!" She groaned. "Except for Karate." She giggled. "I quite liked kicking some asses." She took another large sip from her glass before continuing,

"But everything else was pure bonkers, and I didn't want to do any of that."

"So, you didn't? That was why you guys were estranged?" I nudged her further.

"No, no! I'm not that rebellious. I tried to do everything he expected of me," she said, chugging the liquid in one swig, and slammed the glass down on the table. "You're seeing a woman who knows Karate, is fluent in Italian and many other languages, is a songwriter and singer and knows how to play the piano brilliantly." She gave her collar a proud tug. "I'm no ordinary woman, you know."

I laughed. "If you did what your father asked you to do, why was there any restatement?"

She sighed, defeated with the conversation. "Because one day, I stopped doing it all." She brushed a hand through her open hair nervously. "I left the University of California, where I was studying a major of his choice, to pursue my dream of becoming a film actress. And he had been angry with me ever since." There was a deep hurt evidenced on her face by now, and I felt my heart quiver for her

"I'm so sorry," I said. "I heard that you met with your father the day before he got abducted?"

She nodded. "He came to say goodbye because he was leaving the city. I remember what he said to me as he walked away... 'Yifat, resume Law... that's where you belong.' I had denied him quite bluntly, and now that he's not here and I don't know whether I'll ever see him again, I regret ever disappointing him." She paused for a while as her sobs were slowly building up, almost becoming audible, and I realized that she didn't want that. She wanted to stay hidden behind the mask of happiness and pretenses. I let her be as she collected herself before continuing. "He asked me to wait for him. He said he'd be back, and while I had said I would, I remember those hurtful words more vividly than any other we had shared before we parted." She gulped, controlling her cries. "I don't want my last words to him be that he has no right having a word in my future. I want a better ending. I can't let this be our end," she said, gulping down her growing lump again, not to come off as weak.

I took in a sharp breath, making sure my tone would not reveal my sympathies for her because I knew she didn't want that. "You'll get to rewrite your story. I promise you that."

She warmly looked at me and smiled. "Can I confess something?"

I nodded. "Yes, of course."

"This is the first time I'm seeing you as a component partner since we met. It's the first time I feel like I can trust you," she said honestly, and I could hear the sincerity in her voice.

I smiled back. "I know. It's today that this has become an equal partnership."

She lifted her empty glass from the table and raised it in front of me. "I am not going to drink anymore, but here's to a victorious tomorrow."

I smiled and clinked my glass with hers. "Here's to bringing Aaron Cohen home."

Chapter 10

"This place is hauntingly dark," Yifat exclaimed, looking out the window as we drove through a jungle of semi-built, cheap cottage-like adobe houses.

While the main road leading into the residential area was perfectly constructed, we drove deeper into the area of Pok Fu Lam, toward the deserted hiking trail in the overlooking mountains. The road started to show cracks, which caused severe bumping of the car. The concrete had given out, probably due to harsh weather conditions and lack of attention from the government in the area's reconstruction. The drive was anything but uneventful, and the darkness outside was only adding to the horrors of our journey.

"The devil lurks around in the dark and dances on the broken deserted lands. It had to be a haunting place," I replied, keeping my eyes on the bumpy road. I could see a car following me in the rearview mirror. I made it a note in my head not to stop, for a car on your tail in such deserted roads was not void of dangers. I had no intention of falling prey to an intruder's evil motives before my quest could even begin.

Honk! Honk!

This was not good. I could have ignored the car tailing me from behind and brushed it off as someone going the same way as we were. However, the car seemed to want us to stop. The constant flickering of headlights and nonstop honks narrated a horror story on its own.

"Are we caught or something by the enemy?" Yifat pointed out, voicing what I was thinking but dreading to say it out loud.

"I have no idea, but we can't stop," I said as I pressed on the escalator harder to speed through the broken roads. The darkness of the car following us continued to lurk behind us. It was only a matter of time before the car began to try to overtake us on the narrow crippled road where we were driving.

"We're going to crash," Yifat pointed out as our car skidded to the side, barely maintaining a few inches' distance from the long trail of adobe houses.

I turned to the other side and pressed on my breaks, and the car came to a sudden halt, almost knocking us out. I held onto my gun as I decided to deal with the situation instead of fleeing from it. It was the best option or perhaps the only one we had.

"I'm coming with you," Yifat said, taking hold of her gun and stepping out of the car with me. The car that was tailing us had stopped slightly by our side in front of us, but nobody came out of it.

I extended my gun in the car's direction. "Get out of the vehicle. Come on, face me," I yelled, enough for them to hear behind the closed windows, but not for the residing population to become alert of the commotion.

The car's door opened, and my hand fell on the side to see who it was. "Zhang!" I gasped in surprise, and he came to stand in front of me, laughing out loudly.

"What's up, brother?" He stretched his arms to give me a hug, but I stopped him with my hand.

"What the freaking hell was that?" I asked him, annoyed for causing us this trouble when we were already walking on a thinning time thread.

"Just thought to give you a little scare." Zhang laughed. "Wasn't my intention, though. I honked at you because I meant for you to stop. But when you persisted on fleeing, I went with the notion you had developed that I was some creep following you. I'm sorry, man!" He said, quite sincerely this time.

"How did you know where we were?" I asked him. I was curious about how he came to find us since the second I saw him.

"I know Hong Kong and all of its dirty work, my friend. I have my ways to find intricate information about its evil affairs lingering around in its dark corners," Zhang said, giving a proud lift to his collar. "Besides, I wanted to lend a hand in the mission. This place is dangerous."

"Thank you," I smiled warmly at him.

"Guys, can we keep the reunion bliss for some other time?" Yifat said, sounding almost annoyed at our compassionate exchange.

I nodded. She was right. We needed to get to the hiking trail before it was too late.

"Park your car here and get in with us. Two cars might attract more attention." I suggested.

Zhang agreed, parked his car on the side of the road, and got in the backseat with us. The rest of the drive went by in silence, for each of us was planning our own strategies in our heads and fearing for different things. Fear of failure for me, fear of losing her father for Yifat, and most likely fear of life for Zhang. Apart from briefing Zhang about our plan, there were no other exchanges during the short drive. Soon enough, we had driven deep into the forest, and we found a board at long last.

"Pok Fu Lam Greenland's Hiking Trail. 2 KM away." I read out loud from the crooked board that was covered in dead branches and tree leaves. The text had faded, displaying the impacts of altering seasons on it. I turned to Yifat and Zhang. "Let's walk from this point. A car too close to the meeting area is risking it." I suggested, and they agreed.

With calculated and slow steps, we made our way toward the trail, deep in the far spreads of the jungle, with mountains hailing on the sides like mighty beasts. Although the distance was not as much, our steady speed restricted us from reaching our destination faster. We were careful with our steps, afraid of stepping over dead leaves and fallen twigs.

"Duck!" I announced as we reached a point where we could see the group a few feet away on the lower level of the hiking trail. "We need to keep at this distance and cause our diversion from here."

"I'll do it," Zhang volunteered.

We had taken the time during the drive to get him to speed about our plan and how we had planned to distract the group so we could swoop in and save Aaron.

"I think Yifat is not in the condition to leave here and do anything else," Zhang said, and I instinctively looked at her, who was stunned in her spot.

Our initial plan had been for Yifat to cause the diversion by taking an alternative route to the trail, head to the rear end of the forest, light up a fire, and shoot a few times to get the group's attention. In that commotion, I was supposed to get Aaron and run away, and Yifat would meet us out back near our car. However, we hadn't accounted for the condition we'd find Aaron in and the fact that looking at his miseries could have an impact on Yifat. Despite the darkness, I could clearly see her tears trailing down her cheeks as she stayed glued to her spot, her eyes fixated on the scene unfolding before her.

The place reeked of horrors and evils. Tall trees were surrounding the once well-constructed trail that led the wanderers and travelers to the peak of the mountains, which overlooked the scenic view of Pok Fu Lam. The leaves had long been shed from the trees and what stood now were dead branches and aging trunks. The mountains had grown wild plants all around, which provided for the scene to look all the more terrifying, casting dark shadows over the space where the group of Pakhans and Triads was currently standing.

There were four men on each side; Pakhans and the Triads. I couldn't spot Cheung among them. With the Pakhans, Aaron Cohen stood limply, with the support of two men, who were supporting his ginger body from falling on the ground due to weakness and extensive beating, I presumed. He was tied in thick ropes, and his mouth was taped with a broad silver duct tape, which was shining brightly in the dark. His hair was a mess, and his arms seemed to be bleeding at various points. A very noticeable scar could be spotted on his forehead. The blood oozing out of it was an indication that it was a new one. Perhaps they had inflicted that one upon him during the journey to the mountains here.

"Are you sure you can do it?" I asked Zhang, forcing my attention away from the scene and Yifat's condition. "It's a high-risk task." I reminded him.

Zhang grabbed the duffle bag we had brought with everything one could need to start a fire, and he hung it over his shoulder. "Please, I can handle it quite easily," he said with confidence. "Be prepared. As soon as you hear the gunshots, act fast. We won't have enough time before the group realizes that it was just a distraction to send them away." He instructed, and I nodded, patting him on the back.

"Good luck," I breathed, and he was off, disappearing behind the thick woods. "Yifat, are you ready?" I asked her, and she briefly turned to look at me.

Her silent sobs had by now become audible in the quiet as I could hear her faint hiccups. "What if in the chaos, they take him with them?" She voiced her worries. "We should be doing something now. I mean, he's right there," she said, almost in a pleading tone.

"Look, I know you're hurt seeing your father in this condition, but I assure you, they won't take him along to check where the gunshots came from. They might leave some guard, but his limp body would only slow them down and further diminish their fighting chance." I tried to comfort her, but she didn't respond.

Instead, she focused on looking at her father again. "I can't do this." She breathed amid her cries. "I can't stand idle as they continue to forge deals against my ailing and injured father. I need to save him now." She declared and started marching ahead.

I grabbed her by the arm with force and stopped her in place. "Yifat, just look at me," I ordered, but her downward spiral restricted her from thinking straight.

All she could say was how she wanted to go there and help her father out of this dangerous situation.

"Yifat!" I almost yelled out her name, and at last, it did the trick.

She calmed down under my grip and looked at me with teary eyes.

"We'll save him," I said, assuring her. "Let Zhang cause a distraction first. Okay?"

She nodded but didn't get to answer me as right then, loud gunshots were heard in the air. I looked over to where the exchange was happening, and sure enough, the gunshots had caught the group's attention.

"Where is it coming from?" One of the men asked. "Is someone else here?"

"Look, boss... Fire!" Another one pointed out in a direction, and everyone's eyes darted in that corner.

"Let's go and check out who has come here with a death wish in their hands." The man, who was supposed to be the boss, ordered. "You two, keep guard of this bastard. Rest of you, scurry, spread, and see who's intruding us in this crucial time."

I watched as the group scattered to where the fire was coming from, and I braced myself, turning to Yifat. "Remember, use your full force and bang the heel of your gun into that man's head." I pointed out to the one who was standing over the right side of Aaron. "Meanwhile, I'll simply snap the neck of the other one. Quick and easy death."

Yifat almost rolled her eyes. "Always the show-off." She mumbled under her breath.

I glared at her, and we got in our positions to head up the trail. A few feet away, I whispered to her again, "Don't think, just strike." I instructed her, and she merely nodded.

She stepped ahead. With large leaps forward, she strode her way up and sneaked up on the man. As I had taught her, she banged her gun's heel over the man's head as hard as her karate trained hands took her, and the man fell with a loud crash. Simultaneously, I sneaked up on the other man, and in one fluent motion, I snapped his neck, producing a crackling sound, as the man went down, lifeless like a lump.

I breathed a sigh of relief. "The initial phase is done. Now, let's get your father out of here before they come back," I said as Yifat bent over to open his ropes. "No, wait! We don't have time for this. We need to head out of here." I pointed out, and to my relief, she agreed with much convincing. She held onto Aaron from one side, and I went on the other. As we started walking, I addressed her again. "I think we should head inside the forest, this way," I suggested, pointing out in the opposite direction to where the Pakhans and Triads had gone.

"But they're still lurking around. Isn't it better to just drive out of here as fast as possible?" Yifat argued with my plan.

"The roads are broken. We can't drive fast." I pointed out. "There's a greater chance of us getting caught on the open road, where the sound of the car might lead the group toward us than the thick dark forest where we can find shelter until the group disperses out of here."

Yifat sighed, defeated, or perhaps not having the energy to argue. "Alright, let's go to the forest," she said, and we started walking into the thick bushes of the forest that surrounded the mighty mountains. "Stop! I can't go any further with my father hanging onto us in this miserable condition." She halted in her steps all of a sudden, disrupting the pace we had both set along with the limping Aaron. "I need to untie him."

I could sense an urgency in her tone and see the pain in her eyes. The moon casting its shadow over us made the dried tears in her eyes shine like tiny droplets of water on a clear rock. I knew there was no point in arguing with her now. I nodded in agreement, despite my disapproval. This was important to her. I watched her as she bent down, made her father sit on one of the nearby rocks, and took off his tape. He breathed out heavily as a reflex when he was given an open outlet of air to breathe in. He shivered from the cold hitting his face and all his open wounds and tried to stabilize his huffy state as she proceeded to untie the ropes gradually.

"Yifat, listen to me..." Aaron spoke, stuttering his words out. "I need to tell you something."

"Dad...shhh!" Yifat placed her hands on his cheeks and gently caressed his forehead's wound. "We'll have plenty of time to talk. I need to get you out of these restraints first," she said as she focused her attention on opening a persistent knot that refused to cooperate with her.

My heart warmed at the sight, but my mind that often worked as an agent's immediately perked up as I heard the urgency in Aaron's tone. What was it that he was trying to tell her?

"No, sweetie, listen to me... There's just too much at play here. You have no idea of the kind of people involved here." Aaron tried to get her attention again, but she was still fighting with the same knot.

"I know, dad! I know it all. Just save your energy, please, for me! You need to run with us." She pleaded with her father.

"Yifat, whatever you know is just the tip of the iceberg. I assure you, it goes deeper... way deeper than you could ever imagine."

That caught Yifat's attention and mine as well. She looked up at him but never faltering from loosening the ropes. "What do you mean?" She asked him while struggling with another knot.

"All of this...it's much bigger than what it seems, Yifat... it's..."

Aaron's words were caught in his throat as I heard Yifat's scream at the sudden impact. I looked on in horror as I saw Zhang standing over Aaron's head, having knocked him out with his gun's heel, grinning like the maniac I could never have taken him for.

Chapter 11

"Bigger than it seems, huh!" I watched in sheer shock as Zhang circled around the fallen body of Aaron like a wild beast, priding itself for the prey it had just caught. He walked slowly toward Yifat, who stood numb in her place, still processing what had happened. With a crooked smile, he brought fake sympathy in his eyes, "I'm sorry, Yifat, but your old man was about to disclose some intricate details to you that I'd rather not have revealed to you.... At least not just yet."

"Are you..." Yifat shivered to say the words and stuttered, "Are you working with..." She couldn't finish the sentence, making Zhang laugh at her state.

"No, sweetheart, save your breath. Don't stress yourself over such minuscule turbulences. You have a storm waiting for you ahead. Save yourself some energy to endure some darker days." He said in a sinister mock, "I'll tell you everything. No need to form coherent questions on your own and tire yourself out."

"You were working against us," I said, stepping forward to stand in front of him. "Or is this part of a grander plan? Knocking Aaron out?" I couldn't believe that I was still giving Zhang the benefit of the doubt. I wondered when I got so trusting, but Zhang's betrayal was hurting me to no end. I needed what was unfolding before us to be untrue, some kind of a ruse, a pretense for the betterment of the case; anything. I couldn't have been fooled so mercilessly.

Zhang laughed out loudly, "Tsk! tsk! Oh, naive little Specialist." He trotted his way towards me with slow steps and a menacing pace. His persona had changed so drastically in a matter of minutes since I last saw him that I would even believe it if someone told me that the man in front of me, who had an evil aura lingering around him, was a clone of Zhang and not really him. He brought his face close to mine as a sinister laugh escaped his lips, "Is it that you see the best in people, or your detective skills are getting rusty? I believe it's the latter. Your glory days are long gone."

I felt my fists tightening, and an uncontrollable urge to punch him across his jaw riled up inside. However, I refrained myself, for I intended for him to finish. Maybe he was right! I did like to see the best in people.

"Little Aaron over here was right, though." Zhang gestured behind him to the fallen body of Aaron, "It is bigger than what it seems... much bigger!"

"Why did you help me get to this point if you were not on my side? Why help me in the case at all?" I had to ask, ignoring his threatening words. I knew from the start that this case was not a simple kidnapping case. It went deeper, which was what had intrigued me to take it up in the first place. I was more interested in knowing how this man fooled me.

"Ever heard of 'Keep your friends close and your enemies closer?' You shouldn't be calling yourself 'The Specialist' if you have to ask why I was helping you." He said, using air quotes to mock the titles given to me, "I was spying on you since the time you first came to Atlanta." Another loud laughter came out of him, and this time, I felt my restraint slowly giving in, "You thought another 'agent' bumped into you on the street willy nilly. Wow! You're a fool."

That was it! My patience gave out, and I landed a strong blow at him as my tight fist made contact with his jaw, and he stumbled over with the impact. In no time, however, he had stabilized himself, and his evil laugh came rushing back.

"You should not have done that. I know Karate," Zhang proudly stated. Before I could respond, I saw Yifat held on to his shoulder as she turned him around in one swift motion and kicked her knee in his stomach with a strong force, not letting him go just yet as she threw a punch to his nose, making him bleed and fall on the ground.

"And I have mastered in Krav Maga, you massive tweep," Yifat said, bending over to look at him. He seemed to be pretty out of it... doubled over in pain, holding on to his face, and out of breath as the stinging in his nose had almost cut his supply of air.

Yifat, who was more concerned about her father and taking him out of that place, bent over to shake him awake. "Sheppard, he's not responding." She called out to me as even her harsh shakes were not working. I rushed over to her side, giving a fleeting glance at Zhang, who was still reeling in pain. As I sat beside Yifat, I could see pain so vividly apparent on her face. Her hands were shaking, and I couldn't believe they were the same hands that had just collapsed a man double her size a few moments ago. It was like her senses had gone numb, thinking about a potential prospect where her father might never wake up, or we might not be able to rescue him out of here.

"Yifat, let's take him out of here, and we'll figure..."

My words lingered in the air, never making it to her, as I witnessed Yifat fall on the ground with a howling thud, almost lifeless, limp, and unmoving. Zhang had used a karate chop across her neck, and her body had dropped down like a sack, knocked out instantly due to the harsh impact. I looked up at him, and I saw a smiling maniac - the face covered in blood, which he had smudged all across in an attempt to wipe it off, bloodthirsty eyes, displaying hints of rage, embodying evil, sinister humor within it. His injured, hunched body stood over me like a coward animal, picking on the weakest in the herd.

"Now, it's just us men. None have an edge. Come on, get up." Zhang spat, venom in his words, and a subtle hint of fright resided in his eyes that I knew he was trying to keep under wraps and mask with his witty remarks. I briefly looked over at Yifat and Aaron, knowing they would be revived. At this moment, I could not let Zhang take on the victory. Not even over my dead body.

I stood up and flipped my suit's jacket in place, "If my suit tears during this worthless debacle, you're paying for it with your blood."

My words seemed to have riled him up, which I had wanted. As he stepped forward, I judged by his actions that he was about to sucker punch me. Instinctively, I ducked my hand down, and his hand found nothing but air. Taking the opportunity, I whirled around him and came to stand behind him, ready to hold him by his throat and force some answers out of him. To my immense surprise, Zhang was just as quick as I was in combat. In no time, he had turned, balanced himself on his one foot, as he swirled a kick in my direction, and it landed right across my torso. I found myself stumbling backward, my foot entangling with a fallen branch. A scream escaped my lips as I saw a shortfall from where we were standing at a height in the forest, which was sure to cripple me, I concluded.

"You're not going that easily," I heard Zhang's words, right after I found my hand in his firm grip, pulling me over. I stumbled slightly to stand on my feet again, and I had barely balanced myself when another punch landed hard across my face.

Falling flat on the ground, the impact of my head hitting one of the rocks had me losing my consciousness, and as my eyes shut, Zhang's sinister face was my last sight.

"Look, do you see?" Zhang asked me to come over to the railing of the ship in urgency, "Hurry, you might miss this."

I went over and stood straight by the railing, "What am I supposed to be looking at?"

Zhang rolled his eyes, "Not my face," he said, "Look down...the dolphins. It is like that scene from the Titanic."

I sighed, not having the patience for Zhang's silly antics. I turned around to leave, but Zhang stopped me. I glared at him for daring to lay a hand on me, and he merely brushed my rage off with a smirk, "Loosen up, Specialist. A little fun won't kill you."

"No, but you might!" I said with honesty, "I don't trust you."

Zhang laughed, "What? Do you think that I'd push you off the boat if you looked down the railing?" He shook his head in disbelief, "I'm not stupid. I know you can swim, better than the fish, I might add."

"Stop exaggerating... and the unnecessary rambling." I dismissed him.

Zhang continued to smile at me, "Oh, the wise one, know that you and I are not ending with a coward stab in the back. No, no. We're going down together in a violent, bloody, and really messy combat where we kill each other."

"Where I kill you." I corrected him.

"We'll see about that." Zhang smiled, patted me on my back, and left.

I felt a harsh kick on my torso, and the intense pain in my ribs shot me awake. I watched Zhang hovering over me, and I saw the same smile on his face that I had seen that day. I felt a pang of hurt wash through me as disappointment settled in for ever trusting him. How could I have let this man fool me so blatantly? Something suddenly hit, too close to home and too intense to let it linger without taking action.

Pushing through the sharp pain in my head, I flipped up, catching Zhang by surprise. He was standing over my head, so when I shot up, my back faced him. In the blink of an eye, I swirled around and raised my leg high enough to hit him across the jaw with my harsh kick. His stumbling backward and losing his balance was all I needed... *an opening, a small opening, and then you don't let your opponent breathe*. That's what people would say about me, and nothing was closer to reality.

Without giving him the time to even blink, I had held his collar in my firm grip, scrunching his shirt in my fists. I brought my face close to him, "Why did you do this, huh? Why did you betray me?" I demanded an answer, and when he laughed in my face, his bloodied teeth made my own blood boil with rage. I punched him in the nose as a painful screech escaped his lips. Blood, his face showed nothing but an endless stream of blood, sourcing from various ends.

I held onto him again and gritted my teeth, "Who are you working for? Who had sent you to spy on me?" I tried it again. Although he was pretty out of it now, he still refrained from giving me any answers and continued to laugh. I landed another punch across his jaw and saw him spit some more blood out. "Tell me, or I'll end your life right this instant."

I had just finished my thought when I felt the air around me get tensed. The ground started to shake as if there was an earthquake. My mind was clouded with thoughts of Zhang's betrayal, running rogue with scheming a revenge plan, formulating a strategy to sneak Aaron out of here, and worrying for Yifat. This left me hazy and in a daze, and it wasn't until I physically saw the helicopters approaching in my line of vision that I realized what was happening.

"And boom, you're finished, Specialist," Zhang whispered with a grin. "You didn't think I'd confront you without a backup, did you?" I stepped back, letting go of his shirt in haste as I looked up to really examine the situation... two, no three! Dear lord, three helicopters were circling over our heads. Men were ready to jump out and charge at us, possibly with guns or even worse. I took a few minutes to see if I could spot what kind of weaponry they had: Assault rifles? AK47s? or were they M4 Carbine? I couldn't tell. I just knew that whatever they had, my one lone Shadow 2 Pistol would not be a match. As questions bombard me regarding the kind of arms those men in the hovering birds could have in their possession, things only took a darker turn. I spotted the fire that Zhang had initially started, slowly spreading wide enough to come in our sight.

"Fellows, take hold of Aaron."

"The fire was a distraction. I knew it was."

"Never mind that. Focus on what's essential at the moment."

I heard the ramblings of the fast-approaching group midst the howling sound of the roaring flames of fire. I gulped in fear as I assessed the situation. Aaron still laid unconscious, not stirring or responding to the chaos prevailing around. I could see Yifat slowly moving. Her hand reached his head as I imagined she must be having a throbbing pain. There was Zhang's backup right above us, prepared and most likely equipped to end our existence, and both the Triads and Pakhans were also strolling their way back to the scene.

I looked here and there in a hurry. As the Triads and Pakhans spotted the swirling helicopters and began to speculate amongst themselves, while Zhang still reeled in pain standing in the distance, I made a decision in sheer panic. I took the distraction that the gangs were facing due to Zhang's "army" as my opening window. I walked towards Yifat, who was still not in her senses despite regaining her consciousness. I held on to her as I dragged her out of there, with the burning forest left behind us. I ignored Yifat's cries of "but my father," as we escaped the scene. She would understand... I had no choice.

Chapter 12

Flashback

The pages sitting before her eyes showed some of her shed tears... tiny drops of salty water stained the inked pages of her book, which shone like pearls on the shore under the dim night's lamplight. She often cried, wept for a few minutes, and shed some tears when the pages revealed the harsh realities of the world she lived in. Her heart would break so easily and so badly for the people of history and for what they had endured.

"You're so strong, Yifat." People would tell her, and it was the truth. Someone who was an expert in the form of self-defense, Krav Maga, that was the image she bore for the people who didn't know her heart and were not rightly acquainted with her soul. It was in the lonely moments when she cuddled herself in her cozy blanket that her real self made an appearance - vulnerable to the tiniest of emotions and broken by others' sorrows.

She felt her eyes getting heavy. She glanced at her nightstand; the table clock displayed it was past midnight. A yawn escaped her as she shut the book. Her fingers danced over her engraved name on the cover before she put it aside. She had a thing with making her belongings personal, especially the books she read. The literature in her possession was her most prized treasure, and she wanted to feel a connection with it, so she would have them encrusted with her name.

"Your name is so... musical. It is like a song of love and serenity. That is why you proudly display it like a badge of honor on everything." She recalled many who had said similar words about her name as she laid down and closed her eyes. Yifat Emuna... it really sounded like a serene song. Oh, how easily it laced out of one's lips like a hymn for God. She loved it, perhaps the only thing she loved that came to her from her father.

"People ask me what my name means, father." As a little girl, she had asked her father once, "Everyone loves it. What does it mean? Why did you name me Yifat Emuna?"

Her father had sat her on his lap, caressed her long silky hair, and smiled the warmest smile. He looked at her with the kind of unconditional love that still, to this day, remained unfound. "The day you were born and handed to me in this cozy white blanket, my world became an unknown reality that looked better than every dream my subconscious mind could ever conjure up." He continued, "Holding you in my arms, seeing your beautiful eyes staring back at me..." a word laced out of my lips... "Yifat!" I breathed. It meant 'beautiful' in Hebrew, and I have no idea why my mind praised the beautiful creation before me in my native language, but it did. So I named you Yifat."

The little girl was pleased. "Why Emuna?" She had asked further, "Why not Cohen?"

"Faith... it means faith. You restored my faith in goodness, kindness, and love. You are my faith, my beautiful Yifat."

Yifat felt sleep taking over her as the words of her father echoed in her subconscious mind. As she entered the world of dreams, away from her reality, her heart silently craved for the same relationship with her father... the one she shared while growing up, the one that was lost somewhere in the changing times and altering mindsets regarding life. What laid now between them were uncomfortable silences and dodging gazes. If only she could change that. If only.

***

"Have them send over the script," Yifat breathed out in the phone. "You know I'd not refuse a good theatrical play."

"Miss Emuna, the script is brilliant. However, be warned, the play will consume a lot of your time and energy." Her agent would always try to warn her, "I might never understand why you still follow this tiresome path when your investments had gained you tremendous amounts of wealth."

Yifat toyed with the pancakes on her plate, her fork dancing it around. She never did have an appetite in the morning, but her trainers insisted on her having a full breakfast. Perhaps this was the only downside of the career she had chosen for herself. She plopped the last piece in her mouth as she breathed her words out through the morsel, "If it had been for the wealth, I would have catered to my father's wishes and went into the financial world as he did. Dreams don't bargain with profits and losses, Tanesha." Her fork that was thrown on the plate made an audible noise in the quiet surroundings of her empty penthouse, "Send me the script and let me review the role." She added and hung up the call. A long morning routine awaited her.

Weaving her way back to her bedroom upstairs in her spacious penthouse, she passed by the grand white piano that her father had gifted her on her 16th birthday. Her fingers subconsciously graced its taintless ceramic surface.

This beauty was her father's way of showing he supported her dreams of going into acting and music without actually tangibly supporting it. Although he was the one to enroll her for daily piano lessons, he never wanted her to pursue that or any other related careers. She took in a deep breath as she stroke a few keys before heading up; the melody lingered long in the silent air.

Extended stretches of yoga, a warm shower, and a morning routine of skincare later, Yifat felt refreshed, ready to take on the day. She picked up her phone and checked her email. Tanesha had sent her the script and its schedule, so she propped herself on the bed and began reading. Two pages in, and she had made up her mind – it was the tragic love story of a woman who was a warrior and who had to pick her oath to the nation over her heart. It had hit too close to home for Yifat.

"I'm ready to sign up," Yifat called her agent and told her.

"It's a one-month commitment, Miss Emuna. You may take more time to think," her agent reminded her, but she shook her head. "It is final." She declared before telling Tanesha to arrange for a meeting with the producers. Tossing her phone aside, she made her way down to her living room. Her piano seemed to call out to her as it did every morning. At some point in life, it had become a ritual for her to sing and play the piano for some time every morning. It was like her day didn't start without it.

Her fingers began to hit the keys skillfully in the way she was taught and the way she adapted over the years. Slowly, the music picked its pace, and she started to hum the song out loud, swaying her head from side to side, tapping her feet away with the rise and descend of notes. The scene around her disappeared as she closed her eyes, and she imagined herself back on stage, the place that brought her most pleasure and joy. She was in the middle of a performance, dancing before a broad audience, who watched in awe with held breaths and glued gaze as her soul danced to the melody of her heart's contentment.

"Your skilled mind that creates such beautiful melodies could be out there, in the real world, where it is of the most use... multiplying the pennies into big bucks."

She was startled with the words suddenly breaking her trance. Her fingers stopped on their own. She knew the voice all too well - deep, commanding, and often frightening. She took in a deep breath and turned around to find her father standing there. Although she knew another lecture awaited her, she was happy to see her father after a long time. She stood and stayed numb as she took him in. He had aged since the last time she saw him.

His dark brown hair showed some grey strands, his beautiful, expressive brown eyes were covered in noticeable wrinkles, and he had even lost some weight. His tall stature stood in front of her, a little hunched over, exhausted, and spent. Yifat felt like hugging him, but she was reminded of what he said. Even when they were meeting after so long, he still didn't refrain from a taunt. She sighed. Sometimes, she really regretted giving her father the key to her penthouse.

She kept aside the love she felt for her father and gave him a hurtful smile, "I've made bucks...big enough to afford this house and a lot more." Yifat stated proudly, "All of that by following my dreams."

"Would law or finance really have been that bad, Yifat? You should not have quit." He stated, stepping closer to her.

Yifat stepped back instinctively, as if she was afraid that she would catch a glimpse of the same love in his eyes that she used to see when she was a little girl... when she was the girl who abided by everything her father told her to do. Not anymore! She didn't want to get sucked into the same rule-following regime ever again. She tucked her hair behind her ear, nervously, "Is there a reason why you're here?"

"Yes! I'm leaving the city for a few days. I just wanted to come and see you before that... to say goodbye."

Yifat was taken aback. He had never done that before. As someone who worked in JPI Securities, he was out of town quite often, but he seldom made it a point to bid her goodbye. She raised her eyebrows, "Goodbye? You have never done that before. It's not the first time you're leaving the city."

Yifat could see his features tense up. He looked away as if he was trying to hide something. "I'll be gone for a long while this time. That is why I wanted to come see you."

"Oh," Yifat still had her suspicions, but she decided not to voice them. Reluctantly, she stepped forward and gave her father a hug, "Have a safe journey. I'll see you when you get back."

"Resume law, Yifat! That's where you belong."

Yifat released herself from her father's grip. Her eyes were filled with tears, and her lips trembled. "This wasn't goodbye. This was your last try before going on this long trip of yours."

"No, Yifat, listen…"

"No, father, you listen to me." She almost yelled. It was quite uncharacteristic of her to do so, but she felt her rage gripping her in a way that she lost sense of her true self. "You have no right to tell me what I should be doing in life."

She couldn't control the outpour of tears; her words started coming in stammering sobs, "I tried, dad, I really did. I did everything you asked me to do. I went on your business trips to learn more about your field. I enrolled in law school. I learned so many languages because you told me to. Heck, I even followed suit in your footsteps and invested my income in various things so you'd be happy. But I can't let go of acting… I just can't quit the theatre."

A haunting silence engulfed them, the only sound in the atmosphere was of Yifat's faint cries and the ceiling fan running in a distant corner of the living room. Her father stared at her, his eyes void of emotions yet holding so many. He took in a sharp breath, "Walk me out?" He requested. Despite being angry at her father, Yifat obliged his request. They got into the elevator and out the door. Yifat spotted a man standing by the curb beside a car… he was probably his ride.

Aaron turned to Yifat, and his face turned serious… intense even, "A few weeks at the most. It may take me some more time, but I'll be back. Wait up for me, alright!"

Yifat felt a pang of hurt wash through her. Although she was confused, she didn't ask any questions. There was just something so painful in his eyes that Yifat merely smiled at him, forgoing what had just transpired between them.

"Of course, you would be back, dad. I'll be here." She breathed as her father hugged her again, and they parted ways.

***

"And my heart shall be yours, for as long as I live, it shall beat your name, for my soul is entwined with yours... let the bodies part, but our souls shall never taste distance. Never any separation, my beloved. Never!"

The curtains came close as the crowd stood up in cheers and loud applause. Yifat made her way to the backstage, taking off her wide sunhat and a blonde wig, tossing it aside in haste. She rushed towards her designated station and grabbed her bag. Digging into it, she pulled out her phone.

"Miss Emuna, your phone..."

"Yes, yes, I'm aware. I got it." Yifat cut the sentence in between one of the girls from the backstage crew, who was trying to tell her that her phone had been ringing nonstop during her performance. Another crew member had told her the same thing by holding up signs as she continued to play her scene. She had panicked... This had never happened before. All of her friends knew she was performing that night; many were even present in the audience. Who could be calling her so much? Her heart only sunk deeper when she saw an unknown number. Could it be? No!

"Wait up for me, alright!"

No, no! He must be fine. She assured herself as she hit call on the same number. After a few rings, a man's deep voice came alive in the earpiece.

"Miss Yifat Emuna." The man greeted. His tone held sympathy, almost as if he had some bad news.

"Yes, speaking." She said with a racing heart.

"This is Detective Richard Hans. I am sorry to be calling you after a few days of finding this, but your number that was listed as Mr. Aaron Cohen's emergency number in his office was out of reach, and it took us some time to retrieve this number."

Her heart started to beat at a speed that she felt it would burst out of her chest, "Emergency? What's going on, officer?" She asked him, crossing her fingers.

"I'm afraid I'm not calling you bearing good news."

Yifat gulped down the lump of fear, "Just tell me, please! Is he okay?" She insisted.

"We can't tell, Miss Yifat."

"What do you mean?"

"Your father has been kidnapped. He was seen boarding his train from Munich, but he never made it to his destination. Those who were waiting for him on the other end at Harrisburg came to us with the complaint."

Yifat had long stopped listening as she had slumped on the little plastic chair present backstage.

Her senses had gone numb, and she couldn't think straight. Her mind was clouded with a million questions, but none made it out of her. She was shell shocked in her place...still, seemingly lifeless.

"Miss Yifat?"

It had to be the hundredth time that the detective must have called her name. The light bulb hanging above her head had swung from side to side with a passersby impact, and that had jolted her back to reality. Alas! The reality was dark and lingered with guilt and shame. Her parting words to her father were anything but pleasant, and now as she sat, with uncertain circumstances before her, regret washed over her, and no hope seemed to be in sight.

"Miss Yifat, we got to know that you were really close with your father. We could use your help."

Yifat stood up at the detective's words. Yes, she was close to her father. He had always been her hero. He had taught her so many valuable things and how to play a smart agent when need be was just one of them. The detective was right; they could use her help. She would help. Aaron Cohen had trained her for this very moment. She would give her all and bring her father back home, whatever it shall take.

"Detective, let's meet and discuss the case."

***

"Four days," Yifat exclaimed in rage. "My father got abducted four days ago, and yet this is all the information you have collected so far?"

The two detectives that had come over to brief her over the case and of everything they had found out so far of her father's kidnapping sat back. Slowly, fear became evident on their faces. Yifat Emuna had a reputation of being a tough woman – someone who instilled fear in her opponents during her karate practices, and even when her father took her on business trips. She would often speak in the meeting with a commanding tone and presented compelling arguments, which would get them to agree to her terms quite smoothly.

"Miss Emuna, the case is slowly slipping out of our grip," one of the detectives said, gulping down, "We have tried to find clues, look for eyewitnesses, gather as much intel as we could. Unfortunately, this goes deeper than just a simple kidnapping, or else at least you would have gotten a call for ransom."

Yifat tossed the file on the table and brushed a hand through her hair; it was still a tangled mess from how many times it was styled through the course of her performance today. She looked at the detective sternly, "What do you suggest then?" She asked, trying to hold back her anger at bay.

"We hire additional help... a federal agent perhaps," the man said, "And not just any agent, we present you... him!" He said, extending a file in front of her, "Take a look; here's everything you'd need to know of him."

Yifat picked up the file and read the name out loud, "The Specialist... I have heard of him," she said.

"Everybody has Miss Yifat. He's the best in the game."

"I have also heard that he has retired. How would he work the case then?" Yifat pointed out.

"Yes, but now he takes up some special cases on request of old friends or family... anything that intrigues him really." The detective explained. Yifat flipped through the pages of the file before she stood up, "I'll study about him in detail and get back to you shortly." Yifat told the detectives as she took her leave.

She walked up to her bedroom and immediately pulled out her laptop. A single search of his name brought many results on her screen – cases upon cases, those that were brilliantly solved, and thus were written about by his admirers. On just a first glance at his work, Yifat knew that he was a wise man. One thing, however, stood out to her... some details about his girlfriend.

"Could she be..." She breathed out as she opened a link, "A financier with this amount of knowledge is a lethal person. Many believe that she could be involved in a string of cyberattacks on the Swiss bank. Experts further claim that even if she did not commit the crimes herself, she most likely aided them by sharing intricate inside information. The investigation is still underway regarding the exact nature of her involvement with the incident."

One of the articles read. She closed the lid of her laptop as she felt her eyes getting heavy, and her mind was left in a haze. The words on the screen no longer made sense to her. She had no idea what to do. Perhaps catching some sleep might help her.

***

A week had gone by since her father got kidnapped, and she had spent every waking moment researching about the Specialist and other relating factors of her father's abduction case... that was when she was not on stage. She went through the file a million times over and read up every article she could find online about the special agent. Although skeptical at first, with time, Yifat had realized that Specialist was for sure worth bringing on board with the case.

"Specialist is the only one who could solve cases that reach a dead end," She had heard about him, not from anyone else but her father himself. There had to be something about him that her father spoke so highly of him.

She sighed as she opened the file again, landing on the page that held a picture of the Specialist with one of her father's close friends. She had noticed it the very first time she had seen the file, but because she had her doubts about the Specialist, she never followed that lead. She propped her legs on the center table in the living room where she was sitting, still studying the Specialist. She leaned back on the couch, pulled out her phone, and dialed a number.

"Yifat, how are you doing this fine evening?" A happy male voice came through the earpiece, and she forced a smile.

"Not good, Uncle Michelson," She breathed, "Dad has been kidnapped."

"What?"

"I'll explain everything to you, but could you tell me if you can get the Specialist on this case? I believe you have worked with him before. I saw your picture with him in the file." Yifat tried getting to the subject straight away.

"Yes, of course, provided that he is not busy with something else," Michelson said.

Yifat shook her head, "Nothing is conditional here, Uncle Michelson. I need him on the case. I would have contacted him myself, but two things: you know him better than I do, and I have to honor another prior commitment."

"And Yifat Emuna never falters on her commitments,"

"Please, Uncle... I wouldn't have asked you if I could have done so myself." Yifat requested again.

She could hear a sigh on the other end, "I'll get in touch with the Specialist, but fair warning, he only takes up cases of his choice. So, I can't guarantee if he'll take it."

Yifat smiled, "Trust me, he won't turn this one down."

Chapter 13

"Why did you...drag me out... I was going to..."

"Yifat, not now!" I glared at her as Yifat stammered her complaints while we sat in the car to get to the hotel. I needed to focus on the road, and her voice was distracting. She was still pretty out of it but had come to her senses enough to realize that I had dragged her out of the scene without bringing her father along with us.

"My dad, he should be with..."

"Yifat!" I warned her again. I tried to focus back on the road as I felt my vision getting blurry. All the punches that Zhang had landed on me had me in a daze. It was a rather dangerous bet to be driving back to the hotel, but I could not have left my rental car on the scene, given that it could be traced back to my name. Besides, taking an uber would not be void of risks either. My disheveled condition, as well as Yifat's, was already alarming to a common man. Her stuttering words, revealing what we had endured, would not have helped matters. I released a sigh of relief when silence finally prevailed. I didn't know if

Yifat had lost her consciousness again, or she had listened to me and was letting me drive in peace.

When we reached the hotel that Yifat was staying in, I made sure that we composed ourselves as best as we could. Yifat was not injured, but her senses were still quite numb, which made her tumble over as she walked. Meanwhile, I actually displayed noticeable wounds all over my face. I got out of the car and held Yifat by the arm to help her walk. Fortunately for us, the hotel was busy at the moment... a large convention was checking in, and most of the staff was busy catering to them. So, we were able to make it to Yifat's room without any heads turning in our direction.

While I understood the risks of coming here instead of the hideout, the place that Zhang arranged for us to stay at was no longer an option. I silently thanked myself for my habit of carrying my limited belongings everywhere. Over the years of my career, I started to pack light and travel with my one bag, wherever I went, because I knew that my stays were temporary, prone to being snatched at any time, and unreliable. The door to her room had barely shut when Yifat brushed my hand away from her arm that was holding her in place. She stumbled forward, almost losing her balance, but there seemed to be an urgency in her step as she moved ahead a little towards the center and turned to look at me with rage and frustration evident in her eyes, "Why did you drag me out of there? Why would you do that?"

"Yifat, you don't know how things turned out." I tried to reason with her, but she was not in the mood to listen. She continued to pace around the room. I could see her on the verge of crying out loudly.

"I know everything, but I don't care. I needed to save my father... he was right there." She said. Whispering the last words, she gave up. Her sobs came rushing through, refraining from cooperating with her or staying back.

"So were all the other people... Triads, Pakhans, Zhang's gang, everyone had us surrounded. Had they noticed us, they would have killed us and then your father." I explained to her, and in frustration, she sat down on the bed, holding her head in her hands. I could now hear her faint sniffles. I went over to my bag that I had tossed aside upon entering, and I retrieved a heating pad out of it. I put it in the mini microwave in the room and let it heat up as I went over to her and sat beside her.

"We had no choice." I simply said as she looked up, her eyes red but dry. They were all cried out.

"We could have taken him with us... could we not have?" She reasoned again, refusing to believe that we really were out of options.

I was about to answer, but the microwave beeped, breaking my thoughts. I stood up and went to take out the heating pad. "There were too many people there," I said as I walked back to her, "Dangerous people with high-tech gears, most definitely better than ours. We were outnumbered and lacked the right weaponry.... here!"

"What do I do with this?" She asked me as I handed her the heating pad.

"Your neck must be sore from the impact of that chop. Apply it there." I told her.

"Thanks," she breathed, taking it from me, "Your nose is still bleeding."

"It'll heal." I waved her off. I took in a deep breath, sitting by her side again, "I tried to get Aaron out of there, I really did."

"What happened then?" Yifat asked in a low voice, and the look of disappointment and guilt I saw on her face hurt my heart. I knew then that Yifat was angry at herself and not me. She hated that she was unconscious during the whole event, and she missed an opportunity to save her father when it presented itself.

"You could not have done anything even if you were in your senses." I clarified.

She shook her head and sighed, "I could have tried... we could have tried. I let my emotions cloud over me in the most crucial moment, and Zhang took the better of me."

The mention of Zhang's name stung me with a new wave of pain, but I tried to move past it. For now, I needed Yifat to understand that we had no choice but to escape the scene unnoticed. "We all let our emotions cloud our judgment at times. It only makes us human." I said as she looked back at me. Her hand pressed against her neck, holding on to the heating pad. I inhaled a sharp breath, "I let Zhang fool me as well. It was because of him that we couldn't save

Aaron. But just know that in no way was that your fault. The situation simply turned against us pretty quickly. I saw the Triads and Pakhans focused on Aaron... even with the burning forest around us and helicopters circling above our heads; the members had locked their eyes on Aaron, refusing to look away. That was why I decided that it was best that we got out of there without getting noticed by anyone... we had enough distraction on the scene to escape."

Yifat took in my words, just staring at me for the longest time before she stood up in frustration. She threw the heating pad away in haste and resumed pacing around the room. "I can't sit idle and let them continue to torture my father," she said, almost yelling, "No! I'm going to hit back... with full force. I can't let them hurt my father anymore."

"Yifat!" I called her name in hopes of calming her down. She hardly passed me a glance as she continued to circle around the small space of the room. I groaned and stood up to go to her, "Please listen to me...and listen to what you're saying."

"I told you, I don't care." She shouted, "It could be irrational and impractical, but I need to save my father... now!"

I brushed a frustrated hand through my hair, "I know you're angry. Believe me; I am too. The only reason we failed in this mission is that I trusted Zhang, and he betrayed me." I gulped, "I'm infuriated, and just like you, I plan to hit back with just as much force as well. But do you remember what your father said?"

She stopped and looked down, not meeting my eyes, "It's bigger than what it seems," she breathed, wiping away some of the tears that she couldn't hold back or hide.

"Then you should know that acting out in rage could cost us tremendously." I waited for a sign to see if she understood what I was saying, or at least listening. To my relief, she was, "Look, your father is in captivity, but he's alive. And so long as they need him, they won't harm him. But, if we're compromised because of our haste, they won't waste a second in ending his life to save themselves."

Yifat took some time to think over before she sighed and nodded, "Fine! We'll figure something workable out."

"Tomorrow," I added, "It was a long day. We need to gain back our energies... I'll sleep on the couch for tonight and get myself another room the next day."

Yifat nodded as she went to her bed without saying another word. She looked emotionally exhausted. I saw her lie down, covering herself in a blanket and rolling into a ball. It was only a matter of seconds before the room started echoing with her faint snores. At last, it was quiet, and I relished in the peace as I retired myself to the two-seat couch. It was too small for me, but sleep was already out of the question for tonight. I had a lot on my mind. I closed my eyes as I let myself relax. Zhang's betrayal lurked at the back of my head, influencing a strange set of memories that were dark yet pleasant; in a twisted way, my soul found peace in recalling some of the forgotten moments I had spent with someone I dearly loved.

***

I looked up at the sky. It was a starry night. Wide spreads of twinkles covered the sky's bed, brightening and sparkling. I adjusted the cloth over the picnic basket one more time, afraid that the edibles inside would go cold. I checked my phone for the time, about fifteen minutes late. I took in a sharp breath as I waited and decided to lie down to count some of the stars, perhaps even make my own imaginary constellations.

"A million..." I breathed after the longest wait as I heard footsteps approaching. "A millionth star counted in your absence, my love." I pouted without getting up.

Scarlett, my beautiful girlfriend, came to sit next to me on the blanket, taking off her bright red high heels. She crossed her legs and got comfortable as she bent down to give me a kiss on the cheek, "Oh, stop exaggerating. I'm only but 20 minutes late." She said as she looked around and smiled, "Besides, had I known you have arranged for a picnic in our backyard, I'd have rushed out of the office that much faster."

I sat down and looked into her beautiful dark brown eyes, which often looked hazel under the moon's light. I smiled at her warmly, "As if they'd let you go. You're crucial for them... more than even the CEO."

Scarlett rolled her eyes, "Ever the charmer." She said as she leaned in and kissed me, "Thank you for doing this. You know how much I needed this." She whispered. I smiled at her, tucking her luscious ash brown hair behind her ears. I brought her petite body closer to mine and held her close to my chest. She was wearing a gorgeous, knee-length, red bodycon dress, which complimented every inch of her body. Her hair was left open, and despite coming straight from work, she still looked breathtaking.

"I thought we both needed a break," I whispered, hugging her close. "Case after case, and one financial deal after another, it was time to just... reconnect."

Scarlett looked up at me, enduringly, "I have missed you."

I bent over and planted a feather-light kiss on her lips, "Not more than I missed you."

She smiled, "I can smell tahini sauce," She said, licking her lips, "Did you prepare me some Sabich?"

I nodded at her, pulling out her favorite sandwich and feeding her a bite, "And I have brought champagne." I picked up the bottle and showed it to her.

She sat up, giddy at everything that the little picnic had to offer. She held onto the bottle and looked at me, "May I pop this open?" She requested. I couldn't help but smile at her innocence. She found happiness in the smallest things.

"Yes, go ahead," I told her, and she jumped in excitement as she popped the bottle open, quickly filling up two flutes.

"What are we toasting to?" She asked, scooting closer to me.

"To finding such laid back and beautiful moments amidst our chaotic lives," I suggested.

"And to always be by each other's side no matter what life throws at us." She added to the toast.

I smiled and clinked my glass with hers. "To us... for forever to come!"

Our lips touched each others more than the champagne graced them that night. Our souls had danced together, intertwined and synced as one under the stars. I didn't remember being this happy before. Peace and bliss lingered in the atmosphere, wrapping us up in the blanket of warmth, passion, and never-ending love as we slept with the moon casting its shadow above us that night.

***

My eyes shot open as the memory replayed in my head so vividly as if it was happening for real all over again. I sat up straight and rubbed my face. I missed her. Scarlett never left the frame of my thoughts. Even when I was walking through the roaring flames of fire, I missed her. The last memory I had with her was us promising a forever to each other, and at times, the memory stung. Yet, like an addict, I often replayed it, for the untainted bliss I had felt that night was worth remembering, even if it came with hurt. Its loss caused me extreme pain. I was willing to shatter myself time and time again if it meant living that night, even if merely in a dream.

I looked over at Yifat, who was still sleeping peacefully, and I silently hoped that if she had anyone in her life whom she loved as much as I loved Scarlett, then may she never have to live through what I did. I took in a deep breath to calm my nerves down and bring back my attention to the case.

"When those you trust betray you, it's those few loyal ones who stand by your side in moments of your darkness that are worth your love... worth your loyalty. Keep a lookout for those friends."

My father used to tell me that in life, many would betray my trust, and it was a nature's rule that when one person takes you down, others inevitably join them to knock you over. But, some stay back by your side, give you a hand to stand back up, and help you walk on your feet again. These are the people that you need to put your trust in, even when you have lost faith in everyone else.

I pulled out my phone and scrolled to the one contact that I knew I could trust, for this person had always been there when the world had knocked me over. He had been a true friend. In my darkest of times, he had guided me to the light. If I could trust anyone with this intricate mission, it was him. I knew this much.

"Alexender Abramczyk," I breathed, before hitting call as I stood up to walk to a corner of the room, so I won't disrupt Yifat's rest.

"Specialist, I can presume it's late at night from wherever you're calling."

I couldn't help the smile that escaped my lips despite my melancholic mood at the sound of his raspy voice, reading me like tea leaves. As much of a mystery as I was, there were those rare occasions when I enjoyed being read or predicted rightly. "It is," I answered, "And because it's late, you might also be aware that it must be a crucial affair that I wish to discuss with you."

"Definitely!" Alex said, "Tell me, Sheppard, how may I be of help?"

"Do you remember the case I discussed with you back when I came to Tel Aviv?" I reminded him.

"Yes! I don't forget anything, Specialist... gifted like that."

"Right!" I said, "So, here's what had happened so far in Hong Kong in regards to Aaron Cohen's case."

I quickly briefed him over all the details of our adventures in Hong Kong, and he carefully listened to me, barely chiming in, other than with "hm"s and "uh-huh"s. Finally, when I was done, I waited for him to respond, "I am stuck at a dead-end right now," I said, "I don't know how to move ahead and find Aaron."

Alex waited a while before speaking, "I'm forwarding you the contact details of a man who'll be of great help in the case. Just talk to him with my reference. I believe he is currently residing in Hong Kong. You may arrange a meeting with him first thing tomorrow, or whenever you deem fit."

I listened to Alex carefully, but I had many questions, "Who's this man?" I asked for starters.

"His name is Jack.. everything else, you'll know when you'll meet with him," Alex simply stated.

I was still confused, the name alone didn't clear my doubts, and I didn't want to waste my time with someone who might not even be of help. I cleared my throat, "Give me something to go by, Alex. I need a little more info of the man." I insisted.

There was a long pause on the other end, and I almost believed that Alex would hang up without exchanging any more words. He often did that when he needed to withhold details for a valid reason. He simply didn't talk. To my surprise, Alex told me who the man was, and his words instantly calmed my racing suspicions.

"He's the leader of one of the rebel groups in China."

Chapter 14

"I heard you talking to someone last night," Yifat shook me awake first thing in the morning. I had barely slept at the early hours of dawn, and while I usually slept only for a few hours each night, my body had given out due to all the injuries it endured last night... I needed my proper rest.

I shifted myself in a more comfortable position as I pulled my suit's coat over my head. Yifat might get the message. "Sheppard, wake up." She shook me again, "I'm not leaving here till you tell me who you were talking to last night."

"My precious lover." I breathed, "it was a private conversation, Yifat."

Yifat pulled my coat away and threw it on the table, "I know it wasn't your girlfriend. Now, get up, and talk." Yifat was firm in her demand. Frustrated, I shot up and rubbed the sleep out of my eyes.

Squinting at her, I asked, "how can you be so sure, Miss Emuna. You don't think I can have a girlfriend."

"Oh, I know you had a girlfriend... I just know it wasn't her," Yifat said to my surprise.

I stood up as a yawn escaped my mouth, "elaborate." I demanded.

Yifat shrugged her shoulders and slumped down on the couch. She looked up at me and patted on the open seat beside her, "we have more important matters to discuss right now, I think... let's keep the relationship drama for when I'd host you a celebratory dinner after our victory. We shall bond over personal anecdotes and serious life issues then."

I shook my head, knowing that Yifat had turned into the kind of compass that pointed in only one direction currently, and it was useless to try and navigate her to a different one. I sat down beside her and laid my head on the back of the couch, "So, we're putting a pin in real conversations for now."

Yifat merely nodded, crossing her arms, "The call, Specialist. Who was it?"

I sighed, brushing a hand through my messy hair in an effort to detangle some of the knots. "I have a friend who works in Mossad. In my days with the CIA, I collaborated with him on many of my cases." I started, in between stretches and yawns that escaped me involuntarily, "on my way here to Hong Kong, I met with him in Tel Aviv. He was the one who told me about the initial meeting between the Triads and Pakhans, where we met."

"Yes, the game." She interjected, "you blew my cover that night. How could I ever forget."

I glared at her, "since then, I have made impressive strides in the case, which you gotta admit, wouldn't have been possible for you to achieve alone." I didn't refrain from pointing out.

Yifat rolled her eyes, "continue."

I stood up and walked to the mini-fridge and pulled out a water bottle. "Anyways, I knew that after the curveball thrown by Zhang, if there's anyone who could help with the case, it's him. So, I had called him last night." I said, chugging down the entire bottle of water in one motion. I exhaled sharply before continuing, "he gave me the contact details of a man who operates a secret rebellious group here in China." I said as I walked back to sit on the couch, "I did some more digging last night, and I found out that the sole purpose of these surreptitious operations is to overthrow the current regime."

Yifat sat up straight, her interest peaked. "And because he is a rebel of the regime, he would help anyone who is standing against the very system." She finished what I was explaining, and I couldn't help my proud smile. "Yes!" I simply stated. Finally, in the last many hours, I saw the same hope back in her eyes. A hope that I had witnessed every step of the way since the day I met her, only momentarily vanishing after last night's small setback. It was now back in full swing... twinkling and sparkling, paving the way for us to move ahead with determinant steps.

"When's the meeting?" Yifat asked, standing up and going towards the small kitchen area in the room, which held the necessary amenities. I watched her filling the kettle with water and turning it on.

I picked up my phone and quickly scrolled through my messages. I smiled to myself when I saw that I had received a response, "tonight!" I said. "If you're making coffee, I'll have a cup as well," I told her.

She briefly looked back as she placed two mugs on the counter, "you wasted no time. Was this man even up when you called last night."

"I had sent a text, actually. He got back to me this morning and has asked us to meet with him at Frantzén's Kitchen at 8:00 PM sharp," I explained to her, holding my phone up.

Yifat filled the mugs with water and stirred the crushed coffee beans in. She came over and sat next to me, handing me one of the mugs. Taking a sip, she let out a sigh, "let's hope we encounter only victorious endeavors from this point on."

I raised my coffee mug in her direction, "a thousand cheers to that, Miss Emuna."

***

"This place looks... almost romantic," I said in a mock as I parked my car outside, merely a few steps away.

"Intimate, Sheppard... there's a slight difference," Yifat said, getting out of the car. I locked up and caught up to her.

"I sure hope so; otherwise, I'd seriously doubt Jack's intentions towards me," I said as we entered the small space, and she passed a small smile at me.

The restaurant was dimly lit and intimately decorated. There were wooden barstool-like chair seatings in one corner of the small space, and on the other side, a proper bar was situated, where people were served with food that was prepared live. Those who wished to socialize with strangers would prefer a seat at the bar. At the same time, those with a preference for a quaint sitting arrangement went for the intimate setting.

"Good evening, Sir!" The Maître D greeted us with a warm smile. "How may I be of your service?"

"Good evening," I smiled back. "We're meeting with Jack Wu. He might have a table ready for three here." I told the smiling man.

"Oh, yes! He's actually waiting for his party of two over there at that table in the corner." The Maître D told us and led us to the table where Jack was seated. I took him in as he stood up to greet us; the man was a little shorter than me, his jaw chiseled and sharp, the kind that was often referred to as 'it could cut.' He wore a three-piece suit, much like me. His dark brown hair was set perfectly in place, sleeked back and gelled. His eyes revealed his Asian descent as the deep browns shone under the dim light of the corner table. The man had an authoritative debonair about him, which was always a welcoming aura for me in anyone. As we came in his line of vision, Jack greeted us with an enthusiastic handshake.

"It is so nice to finally meet you, Specialist." Jack smiled at me as we sat down. "I have read your cases... You're truly brilliant."

I nodded. "Likewise, Mr. Wu. Alexander spoke quite highly of you."

Jack waved me off, "Oh, he's a charmer... Order?" He asked, extending the menus towards us.

"Mr. Wu, if you..."

"Call me Jack, please! I don't like my association with a nation whose system I stand so against." Jack said, interrupting Yifat.

Yifat nodded, "Alright, Jack... Could we get to the point? I believe my partner here has briefed you on my father's kidnapping case. So, what could you indulge us with that we don't know already?" Yifat said, sliding the menu away from her, propping her elbows on the table, and leaning forward to hear better. "Food can wait!" She added.

Jack smiled at her, "On the contrary, Miss...?"

"Yifat Emuna," she answered.

"Right, Miss Yifat, food can't wait. You see, our brains work better when there's food in our stomach." He said, sliding the menu back towards her. "Please, I insist."

I watched Yifat groan in frustration as she snatched the menu off the table and opened it. I followed her lead, realizing that we had no option but to order something. I quickly glanced at the menu and found one of the items I liked,

"Magret of Duck," I said.

"Veloute," Yifat also pointed out to an item in the menu.

Jack smiled, "excellent choices, people."

Jack called over a waiter and narrated our orders to him. I could see Yifat fidgeting impatiently. Her fingers were tapping on the table as she waited for the man to leave.

"Now, please share any details you have about the case." Yifat turned to Jack just as soon as the waiter left.

Jack leaned forward and looked at us. "This case, it's no ordinary one. I looked into this briefly, and I immediately gained an insight that its connections go deep... really deep."

"With all due respect, Jack, we have heard the very same many times over," I interjected, "we're looking for a lead that could take us to Aaron Cohen."

Jack leaned back in his chair, crossing his arms, "Ahh! Aaron Cohen... everything comes down to him. It all somehow connects with him, doesn't it? Maybe that is why the CIA, Russia, and even China has deployed all of its best agents in pursuit of this one man."

I held onto the fork on the table and danced it on the empty plate in front of me, "we're aware that he's important for everyone. Could you tell us anything that might serve as a lead to get to him?" I said, trying to divert Yifat's attention. I knew that she was ready for anything, but I still feared how she'd feel if she got to know her father was involved in various illegal activities.

"But why? Why is my father so important? How come he became the most wanted man on the face of the planet? Why is it that such big economies are all pursuing him?" To my dismay, Yifat asked the questions whose answers I had tried so hard to keep under wraps.

"Your father was stealing for the Russians." Jack began, and I could see Yifat's face change colors... her impatience turned into hurt and disappointment so quickly that it was hard to keep track of the altering shades. Regardless, she remained focused on Jack, who continued. "Being in a company as big and important as JPI Securities naturally entails you to have possession of many national secrets... secrets that you can manipulate in your favor, to earn a few additional bucks for yourself."

"My father was rich," Yifat interrupted, clearly bothered by the allegations. "He had more than just a few bucks."

Jack smiled, "money is addictive, Miss Yifat... for those that take a high in it, can never be satiated."

Yifat shook her head, brushing a hand through her hair out of nervousness and frustration. "So my father was a dirty financier, I get it. But does that mean I quit looking for him?"

"No, Miss Yifat, not at all." Jack smiled, "I'm merely explaining everything to you from the root up... You know, if you familiarize yourself with the tree that bears the fruit, it tastes much sweeter when you finally have it in your hold to taste and devour."

I sat up straight and leaned forward, "we're listening, Jack. You have our full attention."

Jack picked up the napkin from the table, opened it, and gently placed it on his lap. He gestured with his eyes in a direction. "Our food's here." He said, and sure enough, the waiter brought our order, set the table neatly for us, and left.

I watched as Jack dug into his plate right away... the crackling sound of knife and fork hitting the plate now lingered between us. Jack propped a bite in his mouth before turning his attention back on us. "Like I was saying, the reason why China wants Aaron is that they wish to launch an elaborate attack on the United States."

"What?" Both Yifat and I gasped, "wow, does my father play a role in it?" She asked.

"He was going to quit the job he had taken up for the Russians." Jack began again, simultaneously eating a bite or two. "This didn't sit well with his bosses. They started to threaten him... with his life, and the life of the only other person he truly cared about."

"Yifat!" I breathed, and I saw Yifat gulped down. Her hands were tightly closed in fists, and she was biting her bottom lip to refrain herself from crying.

Jack nodded, "Aaron Cohen was compromised. He made some bad decisions in his life, and those who asked him to do these evil deeds refused to let him go even when he wanted to quit. Now, China knows that they could manipulate him by using his past against him, and with everything that he knows, he could be of great help to China for the cyber-attack they are planning to launch."

Yifat had balled the white napkin into her fist, and she had not touched her dish at all. I could hear faint sobs coming out of her as she held back her tears. I handed her the glass of water, and she took it, mouthing a small "thank you." I turned to Jack again, "what is this attack you keep speaking of?" I asked, taking a sip of my drink and a fork full of the duck I had ordered. "I'm aware of the tension between the USA and China, but has it really escalated to this extent?"

"Yes!" Jack simply stated, "blown out of proportion actually." Jack bent over to pick up his bag. He retrieved a piece of paper out of it and handed it to me. "Here, go ahead, give this a read. I know your life keeps you busy. This would bring you up to speed about everything."

I took hold of the paper and glanced over it. It was an article entailing the prevailing tension between two powerful countries. I inhaled a deep breath before I started reading.

"Read it out loud. I want to hear," Yifat managed to say, in between her faint sniffles. I nodded as I began,

"Fear lingers and continues to mount high among the Financial Markets, amid the escalating tensions between China and the U.S. China may extensively sell the U.S. government debts it holds in order to cripple the world's biggest economy. As of now, Beijing owns more than $1 trillion worth of U.S. Treasury bonds. If China were to really take such an action, it would result in debt prices plummeting down and interest rates hiking up in the United States. This would diminish investment and consumer spending's even further. Additionally, as a retaliatory action, the USA has taken an offensive approach against China, which pertains to China's enforcement of a controversial national security law regarding its territory Hang Kong. China has been criticized greatly for ending freedom and human rights in Hong Kong, which the USA is using against the country to cause a dent in its economy."

When I finished reading, Yifat released an audible sigh. "In the war of these two countries, my father became a bait." She said, finally taking a bite from her plate, "I wish my father hadn't done all of that."

Jack wiped his face on the napkin and tossed it aside on the table, "it's not the best time to get emotional. There's a lot to be done that requires our focus and undivided attention, Miss Yifat." Jack suggested, and Yifat seemed to have understood right away, as she refrained from voicing any more of her emotions. "Now that all of us are on the same page regarding what has happened let's discuss what's about to happen."

"That's exactly why we're here." I said, "To look ahead. So, what do you know about this attack you mentioned earlier?"

"Care for some dessert, Sir." Jack was about to answer me when the waiter came over. I quickly shook my head negative, and the waiter left. I gestured for Jack to continue again.

"As per my intel, China is planning to launch a major hack attack on the treasury of the United States, which could not just cripple, but dismantle the economy of America completely," Jack explained, and I fell back in my chair, stunned and out of breath. Yifat, however, remained on the same tangent; her father.

"How does Aaron Cohen come into this picture?" She questioned.

Jack looked at her with a tuck to his brow, "We have been over this. Your father holds intricate inside information, which China will get out of him by instilling the fear of ending your life." Jack repeated himself.

Yifat sighed as she stood up, "I think I can't take any more information today. I need some time to think over a strategy," she said.

Jack gestured to her still full plate, "you can eat in silence... We won't say a word." Jack said.

"I've lost my appetite." She said, "I just want to leave for now."

"Very well," Jack said, turning to me, "you have my details. Contact me when you guys are ready to take the next step." I saw him gesturing the waiter over. "I'll take care of the check. You guys may leave."

I stood up and shook Jack's hand, "thank you for indulging us with all the details you knew of. We have a lot to think over now." I said.

Jack smiled back at me, "It's just the start of a long and hopefully a victorious journey. Brace yourselves, people. This shall be an adventure."

***

I failed to arrange for a room of my own in the chaos of the day, and I found myself back in Yifat's hotel room. Sitting on the couch, I watched as she sat on the bed; her back leaned against the headboard, and with a book in her hands. But her gaze was diverted to a different direction. She was distracted, and I knew why. I stood up, went to the kitchen, and turned on the kettle. Quickly, I made a steaming cup of tea for her and handed it to her. She looked at me and shook her head, "thank you, but I'm not in the mood." She said.

"Have it anyway. It'll help to relax your nerves," I said, and she nodded, taking the cup out of my hands. She looked numb to everything else, and I decided to let her process it on her own.

"I said I didn't care what my father did," I was about to go lie down when her words stopped me. I turned around and went back to her and sat down on the edge of the bed. She looked up at me before continuing, "I do care. My father's deeds of the past have caused me great distress."

I nodded, "I know... It's only natural to feel this way, Yifat."

"It's clouding my thought process. It's like my senses have gone numb. I don't know what to think or how to proceed with the case." Yifat said, taking a small sip of tea and putting the cup aside.

"Yifat, he is still your father. Regardless of what he has done in the past, the fact remains, we need to save him. That's all you need to be thinking about. Isn't that what you said earlier?" I said.

Yifat buried her face in her hands, defeated. "I know all of that. My father always taught me to hold my values and my morals in the highest regard. However, now in a twist of fate, I need to save the man who spoke of morals to me from the trouble he got himself into because he forgot about those very morals. And if I save him, without considering what he has done, it'll be like I'm letting go of all that I've believed in my whole life. It'll be like I'm betraying my own values... what a dilemma."

I took in a deep breath, unaware of how to go about this situation, but I had to try, "if I ask you to treat it like a case, not a mission to save your father, would you be able to do that?"

Yifat stared at me, blankly, "I don't know. Maybe I would."

"There's a lot more riding here than your father's abduction. A whole country's economy and its future are at stake. It's bigger than your father at this point, Yifat." I tried one last time to try and cheer her up. To my relief, she nodded in agreement.

Picking up her tea again, she took a few sips and let out a sigh. "So, how do we move forward."

"We sleep," I suggested, standing up. "We'll start fresh tomorrow."

I went back to the couch and laid down. I picked up my jacket and placed it over my chest as I turned to my side to look at Yifat, "In case you think of waking me up early again by shouting, be warned, my gun is right next to me." I said, at which Yifat merely laughed.

"Your intrigue of what tomorrow might bring will not let you slumber, dear Specialist. Good Night!" She said, pulling the comforter over her head.

I sighed... The morning's sun couldn't come soon enough.

Chapter 15

"Shit!" I exclaimed as the notebook I was taking some points in slipped out of my hands when I was putting it away, and it knocked over the steel vase placed atop the side table beside the couch. While I silently thanked the interior designer for going vintage on the decor, for nothing broke, I cursed the annoyingly loud sound the vase made on the impact of hitting the ground.

"Specialist, why the early wake-up call? Flying out to catch worms, are you?" Yifat groaned, pulling up her eye mask as she looked at me with squinted eyes.

I picked up the notebook and tossed it in my bag. "Yes, precisely. That is the plan... to catch some nasty old worms."

"What are you talking about?" Yifat shot up, dangling her legs to the side of the bed. "You were up snooping around on the bad guys again, weren't you?"

"What else should I be doing?" I said, closing the zipper of my bag shut, "come on, we're leaving."

"Where?" Yifat stood up and came to stand in front of me, "I need more details, Sheppard. You can't play detective alone and have me follow you around like a sidekick... I'm not Watson."

I raised my eyebrow. "There was only one Sherlock." I said as I stepped ahead to walk out of the room, "coming?" I said, turning my head to call her over.

She had her hands on her waist in a stern stance. "Not unless you say that I'm the Sherlock in this team."

"Yifat!" I warned. Frustrated, she slumped her shoulders as she picked up her coat and followed me out.

"You could have let me wash up, at the very least," she pouted as we headed for the elevator.

"You could have woken up earlier," I said as the elevator dinged, and we entered. Fortunately, it was empty.

"Are we meeting Jack again?" Yifat guessed, and I smiled at her.

"Smart! That is why you're my partner." I said with pride laced in my tone.

She crossed her arms and smiled, "just a couple of smart Sherlocks."

***

"Ahh! The Specialist and Miss Yifat... isn't it a pleasure to meet you again," Jack greeted us when we reached The Flying Pan, where Jack had called me to meet with him for breakfast. He had texted me late at night to tell me he had more information regarding the case, and I needed to see him as soon as possible.

The place was small, located in a funkier neighborhood of Hong Kong, and had a rowdy appeal. Long metal stools and hunky sofas provided a seating arrangement, made for an exciting interior that I was sure attracted many tourists and locals alike. Although the old diner-like decor was not at par with my liking, I was more intrigued by what Jack had to say than the place he had chosen to eat the first meal of the day.

"Wouldn't have taken you to be so... cultured," Yifat exclaimed, looking around the diner as we both took our places.

Jack, who was doing something on his laptop, looked away from the screen and smiled, "I'll take that as a compliment." \

"Let's get to the point, shall we?" I interjected. I was in no mood to derail the topic by making small talk and exchanging views on the cafe.

"Always in a hurry, aren't you? I like it." Jack said, turning the laptop towards me, "read up and get up to speed... we have a long plan to forge, people."

I pulled the laptop closer towards us as Yifat scooted near to read as well. The screen showed a long article that went into extensive details about Hong Kong's and all of China's government involvement in various illegal acts, especially pertaining to the American economy. As an oversight, it might look to be a conspiracy theory, conjured up by the minds who took pleasure in telling such stories in their free time, over rounds of drinks at shady underground bars. However, for someone in the field, having worked in the CIA, army, and having political connections, I knew that the article's information held a lot of truth. One thing that stood out the most prominently to me was the article talking about China's Minister of Finance. His involvement in lending a helping hand to top businesses' embezzlement and fraud cases led many to believe that the Minister could be involved in severe financial crimes.

"The Minister of Finance, I feel like he is the key to the treasury hack stunt they are planning to pull," I said, sliding the laptop back to Jack, "he has sensitive information, and he must be an expert on the subject... unlike the dirty agents."

Jack smiled, shutting the lid of the laptop closed. "I had contemplated highlighting the important parts in this long read, but I didn't." He leaned back in his chair, folding his hands in front of his face, "I was right to trust your intuition."

I smiled, "what do you suggest to do then?"

"We take a page out of the criminals' book... Excuse me!" Jack said as he gestured the waiter to come over. I heard him order a few things for all three of us before he turned his attention back on us, "do you follow."

"Yes, we break into the Ministry of Finance," Yifat said, beating me to the conclusion of what Jack had meant.

Jack sat back, with a proud smile displayed across his face, "And here I thought I'd have to convince you both... with morals and all, often the likes of you are opposed to such ideas of bending the rules, even if it means it'd help someone."

I cleared my throat, "for the greater good," I said, picking up the empty glass from the table and raising it, pretending to give a toast. "Let's do it!"

***

"It's chilly," Yifat said, hugging the jacket's flaps close together to gain some warmth. It was quite a look... a leather jacket worn over the thick, brightly colored jumpsuit of an electrician.

"The wind or the mission?" Jack asked, raising his eyebrow as we got out of the car and stood outside the tall government building.

"The wind." Yifat declared, "the mission is exciting."

"Aren't you an adventure junkie," Jack exclaimed as he trotted forward towards the entrance.

"I wasn't recruited by the CIA when I was in college for nothing," Yifat said, giving a tuck to her collar.

I looked at her, my mouth hung open in shock, "I have a lot of questions..."

"Later," Jack interjected, "we have to break-in to this building."

"Yes, about that... How are we going to do that? This place must be packed with security, cameras, and whatnot. Even if we're disguised as electricians, wouldn't the men on guard duty know we were not asked for?" I pointed out. Although we had waited for the night to turn dark and for the streets to become deserted, I presumed it was still a task to enter the official building. All day, Yifat and I had tried to get answers out of Jack, but he had remained mummed about certain details, apparently claiming the aged-old 'the walls have ears,' logic to be true.

"You'll have to lose that slick suit of yours for tonight, Specialist." That was all that he had indulged us with. It wasn't until a few minutes before leaving when he had thrown a pair of jumpsuits at me, "zip up," he had said, and I had gathered a part of his plan when I saw the outfit he had picked for tonight.

Now that we stood outside, having little to no clue of how to go about the plan, I was getting skeptical of what would transpire tonight. And Jack's attitude of keeping things under-wraps wasn't helping my concerns. Jack merely smiled at me as he weaved forward to the gate, and to my surprise, the guard standing at the gate enthusiastically smiled at us.

"Ahh, finally... I was going to snooze off waiting for you, good sir." He said to Jack. "Right this way, I'll show you to the unit that needs repairing." The guard unlocked the door and snuck us inside the building.

Walking through the deserted hallways, I stopped Jack momentarily, "you bribed the guard, that's nice. But how about all the security cameras here?" I said, looking up.

Jack smirked at me, "being a leader of a rebellious group grants certain privileges, my man... I'm a Messiah to many of these common men who are looking to set free from the current regime. I didn't bribe the guard. He merely helped, for he's a follower of my clandestine group. The officer overlooking the surveillance room also voluntarily helped me in disabling the cameras for a couple of hours." Jack explained as he patted on my back, "we're safe."

"Sir, are you coming?" The guard, who had walked to a distance, paused to call us over. We nodded as we started following him again. Soon, going through hallways and climbing the elevator, we reached the minister of finance's office. The guard effortlessly opened the door and let us in.

"That's the most I can do," the guard said regretfully. "I'm standing right outside. If there's an intrusion, I'll signal you." The guard explained before he left.

Now, we were faced with a situation where we had to scavenge the room top to bottom without disrupting the room's order, so it won't come to the notice of the Minister when he arrived at his office the next day. The office was large for an ordinary person, but in contrast, I found it to be a small space for a government official. There was a large mahogany table in the center, with a tall chair standing mighty on its back, while two smaller chairs were situated in the front. A picture frame hung on the wall between the flags of China and the regime. Beside it, a potted plant stood; fake, I assumed. On one corner of the room, two leather one-seater couches were placed on either side of a glass-top round table, which had a fancy vase placed atop. One side wall was encrusted with wooden shelves from top to bottom, holding books, important files, and some decorative pieces. On the other end of the room, I spotted possibly the most important piece... A locker.

"Check the shelves," I asked Yifat as I quickly made my way to go through the drawers of the table. Yifat scurried over and began flipping through the pages of the thick box files while Jack made his way to the locker.

I watched him in between checking the drawers, which held nothing of importance... Just some paperweights, a pair of sunglasses, a diary, and oddly a few pairs of socks. "Weird man," I said out loud. I heard the sound of some keys pressing, and I knew Jack was trying a combination on the locker. I walked over to him and saw that he was denied access.

"Try, 0411... his birthday," I shot an arrow in the dark. Jack obliged, but the locker still didn't budge.

"If we break it, the minister will be alerted," I said. "It might compromise the mission."

"What other choice do we have?" Yifat, who had joined us by now, chimed in, "I didn't find anything in the files... Nothing holds sensitive information, as expected. One does not keep such things lying around."

"Yes, which is why this locker might be our key to finding a lead... some clues, anything." Jack said, "we need to break it."

"These things are sturdy." Yifat exclaimed, "we don't even have much time."

"Not sturdy enough for a laser," I said as I dug into my bag and produced out my laser metal cutting gun. "This baby would cut through any safe." I proudly stated as I held onto the weapon like I would hold my shadow, authoritative and with a sharp aim in sight.

"You seriously have everything in your Pandora's box," Yifat said, excited at the prospect.

I merely nodded at her as I wasted no further time and cast the laser point on the side of the locker, shooting the cutting rays as the metal gave way and a prominent piece came out, allowing a wide opening for us to reach inside.

"Beautiful," Yifat said, smiling. "Let's see what's inside."

"Nothing..." Jack, who was the first one to check, informed us.

"That can't be it. Why have a safe in the first place then?" I was confused as I checked inside the empty locker.

My thought remained unanswered as I heard footsteps approaching in the quiet, followed by the guard's loud voice. "Oh, Sir, I didn't expect to see you here at this hour."

"Oh, crap! Is the Minister here?" Yifat said in a state of panic. "What do we do?"

"Behind the door," I suggested. "We'll hide here, under this desk."

Quickly, we scurried around the room and found our hiding spots, just in time when the Minister opened the door to enter. Through the small crack at the bottom of the desk, I could see the Minister, and I could tell that his eyes had immediately landed on the locker we had just opened with a laser. He weaved his way towards it to examine, but before he could reach the end, Yifat came up behind him, holding an umbrella-like a stick. I saw her in a braced position as she extended her hand far up and launched a hard strike against the Minister's head. With a loud thud, the Minister fell to the ground, knocked out and unconscious.

Hurriedly, Jack and I stood up and came to stand by her side, looking down at the seemingly lifeless body of the Minister, "I'm sorry, I panicked... what other option did we have?"

"Let's get out of here," Jack suggested. "He didn't see us; we can just sneak out."

"Not without him." I said, unsure of what I meant, "If not a document of his secrets in his locker, his own-self would do just fine."

***

Dragging around an unconscious man through the hotel's hallways, we stayed at it would have posed as a challenge if it wasn't for Jack to come to our rescue and take us to his secret location. All hail Alex for sending Jack our way! I had silently said the same words many times over, for Jack's presence had made many things easier. Not only did Jack had a place... a secret dungeon of sorts in the darkest nooks of Hong Kong, but his hideout was equipped with amenities that could come in aid for those who committed a crime of abduction, or even worse... much like we had with the Minister.

"What's the plan?" Yifat asked, "torture the Minister into talking?"

I looked at the unconscious man, tied with chains on a metal chair... His head tilted to the side, and his skin turned pale. Although it wasn't like me to resort to such tactics, circumstances demanded me to walk on the wild side of the road. I had learned in my time with the CIA... was it torture when inflicted on those doing the same to others? No! It wasn't. They'd teach you that at the agency.

"One blow to the face, and another to the ribs... He'll talk like a chatty little parrot," Jack said, walking closer to the Minister, holding him by his chin and turning his head from side to side. "I know the likes of these politicians... coward fools, they are. They don't hold well under torture. Snap your fingers, and they shall sing to your rhythm."

"We'll see about that," I said as I went to the tiny bathroom in the hideout, filled up a bucket of water, and came out. "I can't wait around for him to come to his senses," I said as I splashed a large amount of water on the Minister's face, and he was startled awake in a blink.

Disheveled and confused, he tried to catch his breath, that the pressure of water had snatched away. His bulging eyes darted from one person to another and scanned his unfamiliar surroundings. His dark black hair looked ever darker when damped, and his white skin looked paler out of the fear I was sure he was feeling at that moment.

"Who are you people? Why am I here? Do you know who I am?" The man asked many questions... out of breath and stammering, he merely tried to look tough, as if he had no fear of us or the situation he had found himself in.

I walked closer to him and brought my face closer to him, "no, no, my friend, you don't ask the questions; we do." I said in a deep voice. "Now, tell me, where is Aaron Cohen? Your people have him, I know. Tell me where he is!"

"Who's Aaron Cohen?"

"Wrong answer," I said, without wasting another second as I held onto his head by the back and dunked his head in the remaining water in the bucket. His mouth began making bubbles as he found it harder to breathe with each passing second, and just when I knew he was about to lose his senses again, I pulled him out. Gasping, his disoriented self looked at me with teary eyes.

"I don't know who you're talking about... I don't!"

I didn't let him finish the sentence as I took his head and dunked it in the water again. The Minister started tapping his feet when his life felt inching closer to its ending. I brought him out, and I repeated the question, but his answer remained the same... Oblivious and naive, as if unknown to any hidden national secrets.

"Hey, the man fears getting caught in the act of revealing the truth to us more than he fears dying at our hands. He won't answer." Jack chimed in from behind.

Jack's words instantly gave me an idea... Fear! This was what drove us to do the most atrocious of things, didn't it? If this man didn't fear for his own life, indeed he must fear for those close to him. I looked back at Yifat, who held sympathy on her face, but her eyes oddly displayed rage as well... rage for the man who had some level of involvement in the abduction of her father. I knew what I was about to do wasn't the right thing; I never resorted to this. It was against my moral compass... Never bring family into the equation. I knew this much. But, thinking of everything Aaron did, just to keep his daughter safe, I knew that if I needed to get this man to talk, I needed to take this route... no matter how dark and twisted it was.

I stepped closer to him once again, his damp hair trickling water on my face. I brought my face close to him and started in a whisper, "alright, buddy, listen to me now... I hear you have a beautiful wife and two adorable children... how old are they again? Ahh! The older son is at the prime age of 16, and your sweet little daughter is only but 9. Am I right?"

The man gulped, "yes! How do you know all this?"

I smirked, "you're an influential man, Minister. Your family is public information."

"You can't threaten me with their lives, whoever you are. They are always protected. You can't get to them." The man said, his tone unsure, but a pretense of confidence evident in it.

I laughed in his face, and he flinched on impact. "One would assume that I couldn't get to you either, but I did, didn't I?"

The man gulped again, "look, leave my family out of this... whatever this is."

I smiled at him, "I will. I promise I'm the good guy here. But my buddy over here..." I said, gesturing towards Jack. "He's a rebel... a bloodthirsty, evil, wishing to take down the regime kind of rebel. And he has links that even the likes of you won't be able to track down, and because you're a Minister, he already hates you."

I could now see the man visibly displaying fear instead of masking it with his failed attempts to come off as confident. I took this as a win as I whispered what I hoped to be the words that would hit the final nail in the coffin, "Once, he abducted a little girl... I heard she was of the same age as your precious daughter... He sold her off into slavery and followed her sorry life for two years before he saved her from that place. Only to bring her back and have his men kill her mercilessly. He didn't even give the poor girl a proper burial. No, no... her dead body was cut up...

minced and thrown into the trash." I gave out another laugh, "Two years... imagine, dear Minister, this man does not give a swift death. He makes his victims suffer... long and hard. Imagine if it was your daughter. Think of what he'd do..."

"Stop!" The Minister shouted, unable to picture the haunting image. "Just please, stop! I'll tell you anything... Leave my family alone." The Minister said, on the verge of tears.

My heart felt his pain, but I also felt accomplished. I reframed my question again, "where is Aaron Cohen?"

The man took in a deep breath to try and calm his overpoweringly tensed nerves down. He glanced around the room one more time, his eyes fixing momentarily on Jack before he gulped and answered me.

"He's kept in one of our ghost cities. I'm prepared to give you all the details."

Chapter 16

"Let's regroup tomorrow and think this over," Jack suggested as he dropped us off at the hotel. When leaving for the mission to raid the Minister of Finance's office, Jack had suggested that I not take my car. "Rentals are easier to link to the person. It is best not to take any risks." He had said, so we went in his car, which was oddly not even registered under a legal name... The perks of working with an agent who had gone rogue just kept piling up. I quite liked it.

"See you tomorrow," I said. Yifat didn't say a word as she got out of the car and went inside... she had been quiet since the time we left the Minister in a dark alley. As Jack's car drove by, I went after her. The second I entered the room, I found her pacing around the room, stressed about something.

"Do you think the Minister would know it was us and retaliate it out on my father?" She turned around in haste as I went to stand close to her.

"Yifat, please relax!" I tried to calm her down. "How about I make you some tea?"

"Tea doesn't solve things, Sheppard... just tell me if I'm being paranoid or there's really a chance that the Minister might retaliate?" She asked me. She was clearly in a state of panic; with heavy breaths and stuttering words, she was on the verge of completely losing it.

I gestured her towards the couch and asked her to sit, "Please! Let's talk it out." I said, trying to get her to calm down first before I could explain anything to her.

She sighed and went to sit. I took a seat next to her. Picking up the half-empty water bottle from the table, I gave it to her, "please!" I said, and she silently took it, gulping down a few sips. I looked at her intently. "The Minister has no idea who we are. He was unconscious when we brought him to the hideout, and we wore masks the whole time he was there. We also blindfolded him when we took him out and left him in a dark, deserted alley. How would he know?" I reminded her that we had been cautious about the whole heist, and she had nothing to worry about.

Yifat brushed a hand through her hair in fear and frustration, "I am aware of all of that, Sheppard... I'm afraid that because we asked him about my father, he might have an inkling that we're looking for him, and he might take action and... he might ki..."

I knew what she wanted to say between those stammering words, and I knew her fear was not irrational. This thought had also struck my mind, but I had made peace with it. Ever since starting on this case, and with all the reveals, I had concluded that Aaron was important enough for these influential people, agents more like, to keep him alive. So long as Aaron granted them with inside information, his heart would beat, and he shall breathe. However, I also understood why Yifat feared for his life. It was only natural for her to be afraid of her father.

"The Russians, the Chinese, heck even the U.S... They are all asking for Aaron Cohen. We're no different," I pointed out, standing up and going to the mini-fridge. I pulled out a can of beer for myself and asked Yifat if she wanted one. She shook her head in negative. "This case still has many ambiguities, but one thing that I know for certain by now is this... Aaron Cohen is essential, crucial even. They might torture him, and I'm sorry about that. I know it must be hard for you to hear or picture. But trust me, they won't kill him." I said, popping the beer open and coming to sit back on the couch. "Makes sense, right?" I asked, smiling at her as I took a few sips out of my beer.

Finally, I saw a genuine smile across her lips. "Yes! Makes sense." She said, wiping a few shed tears. "So, when are we heading to that ghost city to rescue my father?"

The words suddenly hit me differently. I had thought about talking about what I had been thinking about the case and its dire consequences with Yifat, but she had started the topic sooner than I'd have liked. I looked away, shifting uncomfortably in my seat, unsure how to voice my opinion regarding the case.

I cleared my throat, "Yes, about that... Yifat, don't you think that by going after your father and rescuing him, we're giving the Chinese a reason to retaliate and pull the trigger on their treasury hacking mission even sooner than they must have planned?"

Yifat glared at me in disbelief, "they would do that anyway. Sooner or later, it shouldn't matter." She said in a stern tone. "My father's captivity or a possible rescue won't cause a change in their plans."

"Yes, but if we find more time, we'll be able to conjure up a working plan and stop it." I tried to reason with her.

She glared at me, tears welling in her eyes, "We might, yes! But it'll happen... regardless if we save my father or not."

I leaned forward, folding my hands together, with my elbows propped over the knees. "That is my point, Yifat. The Chinese seem pretty serious about this. I was thinking, should we not focus our energies on the greater mission? Something that poses the potential of causing tremendous amount of damage to an entire nation, not just one person?"

Yifat got up, throwing her hands in the air. "Seriously? You're switching sides?"

"Switching sides?" I was shocked at how she was taking things. "This is still the same case... This case led us here. As an agent, I am just aware of how one should pick his battles when many things strike at once. You always dedicate your energy and efforts to what might cause the greatest damage. That's just how things need to work in our line of work."

"As an agent, you should also honor your commitment." Yifat pointed out. "You took the case of my father, to save my father... You need to honor your word."

"I also took an oath as an army man, and then as a serving agent in the CIA to serve and protect my nation." I spat, standing up to leave the room. This was getting out of my hands. I was not in the mood to argue with Yifat when she was hell-bent on having tunnel vision and refused to see my side and understand my rationalizing situation.

"This is it then," Yifat yelled after me. "You're choosing to save the U.S because of your affiliation with the country while you risk the life of the man you committed to saving prior to any of this?" I turned around to look at her, and I could see her beginning to well up. "Never would have taken you to be so patriotic, Sheppard. Here I thought you had your own rules... not abiding by what the nation entails you to carry out."

I walked back closer to her as I felt my anger riling up at the blatant accusations. "If you're saying I'm conflicted in my judgment and actions because of my previous association with the CIA, then you are as well." I almost shouted. "Ever since the start of the case, you have only one focus; your father and seeking revenge on those who had abducted him. You have such a tunnel vision that you can't even see past it... at the bigger picture. You can't realize that your need for revenge could cost many lives. You don't realize that what started with your father has escalated into something really large... almost catastrophic. And if we don't try with all our might to stop it, we all will have to suffer dire consequences."

Suddenly, silence engulfed us. The room went hauntingly quiet as my words lingered amid the tensed atmosphere. All that could be heard was Yifat's faint sniffles and my grovels. I watched as Yifat went over to her bed and sat down on edge. Her face buried in her palms... She looked up briefly to pass me a glance of hurt and disappointment before she spoke. "I'm not a sadist, nor am I this selfish, Sheppard." She said. "I just... I figured that if things keep leading to my father, saving him might just be the key to solving it all." She took in a deep breath. "I'm sorry I didn't communicate that well enough."

I sighed as I walked towards her and sat beside her on the bed. "That was uncalled for... what I said, I mean. I shouldn't have." I said sincerely, and she nodded at me with a small smile. "I know your heart is in the right place, but you're wrong in the assumption that the lingering threat would wear off if your father is rescued. No! If anything, it might just multiply in chaos."

"How could you tell?" Yifat was still not convinced. "No matter who we talk to, they all tell us how crucial my father is in this mega heist they are trying to pull. Wouldn't his disappearance out of their hands solve everything?"

I shook my head. "I'm afraid not. The Chinese are quite persistent... They have been at it for a long while now." I took in a deep breath, feeling defeated in the face of my conflicting emotions. "Even if we save Aaron, we can't call it a day, knowing the threat over our heads still lurks, loud and wild. If the Chinese pull the trigger and succeed in doing what we know they are about to do, we'll regret it for the rest of our lives that we didn't make a move to stop it from happening when we could have done something. I wouldn't be able to live with myself if anything were to happen to the US under my watch. I can't let it happen."

"What about my father? What about those people who tortured him relentlessly? Do we let it all go?" Yifat asked. I could hear a raging war in her tone. It was as if there reigned a series of emotions within her, striking at her one after another with a force that left her numb and vulnerable.

At that moment, I realized where the conflict had risen. Moving forward, we had found ourselves at a crossroad, each having a varying driving force that contradicted with the others. I looked down, focused on the carpet's strange pattern, unable to see Yifat in the eye. "I believe there's a problem in what's driving us," I said in a faint whisper.

Yifat nodded, "I'm driven by my need for revenge and my love for my father." She hid her face in her palms, ashamed of her own emotions. "It has blinded me to a lurking threat that could cost a lot more than the life of just one person."

I sighed. "And I'm driven by my prior associations with the States, which has made me numb to the commitment I made to you and your family."

Yifat stood up as she circled the room. "For the greater good, they say." She started, "it is decided, we'll try and stop the Chinese from launching the attack on the Treasury. We'll dedicate all our energy and intelligence to that mission, and if in the process, my father was to get killed, I'll hail him as a hero who was martyred in the cause of saving millions of lives from dying off hunger and poverty."

I was stunned at how Yifat, the girl who was unable to say the word "death" in association with his father, now gave a speech of sacrifices in his potential wake. She was prepared to lose her father if it meant saving others from a more severe threat. My heart swelled with pride at my partner... She did what even I couldn't do. I stood up and walked towards her. I smiled, "you have a good heart, Yifat Emuna. Your father must be proud."

She looked down, turning her head to the side... I knew she was trying to hide her tears. "I hope I'll get to hear him say it one day."

I nodded, picking up my bag from the couch and hanging it on my shoulder, "you will." I assured her, "Thank you for doing the right thing... We'll discuss our next move tomorrow." I said as she merely nodded at me.

"Where are you going?" She asked me as I walked toward the exit of the room.

"I arranged for my room this morning... I'll see you tomorrow for breakfast so we can talk over the case in more detail. I think we both just need to clear our heads for now." I said, turning back around and leaving. I didn't hear Yifat say goodbye, but as the door shut, I listened to a light sob linger behind me.

Gulping down my guilt, I walked through the empty hallway to get to my room, which was only a few rooms away from Yifat's. As I reached the door, I took out my key card to enter... Something held me back. My hands started to shiver, and I felt a daze take over me. No! I couldn't do this to her. Placing my key card back in my pocket, I rushed back to Yifat's room and knocked on the door. She took some time in opening the door, but when she did, I found her to be in a mess, and my heart only sunk deeper; unchanged, but hair in a disheveled stray, eyes puffed up, and voice raspy from the weeps.

"Specialist, did you forget something?"

I took in a deep breath, "you know why I am at the position in this game where I am today?"

"Are you looking for validation at this hour?" She groaned. "I'm too tired, Sheppard."

I ignored her complaint. "It is because I don't falter from my word... ever! People who come to me for help, and then come again, they do so with the blind faith that if I committed to helping them, I will... no matter the cost; small or grand, I'll simply honor my commitment."

Yifat slumped her shoulders in frustration, "what are you saying? It's way too late for puzzles."

"I'm saying that I gave your family my word. I made a commitment to you that I would rescue your father, and that is exactly what I'm going to do." I said, influencing a stunned reaction out of Yifat. "I'll figure out how to stop the attack later. Helping you save your father still remains my priority... No matter the cost. I am all in."

Chapter 17

"*Shh*! Down boy, down!" I bent over to calm the barking dog down, and just like it was taking candy from a baby, the cries eventually satiated when I snapped my fingers and danced my hands around, making funny faces and whatnot. It wasn't the first time that I had tamed a wild dog that was put on guard duty for the possible intruders. I had many such incidents before. *"Is it your natural musk? Or is it your wild charms?"* Many would wonder how I turned the loyal animals against their masters and made them bow down to my commands. *"Maybe just a friendly face who dares to play with the fluffy beasts, instead of barking orders at them,"* I would wave those with intriguing minds off like that. It was just easy for me... rather natural.

The dog now sat calmly. His faint whimpers were the only sound lingering in the quiet. I looked around the deserted-looking warehouse building and took in a sharp breath to embrace myself for what lay on the other end of this shutter door. Coming here without any backup might seem like a stupid idea to many, but I had said so before too many who would question my ways. I work best alone! It was just that simple.

Just this morning, Jack had met with Yifat and me for breakfast as planned. "The ghost city," he said. "The address is of this deserted city outside of Hong Kong... hardly an hour drive away."

"Why was it abandoned?" I had asked Jack when my little Google search had revealed that the city was once a significant site of the grand hustle and bustle. Life boomed in its streets, and colors danced in its nooks and corners vividly. Although small, the city was once a tourist attraction site, and those with an itch for adventure hiked its hills and dove through its cold waters. It was rather sad to learn how the city was slowly abandoned as more and more people started migrating to far and wide areas.

"Infestation of a disease," Jack said. "That's what you'd find online, but the reality is different."

"What is the reality?" I was intrigued.

"The freedom movement, or as they like to call it, 'the rebellion,' against the regime originated from here when a small group of locals stood firm for their rights. However, they were shunned away, detained in concentration camps, tortured to bend the knee to the heinous rules of their commanding overlords, and eventually killed for daring to sin in the land of pure." There was sarcasm evident in his last words. "Slowly, people started to take notice of the sudden disappearance of the residents of the small city, and as conspiracies rose, so did the fear in the city's inhabitants. The migrations began steadily, but a time came when the tortures reached a deadly peak, and population began to tank down deep into the ground... eventually turning the once lively city into a ghost town."

The story had managed to tickle my bone, which had a taste for mystery. It had only grown my impatience of going to the city and rescuing Aaron. "Tonight!" I had said when Jack had asked when would it be best for us to leave for the city. To my relief, Jack and Yifat agreed to the proposition, and we set our wheels in the direction of the ghost city.

"We don't know what we'll find inside," Jack had pointed out when we reached the warehouse that the Minister had told us about. "It's best if we have an exit plan set in motion." This was why it was mutually decided that I would tackle the situation head-on in the warehouse, while Jack and Yifat would make arrangements for our fast escape. And now that the plan was set in place, it was time to attack... direct and offensive, soaring ahead without looking sideways or back. It was a 'Do or Die' moment that I was trained for in the CIA. It was what I lived 'for.

I looked down at the guard dog, who was merely pouting at me. I petted him on his head one last time before I grabbed hold of my Shadow Pistol tightly. I embraced the position and hid on the side, knowing full well that anytime now, someone would be opening the shutter-gate, granted that the dog had barked pretty loudly earlier. Ducked and hunched over, I waited in my braced stance, and in a matter of few more seconds, the door came open with a loud noise.

"Hound, is someone out here?" The tall man wearing a dark black half sleeve t-shirt with dark-wash jeans came out and inquired the dog. I didn't have the time to make out the man's face, as it was only a matter of seconds that I had under my belt to act on before the man noticed me. As the man talked to the dog, I came out of hiding and smacked the butt of my pistol across his head with a strong force, and the man fell, crumbling to the ground like dust. I could've shot him, but shooting the first man out the door would have alerted. However, many men were lurking around inside, and it would have ended badly for me before it could even have started.

"Shh!" I said to the dog again. "Keep guard for me." I mouthed as I stepped inside, with my gun out. I stepped from corner to corner, tiptoeing my way forward, not to alert anyone. The inside of the warehouse was like any other... The walls on either side had shelves mounted in them, which held a countless number of boxes. I could spot another room at a distance, the door to which was slightly ajar, and while the open space that I was in currently was empty and void of any men, the other room had a few that I could see from the slight opening in the door.

First thing's first... I needed to check what these boxes held. Drugs? Weapons? Or merely some ordinary commodities. There was a chance that the warehouse could be a front to their hidden sins, which they carried out behind closed shutters, in the dark dungeons of an abandoned city. Carefully, I weaved my way towards the left and picked up one of the boxes. Fortunately, it was open, and my luck only served me even better when I found many guns inside.

Jackpot! I breathed as I picked up another pistol, similar to my own, and held them both in my tight grips. I was ready to go inside. Slowly, ducking my way through the open space, I walked towards the room with the men who were currently quite engrossed in a conversation. I took my time before barging in as I stood back by the side and observed the scene.

The three men who were discussing something intense were still oblivious to my presence. All three of them were wearing the same clothes as the man I had knocked out previously before entering; perhaps it was a uniform? I wasn't sure. They were all tall and well-built, and I could see their jeans encrusted with a holster, each carrying a revolver. I braced myself. This would have to be quick, or else I would get killed in a blink... I knew this much. Speed was always the key in such missions that one carried single-handedly.

Planning my move, I opened the door with a loud thud. Without giving my opponents any chance to think or make a move, who was a lot more superior to me in number and power, I shot two of them with each hand. In the very next second, I shot the third one right before he was about to retrieve his gun to defend himself. In a fight where you were outnumbered, only two things were crucial—timing and being a good shot. I was gifted in both - quick as a tiger with speed soaring through the paws, and as accurate in taking the headshot in one bullet as the eagles preyed on their victims.

I tiptoed and found a spot in this room to hide behind a series of wall-mounted shelves as I saw another door leading to another room. I knew that after the gunshots, someone would be on their way out. Hiding behind a counter, I didn't have to wait all that long as the wooden door swung open and two men came rushing in.

"Holy hell," one of them exclaimed. "Fuck! Someone's here."

I grinned. Oh yes, someone was there. I held onto my guns and targeted their heads as they began to look around... And boom! Two headshots simultaneously, and the two men fell like tiny worms, oozing blood all over the already dirty and stained floor. Getting up, now I hid behind the door. If there were anyone else left inside, they would surely make their way out.

I waited for a while, but when I started hearing movement inside, I figured out that this was the room that they must be keeping Aaron in, and whoever was left inside had thought it was best to escape with him than to fight the intrusion. Not on my watch, folks! I exclaimed to myself as I trotted to the other side so I could glance inside the room. I peeked in, and I could see there were five other men inside. I also spotted Aaron sitting on a metal chair, tied with ropes, with tape wrapped around his mouth.

I gulped down... This was risky. There were too many men. These men had become alert by now and were preparing to not only escape but to defend themselves with full force when faced with an attack. A sneak attack for a single man, when outnumbered by the enemy, was relatively simpler. It got real when the defenses came up, and the fighter in your opponent was ignited to life. This was not going to be as easy. I took in a sharp breath. I was here. There was no turning back. It was a do or die moment, and when had I ever been afraid of death? Never!

I watched as the three men were trying to lift Aaron while he was still tied to the metal chair, and two others were guarding them from behind. I made a plan in my head. I would shoot the two who had their hands free first. It would take the other three sometimes to put down Aaron's chair and react. The time that I'd be using to shoot all of them as well. Perfect! The scene played out without a hitch in my head. I was ready to attack; finish this once and for all.

Stepping inside with my arms stretched out and my targets locked, I shot twice and down came the two guarding men, crumbling to the floor like lifeless sacks. My target immediately altered as I took hold of the other three men. However, this time, one of the men had let go of Aaron's chair and locked me as his target. Oh crap! In taking pride in my efficiency, accuracy, and right timing, I probably didn't account for someone else to possess the same.

Before I could shoot, I sensed that the man had taken a shot at me. I instinctively ducked, and the bullet missed its target as it hit the wall behind me. The man, who had thought that he had shot me, seemed to relax under the false notion, and this was the window I had needed. I stood up straight, and faster than the men could blink, I shot three times; two of them at once, and one right after, as the last set of my opponents fell on the ground... lifeless and displaying a picture of my victory.

Releasing a sigh of relief, I put my original gun in its holster, and the other one went in my back pocket for easy access, in case there were any other enemies I'd need to fight off before I could escape this place. I ran towards Aaron, who was tossed aside in haste when I had entered, and the group tried to defend themselves. I picked up his chair, removed the tape from his mouth, and started to untie his ropes.

"You're... you're The Specialist... I..."

"Hey, save your energy," I said, stopping him from voicing his thoughts into stammering words. "Can you walk?" I asked him.

Aaron gave me a tired smile, "I don't know. It's been a while since I last walked. After being dragged around so much, I'm not sure if my legs even work anymore."

My heart quivered for his pain, but I was running on a thin time thread, which was why I needed him to stay strong and put effort into walking. "Listen,

Aaron, your daughter is out back, arranging for our swift escape. I need you to stay strong for me and try to walk, okay?"

Aaron nodded as he tried to stand up with all his might, despite his injuries. "Yes, you're doing great," I said with a big smile, but my praise was cut short as I heard loud noises at my back. Footsteps and grovels, followed by orders of spreading out, came rushing through.

I immediately retrieved the gun from my holster and my pocket and stretched out my arms as I pushed Aaron down. My intention was for him to lay low so I could save him in the event of a crossfire. However, astonishingly, Aaron's limp body collided with a wall at the back, which opened up and swallowed him in. A secret passageway! I gasped. I could barely think over the new development, for the room was soon filled with many men... four, no six, oh crap, eight men! I breathed out.

The man in the front was the same guard I had merely knocked out earlier instead of killing, and I inwardly smacked myself in the head. A few others stood behind him, but one that caught my attention the most was the giant man standing behind all of them. A juggernaut! He had a body that reached the ceiling and a size that mirrored that of an elephant. The man was the spitting image of a rumored mythical giant, and I felt like a peasant compared to his large and mighty form.

"Where is he?" One of the men extended his gun towards me and yelled. "Did you already sneak him out? Tell me where is he, or I'll shoot."

I gulped, counting again. I could start shooting, but I knew if I did, they would do the same and probably have their juggernaut stomp over me. I needed to play it safe. They wanted information out of me. They would let me live till then. "He wasn't here when I got here. I believe your men have sneaked him out."

"He's lying." The guard I had knocked out initially chimed in, "The helicopter is still standing. Aaron was here, and nobody has left the premises."

"Are you sure, though? Probably he has his team lurking around somewhere outside, who must've stashed Aaron in a secret place."

"We'll send some men out to scavenge the place."

I watched as the men argued amongst themselves, and I took that as an opportunity to defend myself against them. I spotted a shield earlier when I got here, and I used their distraction as my window to retrieve it from the corner. I bent low, hiding my body behind it. I started doing what I had been doing since I got here... Shoot with accuracy and speed. Despite facing retaliatory bullets, I managed to down all men except for the Juggernaut, who thankfully didn't have a gun. I shot him a few times, but the bullets seemed to sink in and disappear into his flesh as he charged his way towards me. I had no other option left.

I looked back to where the wall had opened up and quickly evaluated in my head if the impact of what I was about to do would reach that point. For now, the Juggernaut was standing in the other room, slowly marching towards me. I took in a sharp breath as I pulled out the hand grenade from my jacket, walked closer to the door, took out the pin, and threw it towards the Juggernaut, quickly shutting the door behind me and running towards the wall opening where I had thrown Aaron.

When inside, I found a staircase leading up, and I was reminded of what the guard had said. The only way out of here was through a helicopter. The stairs might lead to the roof. I grabbed Aaron and quickly started to drag him up the stairs, hoping Yifat and Jack would have managed to get a hold of a helicopter. The grenade blasted behind us, shaking our ground, but the fiery ball never made it out to where we stood. Sighing in relief, I continued to climb up the stairs and let it take me where it shall.

***

As the stairs looked to be coming to an end, I could hear the sound of a helicopter's rotors running. While the optimistic part of me relished in that melodious white noise, my more active realist self-forged plans to take on the awaiting enemy on the roof.

Stash Aaron here on the dark stairwell and fight the men off? Throw them over the roof for them to plummet to their deaths? Throw Aaron in the helicopter and tell him to fly out if he knows how to fly? I thought over my strategy if I'd find more men on the roof before I stepped ahead.

The iron door was heavy to open with me trying to balance Aaron into a steady position, but once it swung open, the sight on the other end made me release a sigh of relief. Yifat and Jack stood over a bunch of dead-bodies beside the running helicopter. As we entered, Yifat came rushing to her father,

"Dad, are you okay? You're okay... I know you are." Yifat asked and answered all on her amidst her overpowering emotions. I gave them a few moments alone as I walked forward, climbing over the fallen and bloodied bodies, and went to stand in from Jack.

"Quite a bloodbath you guys drew here, I see," I said with a smile.

Jack patted me on the back, "we heard the gunshots, specialist. It sounded like you partied hard downstairs."

I tucked up my collar, "guilty as charged... Let's get out of here." I said. Yifat heard me as she helped her father walk towards us and then into the helicopter. Once we were all seated, Jack took the pilot seat, I sat beside him, and Yifat sat at the back with her father.

"Let's roll," I announced as the helicopter's rotors started to spin faster, and in a matter of seconds, we were up in the air, heading out of the ghost city, having successfully rescued Aaron Cohen.

I had internally celebrated, but it only took a few more minutes for me to realize that I celebrated a little too early. About ten minutes into our flight through the low skies, flying just slightly above the aged trees that had long shed their leaves, we spotted another helicopter following us. "Maybe it just has the same route as we do," Yifat said, closing her eyes to our grave reality.

"It's not possible..." I said, looking back, "Yifat, see if you can tell who's in it. I thought we finished them all."

Yifat looked out to see who was flying the other bird, but before she could answer me, suddenly, she started shouting. "Descend, sideways... to the right! Now!"

Jack followed her hasty instructions and lowered the helicopter, and hurried it to the right. We barely missed the fast missile targeted at us as we watch it soar ahead in a distance and blast in the trees, causing a roaring fire to ignite. I watched as the other helicopter descended to come down to our height, and Yifat yelled another instruction. "Ascend." Once again, Jack followed, and we successfully missed yet another strike.

"Who's flying it?" I asked again. I liked knowing my enemies. It made me more satisfied when I made them my victims.

Yifat, who was too busy giving us instructions, forgot to see the person inside, but when she did, a loud gasp escaped her. "Zhang... oh my God, it's Zhang."

"The traitor, I see!" Jack chimed in. "I did not see that coming."

"Oh, but I did. I knew he'd be back... Yifat, switch." I said as I climbed to the backseat, and Yifat hopped on the front. "Hunch down in a brace position," I instructed Aaron, who listened to me and took cover. "Soar ahead, Jack... full speed."

The helicopter picked up more speed as we created a reasonable distance from Zhang's helicopter. "To the right," I said, judging another attack timely, and Zhang missing another shot. "Up, up, up," I shouted again, but this time, the bullet touched our helicopter's landing skid, and our bird shook harshly.

Jack took over the control and stabilized it again in no time, "close call." He breathed. That was it. I was done playing around. If Zhang wanted action, he should be granted action. I pulled out my gun, my trusted Shadow Pistol, and I opened the door of the helicopter. "Brace yourselves," I ordered as I bent on one knee and leaned my head out of the helicopter. The cold air hit me, shooting needles through my whole body. I took in a sharp breath as I felt difficulty in breathing with the rasping wind soaring through. I stretched out my hand, tilted a little upward, as I gripped myself inside the helicopter by holding on to the passenger grip situated on the ceiling of the copter. I locked my target, and I shot.

Much like any other time, my shot didn't miss the target as the bullet landed right at the rotor mast. The blades of Zhang's helicopter started to wobble and spin in a haywire fashion, and in a matter of a few minutes, one of them fell to the side, halting the blades from rotating altogether. The next thing I saw was his helicopter doing a nosedive, descending at full speed, and eventually plummeting to the ground.

I took a sigh of relief as I came back inside and shut the door behind me. Yifat was clapping for me, throwing me her little celebration. I took a bow in front of her, and she laughed. I laid my head back and closed my eyes, relishing in our triumph.

"This feels good!" I exclaimed, "this is what victory tastes like."

"Yes, we did it! We managed to rescue dad and kill Zhang all in one night. I guess we're both avenged." Yifat said, smiling in excitement.

"It's not over yet." Aaron, who had been quiet until this point, spoke up even during the chaotic chase. "Things are only getting started."

"What are you saying, father?" Yifat asked, turning around.

"The attack..."

"Yes, Mr. Cohen, we're aware of the attack, and we already have a plan set in motion to prevent it from happening," I said, interrupting his sentence, for I figured where he was going with it.

"No, Specialist, you're too late."

The air around us that echoed with excitement and celebration just a few seconds ago now reeked of alarming notions and messages of our impending doom. I cleared my throat as I turned my full focus on Aaron. "Please elaborate. Tell us what you know."

"The program..." Aaron started, in between some uncomfortable coughs, "I heard them say it right before you came over to rescue me. The program is set in place already, and it's functioning. It's only a matter of time now before it hits the mainframe."

"What does that mean?" Yifat questioned.

Aaron passed a glance at all three of us before he answered. "In a matter of next forty-eight hours, they'll be in... The treasury will be wiped clean. Just forty-eight hours... That's all you have to stop the attack if it's even possible to do so.

Chapter 18

"Here, you must be thirsty," I said, handing Aaron a glass of water.

"Parched, actually. Thank you!" He said as he took hold of the glass with shivering hands and drank it with haste. Lips trembling and teeth-gritting, he posed an image of what's left after a grave disaster strikes.

Yifat had brought out a first aid box and was now busy tending to her father's wounds. The poor man had endured quite a few. Gashes on his forehead, noticeable marks on his cheekbones, and his leg still bled from a fresh sharp cut that his last fall had inflicted on him.

"Made you some soup," Jack came from the small chaotic kitchen in his little hideout and brought a steaming bowl of soup, and placed it on the wooded table in front of the leather sofa that Aaron was currently resting on.

"It's alright. You folks don't have to tend after me. I'm fine!" Aaron said, tightening his fists as the dreaded red medicine that Yifat was applying on his open wounds stung him. "May I?" He asked Yifat, gesturing towards the bowl on the table. Yifat nodded and momentarily stopped the process of dressing and handed him the bowl. "I haven't had a good meal in a really long time. I'm starving." He defended himself.

"Go ahead, don't feel shy at all, my man!" Jack said, who had taken a seat on the couch opposite to where Aaron was seated. He crossed his arms and leaned back. "Besides, you'd need the energy to share your story. We have a lot of questions."

"Jack," Yifat warned. "Let him recover a little first, please!"

"There's no time, princess. We have a literal ticking bomb situation." He glared at her. "Your father said so himself. We have only but forty-eight hours on our hands."

"Since when did you start caring about America's wellbeing?" Yifat spat, for Jack's careless attitude was not sitting well with her.

"Since its wellbeing started going against China's regime. I'm a rogue agent, remember."

"Guys!" Yifat was about to hit back with another snarky remark when I put my hand up and stopped the argument, "There'll be plenty of time for this fun little banter later. For now, we need to focus. Jack," I said, turning to him. "We should give Aaron some time. He won't be of use to us if he's not well."

"No!" Aaron interjected, coughing from the impact of just speaking one word. "Jack is right! This ticking time bomb will blast any minute. I'm ready to talk. Each second counts."

I watched as Jack sat up straight on the couch. Yifat took to a more alert position on the wooden table as well, and I, who had been standing up till this point, brought the metal stools out of the kitchen counter and took a seat near Aaron.

Aaron picked up the bowl of soup from the table and ate a spoonful before clearing his throat. "It all started when the Finance Minister, Bingwen Wei, came to see me that night."

***

The blinds were shut, for the outside passing traffic was getting distracting. The sun had long set, and while the world prepared to get back to their homes, work was only starting to look up for Aaron Cohen. Cramped in his office, he was entering the data of some of the accounts he had closed just today... His calculator out to count the commissions he would receive from each closed account, he smiled as the numbers added up, ascending higher in value with each stroke of the key.

"Snap your fingers to my rhythm and the bucks that shall pour in. You'll be surprised... You would not even be able to count it on that little machine of yours."

Aaron looked up at the intrusion to his quiet moments of calculating his profits. A short, well-built, middle-aged Chinese man stood in the doorframe of his office. On his tail, two guarding men stood, overlooking for the man in the center's wellbeing. Aaron raised his eyebrow, "Do I know you?" He asked.

The Chinese man walked in, trotting his way towards the visitors' chair at Aaron's desk, and sat down. The man turned around to look at the guards, "wait outside. This needs privacy." The man commanded, and the guards merely nodded, walked out, and shut the door behind them. Aaron looked at the Chinese man more carefully... Why did he look so familiar?

The man propped his foot over his leg, sat back in his seat, and folded his hands. "You don't watch the news, do you?"

Aaron eyed the man with a keener eye, but he was still unable to place him. He glanced over the digital clock on his desk and sighed. The papers sat in front of him, demanded his attention, and yet this stranger seemed to be in no mood to leave him to it.

Aaron shut the file and cleared his throat, "the night has fallen dark, and I am running late. Whatever it is that you are here to discuss, please do so quickly so I can leave for home."

The man gave out a laugh. "The fact that you don't recognize me makes me wonder if you're even worth recruiting for this intricate task."

The laugh... It came to him suddenly. Aaron knew who the man sitting in front of him was. He had watched him in the news and even read about him in many articles. He was none other than the Chinese Minister of Finance. Aaron suddenly felt a little uncomfortable in his presence, insecure even. He shifted in his chair and looked at the Chinese Minister with a lowered gaze. "I'm sorry, sir, it took me a while." He said, placing his elbows on the desk, "tell me, what can I do for you, Mr. Bingwen Wei?"

"I like it..." Bingwen stated with a smile. "You get right to the point... This means you value time, much like I do."

"Yes, I'm aware!" Aaron said, "you're a busy man. I'm sure if you're here, it must be for an essential reason, and I'm all ears for it."

"That's great!" Bingwen said, pulling a few papers out of his bag and sliding them across the desk over to Aaron. Aaron looked at the Minister before picking up the papers and going through them. His eyes widened when he saw what the pages showed. It was a contract that said that he needed to share inside information of the American economy and investment stocks with the Minister of Finance, which broadly meant that he was required to steal for China... millions and millions of dollars in exchange for getting a payback of his terms.

He gulped as he looked up at the Chinese Minister, "is it really what I think it is? You're here to buy me?"

The Minister merely nodded as if it was the simplest thing. "Yes, but have no doubts... I want you to know that this deal will be a mutually beneficial one. I know what commissions you get out of closing the accounts. If you help China in stealing some finances, your commissions will be multiplied by a number of your choice. Any number... Just say it, and we'll make it happen."

Aaron observed the minister's words as he sat back with the contract secured in his hands. He read, and he read again, unable to come to a conclusive decision. What about the consequences? What if he'd get caught? Oh, but the money sounded good. Good.

The Minister cleared his throat. "Rest assured, Mr. Cohen, if you do decide to help us, you'll be protected. Our government will look out for you." The Minister leaned closer, lowered his head, and neared towards Aaron. In a hushed whisper, he said the final words that would have made Aaron take the final verdict. "In business, the financial ladder is never a straight path up. To make money, you need to get your hands dirty, or else, you'll be left at the ground steps, cleaning off the dirt fallen from the shoes of those who dared to climb high by stepping into a pile of muck."

***

The room had gone silent as Aaron's words sat heavily on all of us, but most of all on Yifat. I could see her eyes... Disappointment and hurt so visibly displayed in them. She was the first one to break the silence by clearing her throat. "So you took the offer? You signed the contract?"

"Yes!" Aaron said regretfully. "That was my first mistake, and everything that followed was just one punishment after another for this one mistake."

"Why did you do it then, dad?" Yifat asked. "You had enough money."

Aaron sighed, leaning forward to look deeply into his daughter's eyes, "Not enough... Money is never enough. Not when you start to compare yourself with others."

While I knew this was a moment between Yifat and her father, I had important questions to ask, so I cleared my throat to get their attention. "You said that you started in this line when the Chinese contacted you to steal for them, right?"

Aaron nodded. "Yes. That meeting with the Chinese Finance Minister was my first dip in the pool of sin."

"Then how come the Russians kidnapped you? How did they get in the picture, and China tried to buy you off from them?" I framed my train of thoughts as best as I could, unsure if Aaron's disheveled mind would be able to keep track of the ramblings.

"Can I get a glass of water?" Aaron asked Jack, who stood up, picked up the glass from the table and refilled it as he handed it to him. Aaron took a few sips before he continued. "Russians came to me themselves, Specialist... There was no involvement of the Chinese. The Pakhans found me and thought I'd do their bidding, so they gave me another offer, even better than what the Chinese were giving me."

"And you took it," Yifat concluded. I could hear the venom in her tone, but her teary eyes displayed a haunting tale of betrayal and hurt. Aaron merely nodded at her as he continued. "The Russian job seemed to be paying me better, but they were also asking a lot more from me. The worst of it was my constant time. Slowly, it got to the point that I no longer got to see my daughter." Aaron sighed, drinking a little more from his glass. "I just... I wanted to be with my daughter more than anything. I wanted to solve our differences and reconcile with her. And I knew that the only way to do that was to quit the Russian job."

"And when you did, it didn't sit well with the Russians?" Jack chimed in with his conclusion.

"Precisely," he said. "They didn't tell me that, though. I remember telling them off one day and the man I dealt with in these matters... a member of the Pakhans, told me to focus on my family. 'Be careful,' he had said, 'anyone could harm your daughter'." Aaron paused as he tried to recollect himself, "I took that for genuine concern, but later figured out that he was actually threatening me with my daughter's life. However, I remained oblivious to the threats back then."

"So, they kidnapped you?" I asked him, still many questions running through my head, which I was hoping would all be answered as Aaron Cohen paced ahead in his story.

"I was going to meet with some Chinese officials to quit their job as well. I remember meeting with Yifat that day, and I remember thinking I might never return." Aaron welled up as I started to hear an audible crack in his voice.

"You asked me to wait for you," Yifat said in between tears as her emotions could no longer stay at bay either.

Aaron looked at Yifat with love evident in his eyes, "I thought that I might get killed. By the Chinese or the Russians. But in the off chance that they let me live, I'd be back to you... really be back this time. This was why I wanted you to wait for me."

Yifat scooted closer and held her father's hands, "That day... I was just..."

"We'll have plenty of time to make amends, my dear. It's not the time." Aaron halted her in mid-apology. Yifat wiped her tears, nodded, and smiled.

"When you left, you made it seem like you might not return," Yifat said. "Were you aware of the threat?"

Aaron looked around the room at all of our confused and attentive faces and took in a deep breath, "It got bad, Yifat. What started as stealing for the Russians and Chinese got to the point where I realized they were planning something big. So, I figured out one thing... If I were to get in trouble, I knew the very best person would be deployed on the case."

"You mean me," I concluded.

"Yes!" Aaron nodded, "I also knew that my daughter would be on board as well, knowing her talents and her ability to rise to any occasion. And I knew if two greatest minds would start working together, it'll bring the Triads from China and the Pakhans from Russia... and their biggest agents put on this intricate mission, all out in the open, and this lurking threat could be eliminated once and for all."

I stood up and went to stand in front of him next to Yifat. "So you had intended for us to find out about all of it? This was your plan? You wanted to lure the Russians and Chinese agents out to play, so we can put a stop at their little party?"

"Not initially, but yes!" Aaron nodded. "And it worked. I knew you and my daughter would be able to crack the final mystery, and now that you have, we have a chance to prevent the attack from happening."

"Except we hardly have the time." I pointed out, "Forty-Eight hours, and we don't even know where to begin or what to do."

"How about Virginia?" Aaron suggested.

"Why?" I asked, confused.

"I figured you'd take help of the CIA, considering you were an agent once," Aaron said. "Plus, I also have one other piece of information that can come in handy in this solve."

"We're all ears," I said, dragging the stool closer and taking a seat.

"There's one very important person in America who's involved in this... He's a Republican, and his name is Mark. He has been helping the Chinese politician, Cheung, to carry out this attack effortlessly by indulging him with sensitive inside information."

I exhaled a sharp breath. A lot started to make sense. The first time when I had found out about the Treasury attack, I had assumed that there must be someone on the inside from the USA helping the Chinese government... It wouldn't be possible without it. Aaron answered almost all of my questions.

"That's why you want us to head to Virginia," Yifat said. "Track down Mark?"

Aaron shook his head. "No. I believe that from there you may head to the headquarters of the CIA, or Specialist might, I mean." Aaron took in a defeated breath, "I'm not sure what could be done from there onwards, but one must try."

"What about Mark?" I asked him. "You don't want us to catch him first?"

"I'm afraid that with the ticking clock of the attack, the Republican will be fleeing the country soon, and by the time you'll get there, he would have been long gone." Aaron elaborated, "you can still stop the attack... There are ways. Time is just of the essence."

"Alright!" Jack stood up, clapping his hands. "I think we've heard enough. Let's get our heads cleared and head to the USA." Jack responded. Without exchanging another word, he went to one of the doors in his hideout, which probably had his bedroom. As he shut the door, the room fell silent. I could see Yifat still sitting by her father's side, and I decided to give them some time alone. I stepped out on the balcony and shut the sliding door behind me. Perhaps a little fresh would do my system some good.

***

"He said he was proud of me."

I had just taken a long drag out of the cigarette I had just lit when Yifat came out and stood beside me. Usually, I didn't smoke, but I wasn't beyond smoking one or two when the stress got a little too high to bear. I briefly looked at Yifat and smiled. "I told you he would."

"You were right." Yifat took in the fresh air and closed her eyes. "Even though the threat still lingers and you still have a lot on your plate, I just feel so happy in this moment. I haven't felt that in a while."

I smiled. "I'm happy for you. And the case is finally over."

Yifat looked at me, confused. "What do you mean? We still have to stop the attack."

I turned to my side to face her. "I have to stop the attack... You just need to head back home."

"We started this together, Sheppard." Yifat glared at me.

"Yifat, this is not on you. For now, I believe I can manage on my own." I sighed. "Besides, you just got your father back. I think you should focus on keeping him safe while I focus on my job. And if need be, I'll contact you."

Yifat took some time to think before answering, "You promise?"

I nodded with a small smile, "yes, I promise!"

Yifat exhaled a sigh. "Perhaps we'll meet in New York when all of this is over." She said, looking out the view of barren land for as far as the eye could see.

"No, not perhaps... We will." I corrected her.

She smiled at me. "It was a pleasure working with you, Sheppard." She said as she turned around to walk away, but I stopped her with what I said.

"You were right not to trust me in the beginning."

Yifat turned back and looked at me with confusion as she came back to stand next to me, "why is that?"

"You found something about my girlfriend, Scarlett..."

"Um, listen, it's all in the past..."

"It was true." I finished my sentence, which she had interrupted, thinking I'd initially take offense to what she had thought of me.

"What?" She gasped.

I merely nodded. "She was accused of having involvement in the Swiss Bank hacking jobs... Her name was linked in the string of robberies time and again by the FBI."

Yifat looked at me with sympathy, that was evident to me even in the night's light. "Did she actually do it?"

I shook my head, "I don't know."

"But you said it was all true." Yifat was confused.

"Yes, it was... but I still don't know if she did it or not, because even though she was declared guilty in the FBI books, I can't seem to accept it in my heart, given that I never got to talk to her about it."

"Why not?" Yifat asked. Her tone was laced with curiosity and empathy.

I took a deep breath, conjuring up the courage to say the words that I had kept hidden in my heart for so long, never daring to speak of them. "Because she went missing all of a sudden... Poof! Vanished into thin air."

Yifat's mouth hung open at my words. She continued to stare at me for the longest time, unsure of what to say or how to comfort me. I didn't need it. I merely wanted to talk. "Was she... um, I mean... Was she kill..."

"Killed?" I let out a laugh despite myself. "That's the harsh reality of my life, Yifat. I don't even have an idea of whether she's dead or alive. And I don't know if she was involved in the crimes or not." I groaned out of frustration, "I don't know how to feel about it. She went missing... Do I hate her by thinking she left me? Or mourn for her departure? Do I bid her a farewell in my heart, thinking she's dead? Or curse her for the evil road she probably took off on?" I flicked my cigarette and threw it off the railing as I held my face in my palms. "These conflicting emotions just never seem to leave... Not even when I'm walking through a roaring fire of chaos amid the flying bullets. She still occupies most of my mind."

Yifat placed her hand over mine and said in a whisper. "I'm so sorry you have to endure such pain daily. But just know that no matter what the present is... whether she did the robberies, whether she ran away, or she was abducted or killed, nothing changes the time you had with her." I looked at her intently as her words hit me. "Phillip, sometimes in life, our reality gets so dark that all we can do to cope is relish in the light that we have had once. Even if it has ended now, we can be happy that we had it at some point in our life."

Memories! She told me to be grateful for the memories, and I instantly felt as though I had found a solution to my problem. I nodded at her with a warm smile, "Thank you!" I breathed a simple word, and she smiled back at me.

"I'm glad you trusted me enough to share." She spoke after a while.

I raised my hand. "Many masks came off today. I figured it was time for you to see my dark reality as well."

Yifat simply smiled as she turned around to leave. "I think I need to catch some sleep." She announced. I nodded at her, bidding her goodbye.

She stopped at the sliding door of the balcony and turned her head towards me, "Sheppard," she called out. And as I looked back at her, she smiled, "for what it's worth... You look better with the mask off."

Chapter 19

"We're here, Sir."

The Uber driver announced as I was engrossed in my phone and didn't realize that the car had stopped a little way ahead of the CIA's headquarters at Langley, Virginia. I nodded at him as I got out and stood in front of the magnificent CIA building, which spread far and wide and looked mighty, serene, and even hypnotizing to the eye of an onlooker. The white spreads of the location always seemed to welcome me in its glorious boundaries. At some point in my career, the place had started to feel like home, and this time it was no different. I smiled to myself as I adjusted my suit's jacket and held onto my bag more tightly. I took a deep breath as I set course to go inside, where my old friend and colleague, Diana Heartley, was awaiting my arrival.

Amid the greetings of 'Hi's' and 'How are you's', from people who remembered me and those who were curious about me after hearing many different stories about me, I made my way to Diana's office. While the hallways and those white walls looked familiar, and I felt nostalgic walking around those same quarters, there was this odd feeling of estrange settling within me. The knowns felt foreign, and the bricks that once upon a time knew of my stories of triumph and tragedy now hauntingly stared back at me as if I was alien to them. Changed, lost, and amount to nothing.

I shoved all of the dark thoughts out of my head as the wooden door to Diana's office approached. Inhale and let go! I instructed myself, knocking on the door. I was expected, it seemed. Her assistant had let me in, and now all I had to do was wait. Wait for her permission to enter, which came merely after a few seconds.

"Ahhh! The Specialist. My main man." Diana greeted me with her arms wide open, an enthusiasm that was so unique that I had come to associate it with just her. It was along the lines of happiness, embodying a strange sense of pride, a rasping voice to reiterate that while she was happy, you should not take it that her guard was down. It was a warning that she would strangle you sooner than you could blink.

I smiled warmly at her as I walked in and let her embrace me for a hug, "Heartley, you haven't aged a day." I said as we broke away, looking at her carefully. Her light raven hair showed no grey evidence in it, still as luscious and catching light as always in the ripe age of 50. Although they showed some wrinkles around them, her black eyes still had the same sparkle and wisdom displayed in them. The bright red lipstick perked up her thin lips that she always wore. It was her signature. Draped in a pencil knee-length skirt, dress shirt, and a blazer, her slim physique was still a dream for many young girls and a fantasy of many boys. Her tall debonair was just as commanding and even had an authoritative and robust aura about it. And her bronze skin still glistened the same under those bright lights of the headquarters.

Diana waved her hand, smiling at me, "oh, aren't you the same charmer as always."

I smiled, "just trying to match up to your high standards," I said.

She made her way across the desk and took her seat, gesturing me to sit. "You should have come to me sooner, Sheppard. You know I would have lent you a hand... Like the old times." Diana said. I could hear a hint of complaint in her tone, and I had to move past it, knowing there were some more essential matters to discuss.

"I retired for a reason. I can't possibly run back to you for every case." I explained. "Not unless it becomes national interest like it has now."

Diana leaned back in her chair, her elbows placed on the handles with her palms folded in the front. "Let's hear your case out then, Sheppard. We got time."

I shook my head, "actually, no, we don't have time." I clarified as I proceeded to brief her over the whole case. She had insisted on refrain the details over the phone, for as a CIA director, she was the most aware of how difficult phone conversations could be.

She listened to me carefully, and I noticed her eyes widening and her silent gasps on many parts of my story. Finally, when I stopped talking, she took her time before speaking.

"Do you want coffee? Tea perhaps? Or scotch neat as you have it." Diana asked, leaning forward.

"You remember it all," I smiled at the thought.

"You don't forget your best agent's habits," She said, picking up her phone to call. "Not what he drinks or eats... and certainly not how he thinks and shoots."

I nodded a thank you at her as she asked someone to bring us coffee, knowing that I didn't take hard drinks in the morning.

"Now, let's rewind... You have rescued Aaron, but are now looking to stop the attack on Treasury, and supposedly Mark, the Republican, is in on the whole plan?" Diana gave me a rundown.

"Yes!" I said, "That's the gist of this whole chaos."

"Chaos is what drives us, Specialist... You and me both." Diana said. Standing up, she came around her desk to open her door with a code as there was a knock. I watched a man walking in and placing the coffee mugs on the table and leaving. Diana came back to sit on her chair and looked at me.

"If I had known that you're working on Aaron Cohen's case with his daughter, I would have taken over and deployed all the best services at your disposal," Diana said, picking up the cup and taking a sip.

"Um, do you know Yifat?" I was confused.

Diana simply smiled, "I recruited her."

***

The building was magnificent. There was no mystery in that. But her presence in the hustling hallways of the CIA headquarters was nothing short of a puzzle, one that, despite her interest in puzzles, she couldn't solve. When Yifat had gotten a call from the CIA headquarters from the director's assistant, she thought long and hard why the director wanted to meet her. Did she do something wrong? Or is it that her father complained of her straying ways from Law School? No! That was silly.

The door opened as soon as she got there, without even her having to knock on it. The office of the Director, Diana Heartley, was a simple but a large one. Expensive furniture sat at various corners in the room, set artistically—a fancy desk in the center with a tall-back leather officer chair and two visiting chairs. A bookshelf in one corner, which almost looked like a mini library, and comfortable seating of leather couches adorned one beautiful side of the room. Yifat took the whole space in as she sighed out of awe.

"Yifat Emuna, if I'm not wrong?" Diana, the director, greeted her with a smile while seated in her chair, breaking her trance of exploring the beautiful space. Yifat simply nodded, and Diana gestured her to take a seat.

She knocked over the pen holder on the table in the process of taking her handbag off her shoulder. "I'm so sorry," she said in heavy breaths. "I'll pick that up."

"It's fine." Diana stopped her. "Let them be. You just talk to me."

Yifat sunk in her chair, embarrassed. "I'm so sorry. I'm just a little nervous."

Diana leaned forward and looked at her with a warm smile. "Don't be. You're here for a reason. Feel at home. You deserve to be here."

Yifat gulped. "I can't unless I know the reason you speak of."

Diana stood up from her chair and walked around it as she came over to sit on the visitor's chair next to Yifat. "You're in your Junior year in Law School, am I right?"

Yifat nodded, "yes, and I know you're like the CIA... so you know stuff... so I'm not going to ask how, but this is quite intimidating. So, can we get to the point?"

Diana smiled. "The urgency... Your father warned me you're often in haste."

Yifat's mouth hung open. "Wait, my father? Did he... I mean, did he put you to this... whatever this is?"

Diana laughed and shook her head. "Oh, no, no, my dear... He merely talked about you. It is I who figured out that you're the right fit for our agency."

Yifat gasped in shock and disbelief, "you mean..."

"That's right. We're looking to recruit you in our agency, if you're up for it, of course." Diana said.

Yifat felt her throat closing up, "May I?" She asked, gesturing towards the glass of water, and Diana nodded in a yes. Yifat gulped the entire glass in one swig and let out a deep breath before speaking, "Miss Heartley, I'm honored, I truly am... But this is not the life I want. If you know my father, he must have told you about my love for..."

"Acting? Yes, he told me." Diana said, finishing her sentence. "You have no idea how many times we look for great actors who can go on about their own lives and just work secretly for us. You're already on your way to becoming an actor, and we want you to continue down that path." Diana paused for a moment as if to think. "In fact, my dear, we'll help you on that road."

"If I act, won't people know me? I wouldn't be undercover then... or an unknown face, if you will." Yifat asked, confused.

"That's your cover. A perfect cover. An actor who nobody could suspect for an agent."

Yifat took a long pause to think it over. This would work out perfectly for her. Suddenly, something hit her, "Does my father know you're offering me this job?"

Diana shook her head, "No! I know your father because I'm his handler as an operator. He talked about you a lot..." Diana said, leaning back. "You sounded intriguing. A girl who knows self-defense karate styles, so many languages, music, singing, acting... Your resume just stood out by a margin that

I haven't seen in a while. That's why I did my research and invited you here. To work for us."

"Work for the CIA..." Yifat gulped, but her face showed a hint of a smile. "Never thought life would bring me here."

Diana smiled, standing up, "unexpected turns lead to the happiest outcomes... Do we have a deal?"

***

"She took it? She really did?" I was stunned as Diana finished the story, "Yifat was an agent all this time?"

Diana smiled and nodded, "That girl is just full of surprises. You should have brought her here with you. Her mind could be useful."

I nodded, taking a sip from my coffee. "Yes, but I figured she needed time to reconcile with her father. They went to New York."

"Right!" Diana said, glancing at the planner on her desk, "Let's not waste any more hours, shall we then? We have a lot to conquer."

"What do you suggest we do?" I asked, leaning back in my seat.

"We find Mark Thompson," Diana said, writing something on a piece of paper and then picking up her phone and typing something away. "It shouldn't take long with our resources."

"Aaron told us he was planning to flee the country." I pointed out.

"We'll see about that," Diana said, standing up as there was another knock on the door. I turned around to see a man clad in a three-piece suit standing in the doorframe. Diana handed him the piece of paper, "deploy what you can... Do a countrywide search if you must. Get him to this location. Fast."

The man merely nodded and left. When Diana came back and sat, I raised my eyebrow at her, and she smiled at me, "Gear up, Specialist... We've got a man to catch and crack... just like old times."

***

"Boys, are you ready?"

I asked them as we stood out Mark's grand mansion, courtesy of his years of corruption and looting of the nation's wealth. The villa was equipped with top-notch security, and we just got lucky that Mark had not yet fled the country, which made it easier to track him down. Diana had set me off for his hunt with a small team, leading for this mission. It all felt surreal. Each step that I took with tactically equipped men trailing behind me, I remembered my days in the force. I would head a grand mission in the interest of national security as trusted agents followed me to bow down and bend over to follow all of my orders. At times, these orders entailed cold-blooded killing, and they obliged to that as well. I didn't think I would feel this kind of happiness in relishing old memories and walking my old paths, but I did. I felt content. Almost enough to wish to rejoin.

"Aye!" The group of six men nodded at me, each one wearing protective gear, bulletproof vests, and holding their guns out.

"Charge!" I said as the men moved forward with calculated steps as we made our way through the security inside Mark's mansion. I had given them orders to knock the security guards out while shooting anyone who retaliates violently, making sure not to kill. We were just here to kidnap Mark. I was not looking for another bloodbath. Scurrying through, my men snapped some necks and head-butted a few, and we reached to the room that we knew belonged to Mark.

One of my men broke down the door, and we found Mark to be escaping out the window. His one leg propped on the windowsill and the other one still touched the room's floor. He was in his robe, which had ridden up, revealing his hairy white leg. His black hair looked darker as it was damp. His big eyes were widened like an owl's and showed hints of fear in them, while his thick lips were trembling in sheer fright.

"Freeze!" I announced in the quiet room, extending my gun towards him. "Nobody has to get hurt. Come down from there and leave with us." I ordered. To his dismay, Mark still tried to make a run for it, and I had no choice but to call my men to grab him by force. One of them dropped a black cloth over his head, the other one smacked him with a stick to slow his moving limbs down, and another one handcuffed him. Once he was in our captivity, I addressed the group again,

"Let's bring him to the decided location. Diana is waiting for us there." I ordered as I walked out of the room, leaving the last bits of the labor work to my team. I smiled. I could get used to working like this again. This was a high that I didn't know I was missing.

***

"Wakey, wakey, Markey." I heard Diana mockingly call out as I splashed water on his face through a pressure pipe, which I knew hurt like tiny needles passing through one's system. The room looked like a dark dungeon. It was made on an abandoned construction site's basement. It held one bulb hanging down the ceiling, many sticks were spread out throughout the muddy grounds, and there was a box of various torture inflicting objects tossed in one corner. The one lone chair was situated in a corner next to a few wires, which I presumed were used to inflict electric torture.

As Diana continued to strike Mark with the pressure pump, I stood back, numb in my place, as I glanced around the torture chamber in its haunting darkness. While being an agent with the CIA, I had been subjected to many such atrocious tortures. In my career, I had witnessed many heinous ways of extracting information out of people. I had heard and given the same excuse many times over that we were the good guys, which was why whatever we did, was right, for actions were always in the interest of good. However, having had my distance with the agency, as I witnessed the cruelty prevailing before me now, I didn't know whether I agreed with the notion of doing the right thing through the wrong means anymore.

Diana circled Mark, taking off the black cloth from his face as she splashed water at him again. She hardly gave him the time to recover from the attack when she held his chin and dug her long sharp fingernails into his skin, brought her face close to him, "I loathe dirty politicians... More than I hate soggy cereal."

"What... are you..." Mark fumbled, coughing between his stammering words. Diana did not have it. She extended her arm out, and her agents instantly knew what she meant. They handed an iron rod in her open palm, and she held onto it tightly, extending it to one end and striking him across his neck with a strong force.

I stepped forward, "we haven't even asked him anything yet," I pointed out, forgetting if it was this bad when I had worked here.

"We don't ask them... They know what we want from them." Diana simply said as she stepped away. "For my man, Specialist, I'm giving you a chance by asking you in a simple way... What do you know about the Chinese attack on our Treasury? I hear you have a buddy there, Cheung. Tell me," Diana said, circling him again, "what have you two lovely friends planned."

"I don't…" He coughed again as he couldn't say the words. Diana didn't wait. She landed another strike, across his face this time, and then turned to her men.

"Take it away… And don't stop till he confesses… or dies."

No! Surely, this couldn't be true. Would the CIA kill someone if they didn't comply with their commands? I watched as Diana walked away and sat down in a corner on the elevated ground to overlook the scene, and the two men trotted slowly towards Mark. Each held an iron rod in their grips. They began striking him at any place they found, and somewhere in the middle of the torture, they opened his robe and cast one harsh strike after another on his bare flesh. Mark screamed in loud screeches, and the empty lot echoed hauntingly of his woes of pain. Writing a dark tale of the tortures.

Perhaps those men were getting tired, or maybe they thought Mark had bled enough, but they eventually threw away the rods. My horror only continued when one of them went to retrieve the open wire in the corner. The man picked up two wires, turned on the current, and sparked the two ends together. The words "stop it!" laced around my tongue, never making it out, when Mark began shouting himself, having witnessed the sparking wires.

"No, no, no, please don't! I'll tell you anything."

Diana smiled from the other end of the open space as she stood up and swayed her way towards

Mark. "Perfect! Now, start talking, and don't make me ask you questions. Remember, I get moody when I have to interrogate... My system is simple; You waste my breath for a question; I serve you with one strike."

Mark gulped down and looked at her with pleading, bloodshot eyes. He cleared his throat, coughing out blood, "I'm afraid you're late. The attack on the Treasury has already been launched. It's operational and working its way inside the system."

Diana landed a strike across his face as his nose bled on impact, "oh, I'm sorry, I forgot to tell you... you also get a hit for useless blabbing. Be watchful of what you say.

Mark gulped, "the kill switch." He breathed. "The only way to stop the attack is to activate the internet kill switch. There's no other way. And you guys better act fast, for there's no time. And their next target is the New York Stock Exchange."

I stepped forward. "The kill switch, you say... Is it even allowed? I mean, the government can no longer do it, right?"

Mark shook his head, "No, it can. The President has the authority. So do the intelligence agencies if it's a matter of national security... which it is currently. Under the Communications Act's Section 706, the head of the State can order a complete shutdown of internet access for at least forty-eight hours, in the event of a national threat." Mark explained.

Diana moved forward and came close to him, "we're keeping you here till we have this sorted... You know, in case we need you again."

Mark didn't dare to argue, and at that moment, I knew that I might never want to work for the CIA again.

***

"Time won't slow down by you looking at the seconds ticking by."

I looked up as Diana entered her office with a bottle of scotch in her hands. She took her seat and smirked at me. "It's nightfall. I believe you may drink now."

"They say that time halts when you start counting down the seconds," I mused, taking the glass she had filled for me. "Why doesn't the philosophical notions ever work in reality?"

"Philosophy is for the weak-minded, not for the likes of us brilliants," Diana said, taking a sip from her glass.

"Ahh! I see the modesty has not wavered even a tad."

She laughed, raising her glass, "I own who I am... Without shame, Specialist."

"And I'm owning up to who I am, Diana," I said. "I know you don't agree with me to activate the internet kill switch, but you know I go to extreme lengths to earn a solve."

"I am aware of your brutal ways, my vanquished protégé," Diana said. "But you have to keep in mind the consequences of shutting down the internet."

"When faced with a difficult choice, you weigh in the losses," I said, leaning back in my chair as I swirled my drink around in my hand. "I'm aware of the economic fall that the country will have to suffer in the two days that the internet would be shut, but it's still a lot less than what might happen if they do hit the treasury and NY Stock Exchange."

"The Chinese win's if there's so much as a penny's worth of loss to the State," Diana argued. "I still think there has to be another way. All we need to do is to dig a little deeper."

"The grave has been set for burial, Diana," I said, standing up as I gulped the drink down and slid the glass across the table. "We don't have the time to dig deeper. There's no more ground left."

Diana sighed, "when have I ever been able to get you to agree with me?"

I passed a smile, "never! I thought you'd have learned by now."

Diana laughed as she stood up. "New York... That's where the mainframe is located. Head out to the Big Apple as I tie some loose ends here and get you that permission to activate the switch in time."

I nodded at her, "thank you!" I breathed. "I'd have preferred if you would have accompanied me."

"Oh, no!" She shook her head. "I have a lot to stream, given that you're taking our internet away for two long days."

I laughed as I hung my bag on my shoulder and walked towards the door. "Get some sleep, Heartley... The dark circles have started to show."

Diana smiled, "see you around, Sheppard." She said, raising her glass as I bid my farewell and left her office, hoping for the next dawn to bring a stop to the prevailing Chaos.

Chapter 20

The sound of wheels rolling over the hard marble floorings in the airport felt like a sharp reminder of where he had landed. The speaker boomed of announcements in English, and he clutched on to his bag.

Welcome to the United States of America.

He mumbled under his breath. In between the hustle and chaotic crowd of one of the busiest airports in the world, the tip taps of his cane hitting the ground came back up as he walked felt screeching and oddly loud to his ears. It was visible proof of what he had been through. But he liked it. This was what told him every second of his waking moment that he needed to avenge the man who had handed the walking stick to him. Paralyzing him from one side for Lord knows how long, the haunting reminder was a welcomed one. It kept him on his edge and only ignited the fire of revenge to a greater intensity inside of him.

Zhang, crippled by the fall of his helicopter, had survived. The doctors had operated on him and secured him in a room, where he had to run away. He didn't have the time to stay. He had to pay his warm regards to The Specialist.

"You're half the man you were once," his people at the little group he was working with told him. "Picking a battle with The Specialist will take away the other half."

"Let him try. I no longer care." Zhang had made it clear. "Nothing flips the Specialist upside down quite like losing a mission, and that's exactly the kind of revenge I plan to serve." He had told them right before he set course to New York.

Now standing outside the airport, he had hailed a cab to go where he knew the Specialist would eventually be arriving. Zhang never doubted for a second that he wouldn't have figured out about the kill switch. He was sure to meet him there. Sitting in the cab, he took out his phone and called a number.

"Not an action goes that does not first go through me from this point onwards," he stated with a firm tone. "I'm coming over. I'll personally guard the kill switch. I have some old skeletons that need burying."

He hung up the phone and laid his head back on the seat, looking out the window. The busy streets of New York at the late hour of the night felt welcoming. He held onto his cane as he looked down at his plastered leg. The Specialist shall pay, and he shall pay hard. Zhang thought, closing his eyes and reminiscing in the visions of Specialist's defeated face and broken watches. It shall be a sight to behold indeed.

***

The cold air of New York hit me as soon as I set foot on its soil. The night had fallen dark, but the streets were just as busy as ever. The city that never slept always held up its end of the bargain to entertain its inhabitants and tourists alike, with wonderful chaos and happenings that had the potential of altering anyone's reality.

Reigning hustle and ringing life of this lively city, dulled in comparison to the storm currently set afloat inside me. My bag hung over my shoulder, and I spent no time taking a cab to the hotel I had made a temporary booking in. The city's exploring would have to wait another day when the time's ticking hands would not be prepared to strangle me to a defeated death.

"Twelve more hours." I breathed as I made my way through the long hallways of the hotel and into my room. My bag thrown in one corner, I pulled out my phone. She must be sleeping, but the matter was of literal life or death. This couldn't wait.

"Specialist, burning the midnight oil again, I presume."

Her sleepy voice came through the earpiece, and I smiled, "as always." I said. "What do you say, one last hurrah before we call it a day?"

I heard a yawn escape her, "what do you want?" She asked, her tone laced with excitement.

"One last favor in our mission together," I told her. "Meet me at the location I'm sending you at seven sharp."

"I can hardly contain myself. Things were getting rather boring," Yifat said with a smile.

I hung up and sent her the address before falling on the bed, awaiting the sun to rise and bring our case's success to our very feet.

***

"Internet Access Center," Yifat greeted me by gesturing at the board behind her when I got there. "If it's an office building you're looking to have breakfast in, I've heard the UN Headquarters offer a far better range of cuisine."

I smiled, "we're here to put an end to the attack... once and for all."

Yifat looked back and looked at me again before she realized what I was saying. "The kill switch," she affirmed in a hushed tone.

"Yes!" I nodded. "The republican told us that it was the only option."

"Sheppard, the main frame's shut down lasts at least forty-eight hours when activated. It is a default setting." Yifat said, and I knew where she was going with this. "The impact would be monumental."

"But not catastrophic," I argued. "I have been doing my own pros and cons evaluation. This is what we're doing. I have made my decision. It's final."

Yifat sighed. "Fine! Let's go then."

I smiled as we headed for the gate. Diana must have informed the department of our arrival, and they would be expecting us. The tall iron gates of the building had two guards outside. When we reached, one of them stopped us from going in.

"We're guests of Miss Diana Heartley." I informed, "Call someone in the building, and they'll confirm it to you."

The guards, however, seemed to have strict orders otherwise. They remained stern and didn't budge from their position. "We're sorry, Sir, we can't let you in. The authorities have asked us to deny access to every visitor for the next few hours."

"What?" I countered. "What authorities are you talking about?"

"Mr. Mark Thompson. Please step aside." The guard said.

"The Republican," Yifat said. "He has reach."

I shook my head, "On the contrary. For now, he has zero reach... He is literally tied to a chair. There must be a misunderstanding... Wait!"

I immediately pulled out my phone and called Diana to check what was going on. I explained to her that Mark had given orders not to allow anyone in the building, and she was just as surprised as we were. However, she asked me to hold for a while as she would gather a little intel to find out who was overlooking the whole operation in the building and using her resources to speed things up. It took her some time, but when she called, she finally gave me the good news.

"I have pulled some strings, Specialist," She announced. "Go ahead. You should be able to gain access now."

"Thank you," I smiled, but before hanging up. I had one more question, "um... that authority the guard spoke of, who was it?"

"Someone named Zhang. He had an internal system running here. Many people work under his wing, which was how he was able to manipulate things so easily. He is probably on the run by now, now that the CIA would be hunting for him."

My mouth hung open at Diana's words, but I didn't get much time to think as I saw a car rushing out of the parking in haste and urgency as if looking for an escape. I put away my phone. "Would you go inside and overlook this for me?" I asked Yifat.

"Where are you..."

"No time to explain. Just go, please!" I pleaded. Without waiting for her answer, I went to my car to chase after the vehicle that had just rushed out—the one I assumed Zhang was driving. I couldn't believe that Zhang had survived the helicopter crash, but I didn't have time to dwell on that. I simply intended to finish this once and for all.

It took me a few minutes, but I caught up to the black Porsche, speeding ahead of me. I pulled out my gun, ready to shoot at the tire to make it stop. However, Zhang must have thought of it first as I saw him peeking out and shooting at my car. I turn to the side, and my car slid on the sidewalk, screeching loudly. I balanced it back into position and decided to give Zhang a taste of his own medicine. I shot his tire, but with the sudden sharp turn that Zhang took, my bullet hit the trunk of the car instead of the tire.

Damnit! I yelled as my car skidded out of balance with the sudden turns that Zhang was now taking at various roads. I was getting frustrated with the chase. None of my shots were working, and my car seemed to be driving out of its own heart. Finally, the pursuit took us towards a subway station, which appeared to be empty. The narrow road granted me a chance to take another shot, for Zhang's car had slowed down and had nowhere to turn. I shot at his tire again, and this time, I hit the target. The tire burst and the car swirled around and suddenly stopped as it hit the nearby wall.

I immediately got out of the car and watched as Zhang struggled to get out of his. I stepped back subconsciously when I saw him limping his way over to me with a cane in his hands. Our car chase had brought us to an abandoned subway, where there was no train passing by and not a single person in sight. In the early morning hours, the place looked quiet and serene, but one could imagine how it must look at the late hours of the night. Haunting and dreadful; I was sure.

"We meet again," Zhang said with a smirk. "I dreamed of this when my helicopter landed in those wild bushes and caught fire as I barely escaped my burning hell."

"Are you are here to claim it now? Because rest assured, I can arrange for your burning hell anywhere." I said, grinning.

Zhang laughed out loudly. "Ahh, yes! You always did have a great sense of humor... I almost forgot about that." He retorted, stepping closer towards me, bringing his face near mine. "You know what the best and the worst part of that accident was?" Zhang gritted his teeth into a smirk, "Getting crippled. It's not fun, but you know, it has its own perks."

"Special treatment, I suppose?" I mocked him. "Must be a first you, given your lack of class and all."

Zhang gave out another laugh, "way off, Specialist." He said, and before I could even respond to him, he raised his stick and landed a forceful strike across my head as I stumbled backward and fell on the ground with a loud thud. I was trying to recover myself when Zhang bent down and brought his face closer. "I know you have a gun, but let's finish this like real men, shall we? Let's combat."

I held onto my head as the sharp blow had sent a jolt of pain throughout my body. I squinted my eyes to clear out my vision and watched Zhang hovering over me. He held a stick in his hand, and hatred plastered on his face. He looked like nothing short of a maniac. I composed myself and flipped up, despite the pain in my head. For a while, we merely stared each other down before any one of us spoke or did anything.

I grinned at him, "you don't want to do this, Zhang. Not with only half of you working."

This seemed to have enticed Zhang as I had intended. He scrunched his nose and landed a punch across my jaw. However, I saw it coming. I held his fist in my palm, and with one swift motion, I twisted his arm to his side, and with my other hand, I sucker-punched him, making him lose his balance and falling backward.

As he struggled to get up, I bent over closer to him. "I warned you... You should not be doing this, dearest Zhang."

Zhang, to my surprise, had composed himself rather quickly. He used his right leg to entangle with mine, and he brought me to the ground. As he tried to hover over me, I quickly got to my feet again, dancing around him as I held on to his arm and twisted it backward. "Give it up, Zhang. You should be tired by now of losing against me." I whispered in his ear.

"I'm not letting you win this time, Specialist," Zhang said as he used his free hand and elbowed me in the face. This one I didn't see coming, and I felt my nose bleeding with a sudden impact. I had barely recovered from the attack when I saw Zhang pull out his gun and pointed it at me, "it's over!"

My years of training came in handy as I predicted his next move accurately. I ducked down, knowing he was about to take a shot. The bullet went ahead in the air, hitting nothing in particular. However, I took this as an opportunity to hold his hand and twist it till he dropped the gun. What followed was a continuous attack as I landed a series of punches on him, and my legs made contact with his ribs, eventually making him fall mercilessly on the ground, doubled over in pain and unable to breathe. Unknowingly, a part of me was holding back, for my subconscious still remembered him as my friend. But him falling back on his word of not using guns instantly reminded me that that's who he was. A liar. A traitor... Unworthy of forgiveness.

"You have followed me around long enough to know that there's no one I hate more than traitors, my old friend," I whispered my words out as I bent closer to him. "You should not have done that... Any of it."

I stood up straight as I pulled out my gun and pointed it at him. "Any last words?"

Zhang looked at me, eyes wide open, but no signs of fear or remorse displayed on his features. He was relaxed, satisfied even, and it made me wonder what he was planning next? It shouldn't matter. I was going to kill him. As I loaded my pistol, my hands shivered a little. Why? It wasn't the first time I was killing someone. Why was I so nervous?

Let him go with a warning! My subconscious seemed to still be on the same tangent, where I felt sympathy for the man lying on the ground at my mercy. No! I had to do it.

"No, Specialist... You have not won this." Zhang coughed his words out. "I won't let you have the satisfaction of killing me."

The words had barely hit me, and I was in the middle of processing them when I saw Zhang slide across the floor, pick up the gun that had fallen earlier, and shoot himself in the head. An involuntary scream escaped me as I saw Zhang's lifeless body on the ground, thrown over on the abandoned tracks with the impact of the shot, oozing blood and staining the sandy rails.

I released a long breath. Never one to not leave me in absolute shock. Zhang had made sure his departure was not even what I had planned for him. The smug bastard... He had been right. I didn't win. Because despite the reality that his body was laid out in front of me, dead and defeated, I still didn't feel satisfied. He made sure of that.

I stepped down on the tracks and rolled his body over. I did a quick search of his pockets to see if I could find something of value. His wallets, keychains, and cellphones now sat in front of me. I opened his wallet and found some cards and cash. A deeper search led me to a small piece of paper, folded into a chit, tucked away at the back of a card. Carefully I opened the form and found a few words written on it:

"In the name of our great leader, I bow to serve what stands against the cruel rule of our overlords. With my life. With every last drop of my blood."

I held the paper tightly in my hands as I tried to make sense of the words. At first glance, it felt like Zhang was part of the group of rogue agents working against China's regime. But if that was the truth, it meant.... No! It couldn't be. I folded the paper and put it away in my pocket. This was a mystery of another time. I needed to see if Yifat had managed to activate the kill switch.

As I walked towards my car, my phone started buzzing. I pulled it out and saw it was Yifat. As I answered, her panic voice ringed in my ears,

"It's done!" She breathed. "But now, the speculations on the internet blackout has reigned chaos on the streets and everywhere."

I sighed. I saw that one coming.

***

"Cheers!" I rattled my beer bottle with Yifat's as we sat on the rooftop of one of the buildings in New York, overlooking the sun setting behind the city's breathtaking skyline.

"Should there be cheers?" Yifat pointed out, taking a sip from her bottle. "The dust has yet to settle. You know you'll have to face the consequences of shutting down the internet?"

I nodded. "I'm aware, and like any other time, I'll defend my actions. I know I did the right thing." I said with confidence, looking out the scene. "It's just for a few hours. We'll recover from this loss."

Yifat looked at me with a smile. "When the dust does settle on this case, where will life take you, oh wise one?" She mused.

I turned to look at her, and I grinned, raising my eyebrow, "You tell me, what other cases you'll be taking?"

"Cases? What cases?" Yifat held up her hand defensively. "This was a one-time thing because it involved my father," she looked away.

I laughed. "Diana Heartley was my first mentor in the field. She tells me things... More than just investigative strategies."

Yifat sighed. "Great! Make a fuss about keeping me undercover and rat it to a big known agent."

I let out another laugh. "Your secret is safe with me," I said, raising my bottle in her direction again.

She gave a tuck to her eyebrow with a grin, "You didn't answer my question."

"You didn't answer mine either." I pointed out.

Yifat groaned. "Fine! I'm going back to acting... At least till Diana calls me again for something."

I looked at her and smiled at her. "I wish you all the luck for your future endeavors."

Yifat glared at me. "It's not the time for bidding farewells, Specialist. I am still looking for an answer."

I let out a sharp breath as I watched the sun slowly setting. The skyline was pained in a shade of orange, cast by the sun's shadow. Overlooking the whole city from this high up, I felt a sense of calm settle within me, one that I knew would only last for a while before I was back to the chaos, soaring through the rushing streets and corners. I closed my eyes briefly to take in the cold air of New York and let it soothe my tensed nerves. Without turning to Yifat, I answered her question.

"I'll be looking into the Secret Intelligence Society of Rogue agents that Jack was heading."

Acknowledgments

I would like to thank the following people who loved and helped me over the years and who have believed in my talents: Theresa Sheppard Alexander, Arthur Theodore Sheppard, Lintonia Sheppard, Lois Winona Sheppard, Hubert Austin Sheppard, Patricia Ruth Sheppard, Phillis Isabella Sheppard, Lois P. Quillian, Hattie Booker Peterson, James Mitchell Sheppard, and my entire family. They are always there in the most trying of times.

These business people have steadfastly supported me, on this journey, over the years and have trusted me and helped me in crucial times in my life: Mr. Dan Zuckerman, Theresa Sheppard Alexander, and Michael H. Alexander, Patrica Ruth Sheppard. Thank you to these very special friends who support me: Joseph Tillman, Lesley Bracker, Diane Hardy, Ellen Cohen and Alex Varhaftig.

I would also like to acknowledge that the image on the front cover is of actress Annie Monroe and on the back cover the image is of actress Blaine Allen.

Special Thanks

I would also like to thank my friends, creative editors, and all the people who helped with research and character development. Your insights have been invaluable.

About the Author

Phillip William Sheppard is a reality TV star in Santa Monica, California, who is famous for participating in two seasons of the hit TV show *Survivor*™. His reputation as a celebrity gave him more than 15,000 *Twitter*™ followers. Learn about his journey as a famous personality and book author. Leaving home at the young age of sixteen, he joined the US Army and later on became a federal agent. He also worked in technology enterprise sales for the last eighteen years of his career. He is a Former Federal Agent and US Army Veteran.

While roller-skating in Santa Monica, he was discovered by TV network CBS to become part of the 22nd season of *Survivor* called *Redemption Island*. He also made a second appearance in the show's 26th season, *Survivor: Caramoan Fans vs. Favorites*. "It's all pretty heady stuff, but I'm never content just to be satisfied. It's not in me. I always look to engage the fans, too. They're really what it's all about," said Sheppard.

On *Survivor Redemption Island*, Jeff Probst, Executive Producer & host, credited Phillip with creating a legendary and iconic character in "The Specialist." Phillip has been very thankful to the network and its production crew for giving him several opportunities to appear on the show. *Survivor* has given him a way to do other things in life like writing a book, giving back to charities, and having a chance at fame and fortune. Phillip is the only Survivor to have written a fictional novel about his persona, "The Specialist." He is also a former author and Associate Publisher at NeworldReview.com™, where he wrote two columns, "A Conversation" and "A Man About Town." Phillip is one of twelve siblings, which include his twin sister. He is a single parent and currently lives in Santa Monica, California.

Find Phillip on Twitter: @PSheppardTV
And on Instagram: @PhillipTheSpecialist.